CHANGING [illegible] WOLFEN HERITAGE

A Wolfen Heritage 3

Missy Martine

MENAGE AMOUR

Siren Publishing, Inc.
www.SirenPublishing.com

A SIREN PUBLISHING BOOK
IMPRINT: Ménage Amour

CHANGING THEIR WOLFEN HERITAGE

ISBN-10: 1-61034-234-8
ISBN-13: 978-1-61034-234-6

First Printing: January 2011

Cover design by Jinger Heaston

Printed in the U.S.A.

PUBLISHER
Siren Publishing, Inc.
www.SirenPublishing.com

DEDICATION

This book is dedicated to my loving husband, who continues to support me in everything I do. His love and devotion make me feel as if I can do anything.

CHANGING THEIR WOLFEN HERITAGE

A Wolfen Heritage 3

MISSY MARTINE

Prologue

"Well, Michael, it was a beautiful wedding, although a little quick." Remus couldn't help but smirk at the newest member of his pack.

"Why waste time when you know what you want?" Michael replied. He was keeping his arm tight around his new bride. "Remus, we wanted to thank you for the piece of land you gave us for a wedding present. It's the perfect place for a house, which, I will add, has already been designed."

"That was fast. When do you plan on starting construction?" His ambitious brother-in-law continued to surprise him. Just a few weeks ago, Michael still hadn't accepted his family's Wolfen heritage. He, and his sister Maddie, grew up without knowing about their ancestry. The shock of finding out his sister could change into a wolf alienated the siblings even more. Then, Michael fell in love with one of his pack members. The fear of losing Ariane to another wolf shifter had finally driven Michael's own wolf to the surface.

"As soon as we come back from our honeymoon."

"What company is doing the work?" Remus figured that it wouldn't be his family's company if Mali had anything to do with it.

He didn't think that Michael had forgiven him for trying to move in on Ariane when she came back from Houston.

"Yours, unless you have an objection. Mali and I had a nice, long talk, and I don't think he'll have any problems working with me now." He glanced at Ariane. "I know I won't have any problems working with him since I got to keep the woman." He grunted when she elbowed him in the ribs. "Actually, he's doing a job for me while we're away."

Remus frowned. "What job is that?"

"You know I rented a small building in town to use for an office. Turns out it has two stories and you don't have any zoning problems about turning it into an apartment. Melissa saw it last week and loved the idea of living over the office. I've got Mali going in the first of next week to remodel the upstairs into a living space for her." He laughed. "She's so excited I can hardly stand to be around her."

Remus laughed at the thought of Michael's little human friend driving everyone crazy. He'd been reluctant to have her at the wedding since she didn't know anything about the shifters and he wanted to keep it that way. "Where's she staying now?"

"I've got her put up in the little bed and breakfast in town. She's comfortable enough, but she'll be happier with her own place." He glanced around the crowd. "I haven't seen her for a while. It's almost time for us to leave. If I miss her, can you introduce her to Mali for me? I think they should meet before he just shows up at the office on Monday."

"Sure, no problem. But you better go and find your sister to say goodbye. That woman will be hell to live with if you get away without giving her a hug."

Both Michael and Ariane laughed. Ariane reached up and kissed Remus on the cheek. "Thank you for everything, Alpha."

He scowled at her. "It's Remus, and don't you forget it. Now, both of you get! You've got a honeymoon waiting. We'll see you in a couple of weeks." He watched as they scampered off.

"Remus, may I have a word with you?"

Remus turned around to find Vanard Wind River standing behind him, accompanied by a beautiful, young woman. She was not very tall, with long reddish-brown hair falling in waves down her back. Her eyes were a shade of green even more startling than Ariane's. "Hello, Vanard. We're pleased you came to Michael and Ariane's wedding today. Who's your lovely friend?"

Vanard smiled. "Kitania, I'd like to introduce you to the Alpha of Wind River Pack. This is Remus Wind River. Remus, this is Kitania. She's going to be our new schoolteacher when classes start in a few months."

"It's a pleasure to meet you, Alpha, but everyone but Vanard calls me Tania." Her voice was soft and almost lyrical as she bowed her head, exposing her neck in a show of respect.

Vanard chuckled. "I'm sorry, Kitania, but I've never approved of nicknames."

"Please, call me Remus. I'm afraid we're not as formal here as a lot of packs." He looked at Vanard, and then back at the woman, and frowned. "I'm sorry. I didn't catch your name affiliation for your pack." Shifters have always added their pack name to their first name for identification. Before she could answer, Vanard spoke up. "Kitania doesn't have a designation because she doesn't have a pack." He turned to the young woman. "Kitania, would you excuse us for a moment?"

She glanced up at him, and then at Remus. "Sure, no problem. It was a lovely reception, Remus. You have a lovely home."

"Thank you, Tania. I'm happy to have met you. I look forward in the coming months to getting to know you better. Please know you're always welcome in my home, and my wife Maddie will probably be calling on you shortly." He looked at Vanard. "Have you put her up in the teacher's cabin?"

"Yes, she moved in yesterday," he replied.

"Please let us know if there's anything you need to make your cabin into more of a home, Tania." The young woman puzzled Remus. He sniffed the air as discretely as possible but couldn't tell much about her from her scent.

"Thank you. I'll wait over by the trees for you, Vanard." She walked away quickly before he could say anything.

"All right, Vanard. What's going on? Why doesn't she have a name affiliation?"

Vanard sighed. "She doesn't have a pack of her own, Remus. Her parents abandoned her when she was very young. The National Council raised her in one of their homes for children. You know they don't attach names to any of the kids they take in."

"Abandoned," Remus said, shocked. "Wolves abandoned a child to be raised by strangers?" He couldn't imagine such a thing happening.

"That's the problem. She's not entirely wolf. She's a half-breed, and that's all I'm at liberty to say. You know as well as I do that she's not required to tell anyone of her parentage."

"Can she shift?" Remus wanted to know as much as he could about anyone coming into his pack.

"I'm told she can, but I've not witnessed it. The people I talked to on the Council say she's quite a loner. She doesn't mix with other pack members much, and she's never caused any trouble. She made high marks in school and is reported to be an excellent teacher."

"Well, that's something. We definitely need a good teacher. What's she going to do for the next couple of months before classes start?"

"I thought she might just spend some time meeting some of the families with children she'll be teaching, and maybe get to know her surroundings."

"All right, just keep me posted on what she's doing. I don't like surprises. I've got my hands full with other things right now. I don't want to be babysitting a new female."

"All right, no need to get huffy. She won't be a problem." He gave Remus a shrewd look. "Is there anything I can do to help with your problems?"

"Not at this time, but I'll let you know if I need anything." Remus meant his words to be a dismissal. He was happy when Vanard nodded and left to go after his new project. He glanced up to see Koril headed his way. He wasn't happy to see the frown on his face.

"Remus, we need to talk." Koril was always a man of few words.

"What's wrong?"

"I fucked up big time with Kaugh."

"How?" Vincent Kaugh had recently arrived from California. He'd been a close, personal friend and colleague of Dr. Richard Constantine. The doctor had known about Michael and Maddie's family history when he treated Maddie after a childhood accident. He'd kept her a prisoner for years while he studied her like a lab rat. His attempt to kidnap her following her mating to Remus had resulted in his death.

Koril sighed and looked disgusted. "We thought we'd found all of Constantine's records and destroyed them when we cleaned out his home and office."

"And you didn't?" Remus was beginning to get angry at getting just a little of the information at a time.

"Apparently, he set up a dummy corporation before he died that we weren't aware of. He rented a post office box in the name of the corporation at the bank." He paused and gave Remus a deadly look. "Yesterday, my man followed Kaugh to the bank. Dr. Constantine had made him an officer of the corporation and forwarded him the key to the safety deposit box. He walked out of there yesterday with an armload of files and computer discs. His three bodyguards were surrounding him."

"That's fucking great. Where is he now?"

Koril stepped back when Remus exploded in anger. "He's rented an office on Main Street in town."

Remus thought for a moment. "Tomorrow, when all this wedding and reception nonsense is over, we need to sit down with the Elders and form a plan. We've got to get those records back and find out if there are any more surprises out there waiting for us." He looked at his longtime friend. "I want your best men guarding Maddie every time she steps foot out of this house. Is that understood?"

"Yes, Alpha."

"I'm counting on you, my friend. She's not only my mate. She's carrying my pup now."

Koril's eyes got big, and he slapped Remus on the back. "I'm so happy for you. Don't you worry. We'll guard her with our lives." He nodded to Remus and hurried off.

* * * *

Vanard walked quickly over to where Kitania was waiting by the forest trail. He was worried that everything was going to blow up in his face.

"Well, is he going to let me stay? Did I pass his test?" She gave Vanard a look of amusement.

"Of course he's going to let you stay. He has no reason to doubt anything I tell him." He glanced back at Remus. "Of course, when all this comes to light, he's never going to forgive me for lying to him."

She patted him on the shoulder. "Don't worry, Vanard. I'm not going to cause any unnecessary trouble. I'll just do my job and then be out of your hair permanently."

He looked at her with pity in his heart. "Don't you ever want to settle down, Kitania? Don't you long for a pack of your own? Family? Pups?"

For just a moment, there was a yearning expression on her face, and then it was gone. "I don't yearn for what I can't have. I'm a half-breed, Vanard. Believe me when I tell you that no one's ever going to want to mate and have pups with me."

"You do shift, don't you?"

She hesitated. "I can, but I don't do it very often." Her tone told him not to question further.

"Oh, I forgot to tell Remus about your cat. Well, it'll be okay. Just be careful about letting it outside. No telling what could happen to it if it met up with one of the wolves out running. At least keep it inside until I can spread the word that you have a pet."

She sighed. "Thanks, Vanard. I'll keep her inside until you say it's safe. I wouldn't want anything happening to her."

"Come on, then. I'll walk you back to your cabin."

She glanced back toward the house one last time before they left. "Who are those two men?"

He looked to see who she was looking at and chuckled. "That's Ethan and Latan, the brothers of Remus." Both men were staring at Kitania as if they could eat her up. "Better watch out for them. They have a reputation with the ladies, and they like sharing." He just laughed when Kitania snorted, and then followed her into the woods.

* * * *

"Who the hell is that creature of beauty, Remus?" Latan grabbed Remus by the arm and jerked him around to point toward the forest path.

Remus looked where his brother pointed and sighed. "Her name is Kitania, but she prefers to be called Tania. She's the new schoolteacher." He already knew what was coming next.

"Hot damn! Teachers never looked like that when we were in school. Is she gonna be staying in the teacher's cabin?" Ethan was positively drooling.

"Yes, and the two of you stay away from her." Remus tried to sound fierce, but knew it was a waste of time with his over-sexed brothers. He sure hoped the young woman knew how to take care of herself.

"In your dreams," Latan replied. He glanced over at Ethan, ignoring Remus. "What do you think, bro? You think the welcome wagon ought to pay the little lady a visit? Maybe take her some wedding cake?"

"Now you're talking. Let's go." Ethan grabbed his arm and walked away before Remus could say anything.

"I feel trouble coming," Remus exclaimed.

"Remus, I just wanted to say it was a really nice party."

He turned around to see Mali standing in front of him. "Hey, Mali, we're very glad you camc. Michael told me that you and he worked things out well enough that you're going to be working together on his house."

"Yeah, there are no hard feelings. I always knew they were mates, so I never really stood a chance anyway." He laughed. "You ought to see the designs for their house. It's even nicer than yours."

Remus's mouth fell open in surprise. He didn't think anything could be better than the house Michael designed for them. "That reminds me, I'm supposed to introduce you to Melissa so she knows who you are when you show up on Monday. Hold on a minute." He walked off in search of Melissa, confident that Mali would wait for him. After a couple of minutes, he found her in the kitchen swapping stories about Michael with Maddie. "Melissa, would you come with me for just a minute? Michael wanted me to introduce you to Mali. He'll be at the office first thing on Monday to start the remodeling for your apartment."

"Sure, Remus. Maddie, I'll talk to you later. Maybe we can get together for lunch one day this week?" Melissa got up and joined Remus at the door.

"That would be great, Melissa. I'll give you a call," Maddie replied.

Remus walked with Melissa across the yard to where Mali was still standing. As they got near, he turned and faced them. "Melissa, this is Mali Wind River. He's a contractor and will be at your office on Monday to remodel the space for your apartment." He glanced at Mali and was surprised to see the man moving closer, obviously sniffing the air. "Mali, this is Melissa Rogers. She's Michael's business partner."

Mali walked closer and took the hand that Melissa offered. "It's a pleasure to meet you, Ms. Rogers." As Remus watched, he pulled on Melissa's hand, moving her closer to his body.

"Uh, nice to meet you, too. Please, call me Melissa." She seemed to be pulling back on her hand, attempting to free herself.

Still holding on, Mali leaned forward and inhaled deeply. "You can call me Mali."

Alarmed when he heard a small growl, Remus stepped up and pulled Melissa's hand from Mali's, earning a look of gratitude from the woman. "Melissa, do you already know what you want done in your apartment?" Remus narrowed his eyes as he glared at Mali.

"Oh, sure, it's pretty simple. There's not much work to be done." Melissa seemed to be in a daze. "Well, I promised Maddie I'd come right back. Guess I'll see you Monday." Without waiting for an answer, she scurried off.

Mali started after her, and Remus caught him by the arm. He stared at him hard when Mali let out an angry growl. "What the hell is wrong with you?"

"She's my mate!"

Remus sighed. "Oh, shit! What next?"

* * * *

Latan approached the small teacher's cabin with a plate of cake in his hand, excitement making him feel as if he were bursting at the seams. His brother, Ethan, walked beside him, probably driven by the same feelings of anticipation. The new teacher was beautiful, and he sure hoped she was interested in getting to know the two of them better.

"Kitania is an unusual name. What do you think it means?" Ethan posed his question to Latan as they hurried toward the cabin.

"Who cares? Let's hope it means available!" Both brothers laughed.

As they approached the porch, Latan looked over and saw a furry, black cat sitting in the window. He poked his brother in the side and nodded. "Take a look." He pointed to the window. "She's got a damn cat. I hate cats!"

Ethan snickered. "Better not say that too loudly. The lady might take offense if you insult her pet." He reached up and knocked at the door. As he watched, the cat scrambled out of the window and disappeared into the house. A minute later, the door opened just far enough for the new teacher to stick her head out.

Latan stared at the beauty that opened the door. She was breathtaking, and his heart sped up when he realized she was dressed in just a robe. "Hi, Tania, I'm Latan, and this is my brother, Ethan. We're the Alpha's brothers." He held out the plate. "We noticed you left without eating and thought you might like some of the wedding cake. We wanted to welcome you to the pack."

Tania reached for the plate and pulled it back inside the door. "Thank you, it was very thoughtful of you to bring it to me."

"No problem, we kind of hoped that you might want to get together." Ethan smiled at her with his request.

"What for?" she asked.

Latan looked at Ethan in surprise. "Well, to get to know each other better. We could tell you all about the pack, show you around, or just sit and talk." Latan was beginning to feel like things weren't going to go their way today.

Tania looked both men up and down and then smiled. "Not today, boys, maybe another time." She closed the door, and they could hear the lock turning on the other side.

Slowly, they walked away from the porch. For several minutes, they walked back toward their house in silence, and then Latan spoke up. “I’m in love. She’s perfect.”

Ethan glanced at him. “I’m in love, too. What are we going to do about it? She feels different than the other women we date.”

Latan stopped and stared at his brother for several minutes while he thought about the situation. “Yeah, she feels different, but does that really matter? We’ve always shared in the past. Why don’t we just share her now? Or are you thinking along the lines of a mate?”

Ethan hesitated before he answered. “No, I’m not looking for a mate.”

“So we share, like always?” Latan asked.

Ethan thought for a moment and then smiled and held out his hand for his brother to shake. “We share!”

Chapter 1

Tania stared down at the plate of wedding cake and grinned. The Alpha's brothers were really hot! She felt her body tingling in places that it hadn't tingled in quite some time. Maybe she could have a little fun while she carried out her assignment. It had been a long time since she'd allowed herself to enjoy the company of a male. There was always a danger that a wolf could decide to mate her, and she'd always avoided that at all costs. She'd revealed her true, half-breed self only once to a potential mate, and it was a mistake she would never make again. But with the brothers, it wouldn't be a problem. *Wolves are very possessive of their mates, and they don't share them with anyone.* As long as the two men wanted to play together, she was safe as a newborn pup.

Tania closed her eyes, imagining two strong, male bodies holding her tightly.

Lips as soft as a whisper trailed down her neck, while a warm, wet tongue darted out to taste the skin they explored. Fingers glided softly over the aching tips of her breasts before returning to roll them gently back and forth. She could feel a second set of hands squeezing her ass cheeks before dipping between them to tease the tiny, hidden entrance to her body. A trail of hot, fiery warmth trailed from the back of her neck, straight down her spine. Lips closed around her nipple and began to suckle, while the heat along the skin of her back returned to her neck. She could feel the moist breath as he pressed his lips to her ear. "You're ours, Tania!"

Tania's eyes popped open in shock. "Like hell, I'm yours!" She laughed at the absurdity of her daydream. As much fun as some really hot, kinky sex would be with a couple of good-looking wolves, she would never allow it to go any further than that. Besides, she already knew they were both only looking for a good-time girl. Very few people knew she had the ability to sense the emotions of others, no matter what their species. It had been vital to keep it a secret since her gift made it easier for her to accomplish the jobs the Council sent her on. The brothers had been very easy to read, which usually meant the subject wasn't trying to hide anything.

Tania took a deep breath and shook her head. "First things first." She left the cake sitting on the kitchen counter and went over to pick up the file on her current assignment. She cringed as she read over the material, wondering how she was going to be able to pull this off without getting caught. The Alpha, Remus, seemed pretty sharp, and it was going to be difficult to stay off his radar. Maybe spending time with his brothers could help her cause. She could use them to keep track of what their brother did or didn't know.

Tania frowned as a shiver ran over her, and the little hairs on the back of her neck stood up. For some reason, the idea of using the two men in such a way was extremely distasteful to her beast. She sighed and looked around the small cabin. "Okay, Kit, my little furball, you're gonna have to help me out on this one. I'm gonna need you to do a little reconnaissance for me. I hope you're up to the challenge because you're gonna have to avoid the big, bad wolves while we're here."

* * * *

Latan looked around the Pack House meeting room as the Elders, and a few other wolves from the pack, gathered. Remus had called everyone together on this beautiful Sunday morning to discuss some problem the pack faced. Personally, he would prefer being curled up in his bed dreaming of the hot, new teacher. He snickered as he watched his brother Ethan slowly shuffle through the door. They had both been up pretty late last night, trying to come up with a foolproof plan for getting on the teacher's good side.

"Did they start without me?" Ethan mumbled as he took the seat next to Latan.

"No, Remus is still talking to Vanard." Vanard was the head Elder of their pack, and Latan had often wondered how Remus kept from killing him. The Alpha was the top ruler of any pack and always had the final word in any situation. Vanard had a tendency to forget who was in charge. Latan stared into his brother's bloodshot eyes. "Man, you look like shit."

Ethan took a deep breath and then glared at his brother. "You're no vision of beauty yourself this morning." He rubbed a hand over his forehead. "Do you know what this meeting is supposed to be about?"

"No, Remus hasn't said anything."

Before Ethan could respond, Remus's voice shot out over the room. "Okay, my fellow pack mates. We have a new threat to address." He waited until every wolf in the room was silent before continuing. "Yesterday, Koril discovered that Dr. Constantine left a bunch of records in a safety deposit box at the bank. They're now in the hands of Dr. Vincent Kaugh."

"What kind of records?" asked Taynor Wind River.

"At this point, there's no way to know for certain. We're operating under the assumption that they're records from his so-called *medical research* on shape-shifting wolves." Remus took a deep breath as a fierce look came over his face. "He's probably now in possession of all Constantine's records on Maddie." His voice was a mixture of pain and fury.

"What do you think he'll do with them, Remus?" Taynor's voice carried a soft growl with his words. He was an extremely fierce wolf, despite being an investment counselor who handled all the pack's finances.

Remus walked over to the window. For a moment, he stood quietly, seemingly lost in thought. Then he turned and growled before answering. "I think he'll try and continue Constantine's work. Hell, he may even try and kidnap Maddie so he'll have the same test subject." He walked over and sat back down, then glanced down the table. "Koril, why don't you fill them in on what you've learned about Kaugh?"

Koril stood and bowed respectfully to Remus before he addressed the rest of the pack. He and Brenner handled all security matters for the Wind River Pack, and it would be dangerous to have him for an enemy. "Kaugh comes from Carsonville, California. He's been involved in secret research for more than twenty years. The National Council believes the research involves shifters, possibly more than just wolves. He showed up here after he learned that Constantine had been killed." Koril grimaced and shot an apologetic look toward Remus. "We were careless and didn't find out about the dummy corporation that Constantine set up until it was too late to stop Kaugh from getting his hands on the safety deposit box. He just waltzed in with a key and took everything there."

"We don't want to just go storming in to retrieve the files until we have more facts," Remus said. "We need to know exactly what we're dealing with and how many others might be involved. We don't want any more scientists showing up after we take this man out."

"Right now, Kaugh has three associates with him," Koril said. "Sean Cross, Marty Dyer, and Calvin Ames. None of these men are scientists or doctors, and they're human. It's pretty obvious that they're his muscle."

"Alpha, what is it you want us to do?" asked Vanard.

"Kaugh has rented a place on Main Street, just across from the building where Michael is setting up his office. I don't think he would have gone to the trouble of renting space unless he was up to something." Remus looked out at the members of his pack. "I want to keep him under surveillance until we figure out what he's planning. I want to find out who else knows about his research and if there are any other test subjects that might need our help." He got to his feet and took on the fierce aura of an Alpha. Shoulders back, canines extended, his inner power snaked through the room.

As Latan watched his older brother, a movement to the right caught his attention, and he turned to look toward the windows. Down on his knees, Taynor was looking at something under the table.

"I want help in guarding my mate twenty-four hours a day," Remus cried out. "I won't let anyone take her from me again." He lowered his head in an unusual show of humility. "I need your help to protect her." He raised his eyes, and they swept the room. "It's vital that we keep her safe. She's expecting our first pup."

As the room broke out in a round of congratulations, Latan watched Taynor crawl under the table. Intrigued, he stood and walked toward the older man. Suddenly, he stopped and watched, incredulous, as Taynor rose to his feet holding a small black cat by the scruff of its neck.

"Well, lookey, lookey! I tink I see a puddy tat!" Taynor laughed, mimicking the line from a children's television cartoon, as the cat hissed and thrashed about trying to free itself.

Latan groaned. He'd always hated cats. "Looks to me like you found a snack, Taynor," he encouraged, with an exaggerated wink.

Vanard came rushing over. "No, for God's sake, don't hurt it. If I'm not mistaken, it belongs to our new teacher."

"Yeah," Ethan agreed. "Latan and I saw it at her cabin yesterday when we took her some wedding cake."

Laughing, Latan walked over and bent down to stare into the eyes of the struggling cat. Pulling from deep inside himself, he let out a ferocious growl in an attempt to frighten the tiny animal into submission. He was surprised when the cat stopped struggling for a moment and seemed to focus its eyes back onto Latan's own gaze. Without warning, the small ball of fur suddenly hissed and lashed out with its paw, claws extended. Latan jumped back, narrowly missing getting injured. Taynor laughed and then screeched as the cat swung those deadly weapons around, drawing them neatly across the wrist that held it prisoner. Latan saw the bright red stripes as Taynor quickly let go of the tiny beast, dropping it to the floor. Everyone laughed as the cat jumped up and fled through the open window.

Latan grimaced, wondering how he was going to convince Tania to have a relationship with him and hide his hatred of her cat at the same time. He turned around to ask Ethan what he thought and came face to face with Vanard. For a moment, he could have sworn he saw relief on the pompous Elder's face.

* * * *

Melissa glanced at the clock for the tenth time in the last half hour. She was waiting for Mali to arrive, and she'd never been more nervous in her life. Meeting him at Ariane and Michael's wedding reception had been the highlight of her whole year. She could still feel the tingles from the electrical charge that had shot through her body when he'd taken her hand. She sighed as she pictured the handsome man in her mind. He was tall, well over six feet, towering over her five and a half foot frame. His large, muscular body had made her feel small and dainty even though she had what polite society called a *plus size figure*. His brown hair, lightly dusted with gray, fell just long enough to make a stubby ponytail at the base of his neck. Melissa shivered when she thought of his mesmerizing eyes. Brown, with tiny flecks of gold, they seemed to stare directly into her soul. They'd made her feel as if he wanted to consume her. She'd never had such an instant attraction to a man before, and she had an inexplicable feeling that he'd felt the same way. If it hadn't been for Remus pulling her away from Mali's grasp, she believed the handsome man would have taken her away from the party. Even more startling was the fact she would have gone with him willingly.

The door opened suddenly, startling Melissa out of her thoughts. She glanced up, expecting to see Mali, and was surprised to see an attractive young woman. "Can I help you?" Dainty, with long auburn hair and bright green eyes, she was everything Melissa wished she could be, and wasn't.

"Hi, my name's Tania. I'm the new teacher at the mountain school."

Melissa stood and walked over to offer her hand. "I'm Melissa. It's nice to meet you. Um, the office is not really open for business yet. We're just now getting settled in and unpacking."

Tania laughed. "Yes, I know. Actually, I'm here to help if I can."

"I, uh, don't understand." Melissa glanced at the clock again. She wanted to get this young woman out of the office before Mali arrived. She definitely didn't want this kind of competition for his attention.

"Sorry, I should have explained better." Tania walked farther into the room and looked around. "My boss is a friend of Michael's, and he thought that you might appreciate some help getting unpacked while Michael is on his honeymoon." She laughed again and lowered her voice. "Actually, I think he's trying to find things for me to do to justify paying me while school's out. I don't start classes for a couple of months, so I'm at loose ends."

It was impossible not to like Tania, and Melissa felt herself softening. She felt just a tad bit guilty for her earlier, jealous thoughts. "Well, there's really not much to do yet. I'm waiting for Mali this morning. He's doing some remodeling for us both here in the office and upstairs. I don't really want to unpack anything until he's finished." She indicated the chairs at the desk. "You're welcome to sit a spell and visit."

Tania glanced out the window like she was looking for something, and then took a seat at the desk, across from Melissa. She turned her chair sideways, and then stretched her legs out in front of her. Her eyes kept darting to the front windows.

"Is something wrong?" asked Melissa.

Tania frowned. "No, why would you ask that?"

"You keep looking out the window like you're looking for something or someone."

A blush rose up Tania's neck and settled in her cheeks. "Oh, sorry, I'm just curious about the town. I'm new here, and this is the first chance I've had to get out and look around."

Melissa laughed. "Join the club. I'm new, too, and trust me when I tell you there's nothing much to see. I should know. I've been over it from one end to the other." She smirked. "It took me about five minutes."

Grinning, Tania relaxed back into her chair. "Okay, so what brought you to this neck of the woods?"

"Well, a love of my boss and a desire not to have to find another job. Then, of course, there was my lack of a life and the hopes that I could find one if I moved somewhere new."

"You worked for Michael before?"

"Yeah, I've worked with him since I graduated college. I helped him, and his former partner, set up their firm in Texas."

"What on earth possessed him to move his company here?"

Melissa sighed wistfully. "Love! He fell in love with a local girl, and she wasn't happy in the big city." She smiled. "Truthfully, I don't think Michael was happy there either."

"That sounds so romantic," Tania groaned longingly.

"It was, and it's one of the reasons I wanted to come with him when he moved here. Ariane told me a long time ago that there were a lot more men here than women. It kind of gave me hope for the future, if you know what I mean." She watched Tania steal a look out the window again. "What brought you to this area, Tania?"

Tania turned back around to face Melissa. "I just wanted a change of scenery for a while. They had an opening for a teacher, so I jumped on it. It's only temporary, though. They have a permanent replacement coming at the end of the first semester. I won't be here long enough to even think about the single men."

"Boy, that's a depressing thought." Both women's heads turned when the door opened.

* * * *

Tania looked up and felt her pulse speed up at the sight of the two men walking through the door. They were even more handsome than she remembered from their visit two days ago. “Well, well, well! What brings the mountain’s very own welcome wagon here,” she teased.

Melissa snickered. “Hi Latan, Ethan, what can I do for you today?”

Ethan walked over and stood beside Tania’s chair. He leaned down and inhaled deeply, then let out a low growl that her sensitive shifter hearing picked up. He turned and met Melissa’s eyes with his own. “Just like the lady says, we’re the welcome wagon, and we’ve come to welcome you to Takoda.”

“Thanks, guys,” Melissa replied. “I was going to ask Michael when he got back, but since you’re here, I’ll just pick your brains.” She flashed them a big smile. “How did this little town get its name?”

Latan took up a position on the other side of Tania’s chair before answering Melissa’s question. “The Indians considered this a safe haven. It was a place they used to trade goods, and they didn’t tolerate fighting here. The name Takoda means ‘friend to everyone’. If you’re really interested in the history of this area, you should find some time to sit and talk with Remus.”

Ethan snorted. “Yeah, he’s a veritable bottomless pit of useless information.”

Melissa covered her mouth and coughed, obviously trying to smother a laugh. “Thanks, I just might do that.”

Ethan leaned over, his shoulder pressed tight against Tania’s back. “Latan and I would like to take you to dinner tonight.”

Tania glanced up into Ethan’s mischievous gaze and smiled. “Dinner, huh?”

“Well, dinner and getting to know each other better,” Latan said. An extremely lecherous look accompanied his words.

Tania glanced over at Melissa before answering the tempting invitation. It surprised her to see a wistful expression on the other woman's face. She quickly looked back up at Ethan. "Sounds great, guys. Why don't you pick me up around six?" She felt a strange, warm feeling wash over her and saw the pleasure echoed in both men's eyes.

Latan grabbed Ethan's arm and dragged him toward the door. "Six, you got it! We'll be there with bells on." He grinned at her, and then focused his attention on Ethan. "Come on, bro, we've got some work to get finished so we'll have time to go home and get cleaned up before we need to pick her up." He glanced over at Melissa. "Oh, yeah, sorry, Melissa. I almost forgot to tell you that Mali is gonna be running late this morning. He had a problem to straighten out on another job. He said he wanted to finish that one before coming here to start a new one. Something about being able to give you his full attention then. Anyway, he'll be here sometime around noon." He pushed Ethan out the door, peeking back over at Tania one more time. "See ya later, pretty lady." The door closed loudly behind him.

"They are a force to be reckoned with. How in the world are you brave enough to take them on at the same time?" Melissa's voice didn't sound like she was jealous, more like she was in awe of Tania.

Tania laughed. "Together is the only way I'd even consider taking them on."

Melissa frowned. "I don't understand."

"It's simple. Together, they're not a threat."

"A threat!" Melissa stared at Tania as if she thought she'd lost her mind. "Surely you don't think either of them would harm you in some way?"

"No, of course not. From what I can tell, neither of them would even be capable of physically harming a woman." Her ability to sense their innermost emotions had shown her that. She laughed. "There are other ways to harm, though. I like the idea of taking on both of them because that insures that I can keep it casual. There's no danger of anybody getting serious."

Melissa looked at her with sadness in her expression. "I guess that's where we differ. I'd give anything to find someone to be serious about."

Tania stood and headed for the door. "Don't worry, Melissa. Your time's coming. I've always believed in fate. Somebody with your honest nature is bound to have a true ma…um, love out there, just waiting to find them." Vanard had warned her to be careful not to reveal anything about the pack to the humans living in the town. She opened the door and looked back over her shoulder. "Just be patient, sweetie. You'll find him. Listen, I'm gonna head out since you're not gonna unpack until after the sawdust stops flying. I'll check back in a few days and see if you need any help, or maybe even before that if you think you might like to have lunch sometime."

"I'd like that a lot, Tania. It was nice visiting with you this morning. With Michael gone, I don't really have any real friends here."

"Aren't you friends with his sister?"

"Well, yeah, I am, kind of. I mean, I've known her for a long time, but we're not really friends. To be honest, I never really feel very comfortable when I'm around her and her husband. For some reason, and I'm sure it's all my fault, I feel like I'm an outsider whenever they're around." The poor woman looked embarrassed, like she regretted saying anything.

"Believe it or not, I know what you mean." She glanced out the door at the building across the street where she knew Kaugh had set up his own office, and then back at the troubled woman. "Consider me your newest friend, Melissa. I may not be around forever, but friendships should be able to stand the strain of distance." She looked back over at the other building. "Just promise me you'll be careful about meeting any new people. Be sure and ask Michael before getting too involved with any of the locals." Before Melissa could have time to question her about the advice, she waved goodbye and shut the door behind her.

Tania walked slowly down the street toward her car. She'd purposely parked it directly across the street from the front door of Kaugh's new office. She was going to have to find a way to get in there and see what he was up to, and fast, before the members of Remus's pack took matters into their own hands. She cringed when she thought about how furious Remus was going to be when he found out she worked for the National Council. He was bound to come to the conclusion that he wasn't told about her because they didn't trust him. She snorted. For all she knew, he might be right. She hadn't been able to pick up any feelings of mistrust from the members of the Council when they'd briefed her on her assignment, but that didn't necessarily mean anything. They knew about her gift and sometimes took great care to mask their feelings.

Vanard would be the one to suffer the most. The Alpha would be very angry with him for lying to him. Tania was leaving and wouldn't have to suffer Remus's wrath. Unfortunately, Vanard wouldn't have that luxury.

Her instructions from the Council had been clear. She was to track down Kaugh, find out what he was up to, and then eliminate him after she uncovered everyone working with him. She'd been close to nailing him in California, and then discovered his ties to Constantine. It was vital that they get their hands on the research material. It should lead them to everyone involved in their activities, as well as help her to free up any unwilling research subjects they might be holding. The Council wanted no stones left unturned and nothing to come back and haunt them after Kaugh was gone.

They'd not been happy after Remus had taken out Constantine. He'd left too many questions unanswered, and they were all paying for it now. His rage over his mate's capture had driven him to make too many mistakes.

Tania was going to have to find a way to do her job and avoid the pack members that Remus had watching the doctor and his associates. She chuckled. “At least my life’s never boring,” she whispered. Opening her car door, she slid inside and thought about her dinner date with Remus’s brothers. “At least for one night, I’m gonna put myself first.” She smiled, started the car, and drove back up the mountain to her cabin.

* * * *

“Damn, that is one hot little number!” Sean Cross licked his lips as he watched the sexy redhead drive away. He turned from the window to stare at the desk where his boss sat, working on the computer. He’d worked for Vincent Kaugh for the last five years and had no complaints. Kaugh paid well and didn’t care what methods Sean used to accomplish his goals. Well over six feet tall, he had dark hair and eyes, with his most predominant feature being the wicked scarring along the left side of his face. He’d gotten those scars courtesy of one of Kaugh’s test subjects several years ago. “She was in that architect’s office for a long time. You think she’s one of the wolves?”

Kaugh glanced up from the file he was reading and regarded the most dangerous of the three men he’d brought with him to Wyoming. “Yes, I think it’s probable that she’s one of Remus’s wolves. From what I’ve gathered from Constantine’s notes, they rarely have any business dealings with outsiders, although things may have changed since Remus became the Alpha. There’s not a lot said about their outside interests once Remus was mated to Maddie.”

Sean snickered. “Do you think we could bring the visiting redhead in for one of your special injections?”

Kaugh pulled off his reading glasses and frowned up at his employee. “What the hell are you talking about?”

Sean jumped forward, in a protective stance, when the back door to the office opened. He relaxed when he saw it was the other two men Kaugh had brought along on this trip. Marty Dyer barely looked human at over six feet tall, with a bushy dark beard and long, stringy hair. He resembled the shifters in their half-formed wolf states. Their companion, Calvin Ames, was what he would consider a *pretty boy.* Although six feet tall, he had a baby face framed by blond curls and deep blue eyes. He stayed as far away from him as he could get at all times. He nodded to the two men.

"Come on, boss. You give her one of your injections so she can't shift, and then give her to me for a couple of hours." His two co-workers snickered.

"I don't think so," Kaugh said, shaking his head. "My formula is too expensive to produce to be wasting it on your love life. Once we get everything in place, you're welcome to take her any way you want, only without the help of my serum." He turned back to the computer. "Of course, that didn't turn out too well the last time you tried it, if I remember correctly."

"Do tell. What happened?" asked Marty.

Sean looked angry for a moment and then shrugged. "I hadn't been working with Dr. Kaugh for very long when he brought in a new female for his studies." He ran his hand along the scars on his face. "Let's just say she had an objection to my loving personality."

"You tried to fuck one of the female wolves?" Calvin's voice held a note of disgust.

Sean looked at Calvin and wondered what upset him more, the fact she'd been a wolf or that she'd been a woman. "No, I didn't try and fuck one of the female wolves. She was definitely not a wolf when I tried to gain her interest."

"That's enough out of the two of you. We have more important things to discuss." He pointed to the computer screen. "All of Constantine's records are here, and lucky for me, he was one meticulous bastard when it came to records. Everything we'll need to finish my work is here. Well, almost everything."

"What else do you need, boss?" Marty asked.

"All Constantine's years of research were based on two subjects. The first was a fully grown female, already mated, with one child. It was early in his career, and the testing was immature and not terribly informative. Years later, when he was better funded and had completed his education, he acquired a second female subject. This one was extremely young and unmated. He had access to her for years, and his testing was broad and produced a great many results. He lost control of her for a brief period, and then was lucky enough to get his hands on her shortly before he died. During that time, he completed a short battery of tests on her, right after she'd taken a mate."

"I'm lost, boss. How does this help you?" Marty was looking more and more puzzled.

"It's simple, Marty. Constantine's work closely mirrored mine over the years. We both had the same goals, but went about proving our theories in a slightly different way. A few years ago, we compared notes and discovered that if we pooled our information and resources, we could both attain our goals a little faster. With all his research at my disposal, all I need is his test subject to accomplish what I've been working toward for over twenty years."

Sean gasped, drawing the other men's attention. "You mean…?"

"Exactly," Kaugh replied. "I need Maddie Wind River to finish my work."

"Hell, I don't see how that's gonna be possible." Calvin paced up and down the office. "She's the mate of an Alpha, and she's always surrounded by wolves guarding her. Can't you just use another female wolf that's the same age?"

"No, using a different wolf would make the tests invalid. I know it won't be easy, but we'll think of something." Kaugh thought for a moment, and then smiled. "Maybe we need to go about things in a different way. The answer might be to grab someone who's less guarded, less important to the pack, but important enough to Maddie to make her come along willingly."

"You got someone in mind?" asked Marty.

Kaugh grinned. "Yeah, I do. Her brother, Michael, would be perfect. He's been living in Texas up until now and doesn't have any close ties to the pack with the exception of his new mate. According to Constantine's notes, Maddie would do anything for her brother. He's the only family she has left." He looked over at Calvin. "Get busy and find us a secluded house or cabin. I need somewhere we can transfer our equipment and not have to worry about nosy neighbors hearing or seeing anything."

"I'll get right on it," Calvin assured him.

"You two keep an eye on that office across the street. I want to know who comes and goes, and more importantly, I want to know the minute Michael gets back in town."

Sean followed Marty and Calvin out of the office and hoped like hell that Kaugh wasn't biting off more than he could chew this time. Something told him that Remus was someone that he wouldn't want to have as an enemy.

* * * *

Mali gripped the steering wheel tightly as he tried to control the mating heat that threatened to consume him. He'd parked his truck down the street from Michael's office to give himself time to get his wolf under control before facing his mate. *My mate! I can't believe I've finally found her!* Her scent had overwhelmed him the instant he'd touched her hand. If it hadn't been for his Alpha interfering, he would have carried her off right then. *Damn, Remus, how could you do this to me?* The pack had strict rules about mating with non-shifters, and Remus had been quick to remind him of that. Mali couldn't mate with Melissa until she knew about the wolves and was in complete agreement with the mating. Mali snorted. *Like I'm gonna give her a chance to say no.* He didn't really believe there would be a problem. He'd sensed Melissa's arousal in the few minutes they'd spent together. Everything was perfect until Remus dropped his little bombshell. He'd told Mali that he would have to wait until Michael and Ariane returned from their honeymoon to mate. His Alpha thought Michael should be the one to tell her about the wolf shifters because they'd been friends for many years, and she trusted him.

He glanced down the street toward the building he'd agreed to remodel for Michael. *How the hell am I gonna be around her for two whole weeks and not mate her?* His Alpha had ordered him to romance her for the next couple of weeks and give her a chance to get to know him. He even went so far as to say it would make their mating stronger, based more on love than biology. Mali laughed as he got out of his truck. *Tell that to the wolf that has scented its mate.* It was going to be a long two weeks.

He walked quickly down the sidewalk and stopped, took a deep breath to gain control, and then opened the door to Michael's new office. Nothing could have prepared him for the sight of his beautiful mate. She was more than a foot shorter than his own frame, making him feel very masculine and protective. Her short, brown hair framed her face in soft curls, giving her an angelic look, while the sparkles in her dark, brown eyes told of her hidden fire. He let his eyes rake her body from head to toe and had to bite back a groan. She was perfect in every way with her rounded, hourglass figure. A man could bury his face between her large breasts and never want to come up for air. Her hips were wide and full, perfect for gripping tightly when their bodies came together. But it was her ample, rounded ass that had kept him up the past couple of nights. He'd had fantasies of having her on her hands and knees, breasts swinging down freely, while he cradled his hips against those luscious, full cheeks.

"Mali, it's good to see you again." Melissa's words startled him out of his daydreams. "Were you able to get your other job finished?" she asked.

He swallowed hard and then remembered that he'd told Latan to give her the message that he would be late. "It's good to see you, too, Melissa." *God, if you only knew how good it is to be here with you.* He laughed. "Well, I guess that means Latan remembered to give you my message." He took a deep breath and nearly dropped to his knees. His mate was aroused! As he watched, her nipples pushed against the front of her thin, white blouse. *I wonder what color they are.*

"So, did you finish your other job? Will you be able to start on the office soon?"

* * * *

Melissa was beginning to feel a little uncomfortable. Okay, she felt a lot uncomfortable. This was, without a doubt, the most handsome man she'd ever met. He only had to walk through the door and she was flooded with desire. Already, her breasts were throbbing, aching to feel the touch of his mouth, while dampness was gathering between her legs. It would probably have been easier to handle all those feelings if the man in question didn't look at her as if he wanted to eat her alive.

"Yeah, the other job is wrapped up. If you can show me everything you want done today, I can be back early tomorrow to get started." Mali flashed her a big smile, and then his eyes seemed to settle on her breasts.

Feeling a little self-conscious, Melissa crossed her arms across her chest. "Sure, that's no problem. Down here, it's pretty straightforward." She indicated the wall alongside her desk. "Michael wants this turned into built-in shelves. He left me the dimensions he wants you to use." She walked farther toward the back of the large room, with Mali following close behind. "He'd like you to make this into a little alcove. It's going to house the copier and some file cabinets."

Mali stood so close Melissa could feel the heat of his body across her back and legs. She tensed when she felt him lean toward her. She could swear the man was sniffing her! *Oh, my God! What the hell is he doing?* She quickly stepped away and walked back toward the front of the office. "Other than that, he wants a partition dividing the room right about here." She indicated a place that would block off about a third of the floor space. "Michael thought we needed a conference room where we could talk to potential clients in privacy."

"You don't want to divide this out so you both have a private office?" Mali asked.

Melissa smiled. "Actually, we talked about that. Neither one of us liked the idea of being segregated in some private space. We decided that sharing would give it a more family-like atmosphere. We've always been pretty close." She jumped slightly. She could have sworn she heard a low growl coming from the frowning man. "Uh, we've both had bad experiences in the past with closed office doors, and neither of us ever wants to go through that again."

Mali looked downright dangerous. His dark eyes flashed with something that Melissa couldn't define. He looked angry. "Okay, is that it for down here?" he growled out.

Melissa hesitated, feeling just a little confused. She wasn't sure what she'd said or done to change his mood, but he was definitely in a snit about something. She decided it would be better to get it out in the open, whatever it was, than to keep worrying, imagining the worst. "Mali, is something wrong? Did I say or do something wrong?"

The large man looked surprised and then embarrassed. As she watched, a slow flush crept up his neck. His eyes softened, and he took a step closer to her. "No, nothing's wrong." He sighed and ran a hand through his hair. Today it was loose instead of in the tight ponytail he'd worn at the wedding reception. Her fingers itched to replace his as they sank into the silky-looking strands. "I'm sorry if I've given you a bad impression. I guess I should've taken the time to clear my thoughts before coming here today. I think I'm still caught up mentally in the problems from my last job." He smiled at her, making her breath catch in her throat. "It doesn't have anything to do with you, sweet lady. I promise, from this moment on, I'm putting all bad thoughts behind me and concentrating on your job and getting to know you better."

Melissa was shocked and, as usual, couldn't control her mouth when something surprised her. "Why would you want to get to know me better?"

He looked incredulous for just a moment and then grinned wickedly. "Do I need a reason to get to know a beautiful woman better?"

Melissa snorted, now convinced he was pulling her leg. *He must think he'll lose this job if he angers me in some way.* "Okay, big man, try to keep the bull to a minimum if you don't mind. I promise the job's yours no matter what." She smiled, trying to soften her words, but from the look of anger on his face, she didn't think she'd succeeded.

Mali clenched his jaw and narrowed his eyes. "I don't say things I don't mean, Melissa. You need to learn that before we go any further."

Melissa felt her anger get the best of her. "Yeah, right. Then why did you call me a *beautiful woman*? We both know that's just not true." The look on his face made her hesitate. "I'm not saying I'm *Elephant Man* ugly, just that nobody in their right mind would consider me *beautiful*, and you seem to be a reasonably intelligent man."

Mali walked over, grabbed Melissa's shoulders with his large hands, and then eased her forward until her taut nipples pressed against his abdomen. He kept silent until she trembled and looked up into his anger-filled eyes. He locked his gaze with hers for several silent moments as if he searched for something, and then his eyes softened, and the corners of his mouth turned up into a slight grin. "You don't even realize it, do you?"

Melissa swallowed. She couldn't pull her eyes away from his intense stare. "Realize what?"

He smiled and cupped her cheek with one of his hands. "How beautiful you are."

She gasped and, for once, couldn't think of anything flip to say. Somehow, she knew in her heart that Mali wasn't lying to her. "You really think I'm beautiful," she whispered. It was a statement, not a question, because she could already see the answer in his eyes.

"I think you're very beautiful," he answered. Mali started lowering his head slowly toward hers, his focus on her mouth.

Melissa panicked, not yet ready for their relationship to go any further. *Wow, Ariane, when you said the men here would be interested in me, you weren't just feeding me a line.* Deciding she needed to regain a little control, Melissa pulled back and slid away from the hand on her shoulder. She almost laughed at the disbelieving look that came over his face. "Well, that's it for down here. Let me show you what needs to be done upstairs, and then you can get back to whatever else you need to get done today." Melissa knew she was rambling, but couldn't seem to stop. She risked a glance up to gauge his reaction to her wily escape and was somewhat annoyed to see the devilish grin on his face.

Mali chuckled. "All right, sweet lady, we'll do it your way, for now. Why don't you show me what you want done on the upper level?"

Flustered, Melissa quickly headed toward the back of the office and then up the short flight of stairs that led to her future apartment. Mali walked so closely behind her their bodies brushed every couple of steps. *If he doesn't back off, I just might come without his ever laying a hand on me!* Reaching the upper level, she quickly stepped away. "I wanna keep this pretty much one big room." She pointed to various places in the large room. "A little kitchenette should go over there with a sink, a small stove, and a couple of cabinets. I want the bathroom there," she indicated a different corner, "with a tub and shower together."

"You would lose a lot less living space if you had just a shower," Mali pointed out.

Melissa grimaced. "No, I'll give up all the other living space to have a nice tub. There's nothing like soaking in a tub full of warm, fragrant bubbles after a hard day. You wouldn't understand unless you give it a try." She hadn't realized how that would sound until she heard him groan.

"Now that's something I just might take you up on, someday soon," he said softly.

She could feel her face heat up and decided it would be better to ignore his statement for now. "I want a closet put in that corner and, if possible, a line of shelves built across one end for shoes and things." She turned and faced him. "That's it. How long do you think all this will take?"

"Are you in a big hurry?" he asked.

She thought for a moment. "I guess not a real big hurry. I'm living in a little bed-and-breakfast on the outskirts of town. It's nice, but it doesn't feel like home, if you know what I mean. I like being around my own things and not having to worry about coming and going on somebody else's schedule."

Mali looked shocked. "They control when you come and go?"

She laughed, and tried to explain. "No, not exactly. The lady that runs it is elderly. I know she prefers to go to bed early, and she's an early riser. She's not a very trusting person, though. She gave me a key to my room, but the outside door to her home stays locked. If you stay out late, she has to get up to let you back in."

"You stay out late a lot?"

Melissa didn't care for his tone at all. "Of course not. Even if I was a night owl, there's nothing in this little town to keep me out late.

You don't even have a movie theater." She cringed when she heard the anger in her own voice and tried to tone it down. "When I first arrived, right before the wedding, I took a drive one evening just to see some of the countryside. I lost track of time and decided to have dinner in Kenyan." She sighed. "It was about nine o'clock when I got back here, and the sight of that poor little old lady coming to the door in her flannel gown instilled enough guilt in me that I've not been out late again." She smiled at the sound of loud, uninhibited laughter coming from Mali.

"Okay, I can scc your problem. I'll do my best to hurry things along. The bathroom and kitchen will take the longest because it wasn't set up to have any plumbing upstairs. Once we get that done, the rest can be finished in a few days." He gave her a sexy smile and a quick little wink. "It would speed things up if you helped me out."

"Help you, how?" she asked warily.

"Make yourself available to spend some time with me. I'll need quick decisions if there's a problem. You'll need to pick out your colors for painting and any other personal touches you want. It would just make things go faster if you stuck around while I'm doing the job."

Melissa chewed on her bottom lip and thought for a moment. *What harm can it do? It's not like he'll be paying much attention to you. There's all this work to keep him busy.* She almost groaned out loud. *Why the hell are you hesitating? You want to be with him, you know you do.* "Okay, I'll make sure to stick around where I'm here every day you work." She hesitated for a moment. "Do you have any paint chips or samples that I could look through so I can make my decisions, or do I need to find a paint store?"

"I have everything you need, sweet lady, and I'll bring it all with me tonight when I take you to dinner."

"When you what? Take me where?" Melissa's voice had raised a couple of decibels.

"Take you to dinner tonight." He grinned. "I'll pick you up around seven."

She didn't think she liked the predatory look on his face. "Why do we need to go to dinner just to look at paint samples?" She wasn't going to give in too easily. She wanted him to have to work a little before she agreed to go. His interest in her was doing wonders for her ego.

"Everybody knows you need to keep up your strength when you're picking out something as important as the color of paint to go on your walls. Hell, that's something you'll have to look at day in and day out for years to come. It's important to be in the right frame of mind when you're choosing them." He walked over and took her chin in his hand. With firm pressure, he tilted her head until they were almost nose to nose. He hesitated just a moment, and then pressed his lips lightly to hers. "I'll pick you up at the bed-and-breakfast at seven." He looked into her eyes and groaned softly before walking swiftly toward the stairs.

Melissa stared after him in shock, still feeling the pressure of his lips against hers. She started when she heard him grumbling as he walked down the steps, clearly hearing him say, "I'm gonna make Remus pay for this!"

* * * *

Koril paced nervously as he and Brenner waited near the river for Remus to arrive. They'd both received messages from their Alpha ordering them to this meeting, and he was pretty sure he knew what Remus wanted. Unfortunately, his Alpha wasn't going to be happy with the answers they had for him. He looked over at his friend and the other half of Wind River Pack's security team. "He's gonna be pissed."

"I know," Brenner sighed, "but it can't be helped. He only gave us two days to gather information, and it wasn't enough time. These people are organized and, apparently, well funded. I keep hitting walls no matter which direction I search in. Remus is just gonna have to understand that we need more time."

"Fine," Koril said dryly. "I'll just let you tell him."

"The hell I will," he barked. "You're the leader of this team. You tell him."

"Just when did I become leader?" Koril asked.

Brenner frowned. "What time this morning did you get the message for us to meet here?"

"Around ten o'clock, why?"

"Then you became leader of this team around ten o'clock."

"You're such an asshole. If you think—"

"Here he comes," Brenner interrupted.

They watched as Remus came running along the riverbank in his wolf form. When he reached the two men, he shifted, seeming unconcerned with his state of undress. Remus gave them both a hard glare. "Gentlemen, report. What have you learned?"

"Not much, Remus," Koril replied. "Kaugh hasn't left his Main Street office since yesterday. He hasn't made any phone calls, but did have internet service installed. I've got people tracing any online activity, but so far, there hasn't been anything other than e-mails. Earlier today, Calvin Ames left the office and drove to Kenyan. We found out that Kaugh and all three men with him have hotel rooms there." Koril ran a hand through his short hair. "While Ames was there, he stopped in to see a realtor." He consulted his notes. "Her name's Alice Mitchell. We don't know what business he had with her, yet. I had their hotel rooms searched but came up empty-handed."

"What about the other two men? What have they been up to?" Remus asked.

"We're watching the place day and night, and we're fully prepared with enough manpower to follow anyone who leaves the premises," Brenner added. "It's weird, Remus. One of the men with Kaugh, Sean Cross, has spent most of his time staring out the window toward Michael's office. My guy said that our new teacher visited Michael's assistant this morning and Sean was practically drooling on the windowpanes watching her."

"Why was Tania visiting Melissa? I didn't even know they knew each other. Did she make any contact with Kaugh or any of his men?" Remus asked.

"No, she didn't have any actual contact," Brenner said, "but she spent an unusual amount of time standing next to her car staring at Kaugh's office."

Remus growled and paced back and forth in front of the men. "Something's not right with her. I can feel it, but I can't quite put my finger on what it is that's off. Keep an eye on her until we learn more." He looked at Brenner. "Is that it?"

"We ran checks on Kaugh's three associates. Dyer and Ames have nothing remarkable in their backgrounds. Neither of them has ever been arrested, and they don't have any family to speak of. Sean Cross is another matter entirely. He's bad news, Remus. He has been Kaugh's muscle for the last five years, and the man enjoys his work. He's a sadist through and through. The police picked him up numerous times, but no charges were ever filed against him. He bragged to more than one individual that he got the scars on his face from an intimate encounter with one of Kaugh's test subjects."

"Damn, now we have to worry about our females," Remus bellowed. "You said he was drooling over Tania?"

"Yeah, that's what my man said," Brenner confirmed.

Remus stopped pacing. "Double the guards on Cross, and put men on every road leading into pack territory. I want to know their movements twenty-four hours a day. Find out who their outside contacts are. If he needed internet access, he's in contact with someone." Remus was quiet for a moment. "Do a complete background check on our new teacher. Her name's Kitania, with no pack affiliation. She grew up in one of the National Council's homes.

I don't trust her. It seems a little too coincidental that she showed up at the same time as Kaugh and only wanting a temporary position."

Brenner looked surprised by the information. "I'll get right on it, Remus."

"What the hell!" Koril's cry caused both men to follow his gaze. A small black cat had just come sauntering through the trees and was slowly approaching the three men.

Remus laughed. "Easy, guys, it's the teacher's pet, if I'm not mistaken. Vanard requested that we not let anything happen to the little guy, since apparently she's quite fond of him."

Koril grimaced. "I hate cats! The damn thing tried to take Taynor's arm off the other day." He growled when Brenner laughed. "You won't think it's so amusing if he gets his claws into you." He stared at the small cat and felt the hairs on the back of his neck stand up. "The only good cat is a dead cat." Koril stomped his foot toward the tiny animal and growled loudly in an attempt to scare him off. He was shocked when, instead of running away, the cat walked right up to him, hissing. Before he had a chance to back away, a small, furry paw swiped toward his leg, the razor sharp claws slicing through his jeans and lodging themselves into the calf of his leg.

Koril yelped and jumped back, swearing as Remus and Brenner broke out into laughter. The black ball of fur continued to hiss, every hair on its back standing on end. Koril growled again. "You better watch it, cat. I'll knock your furry ass out and pull your damn claws out one at a time!"

Brenner was laughing so hard there were tears in his eyes. "Gee, Koril, do you think you scared it?"

Before he could answer, Koril watched as the cat calmly sat down in front of him. With a look of utter disdain on its face, the tiny beast began licking its paws clean. After just a few moments, it got to its feet and meandered off into the woods, seemingly unconcerned about anything.

Remus cleared his throat. “Okay, guys. I think that’s enough entertainment for one day. Get moving on those extra guards right away, and let me know as soon as you get anything on our new teacher.” He gave Brenner a sharp look. “Keep this quiet, Brenner. Vanard seems to be very fond of Tania, and he won’t be very happy if he finds out we’re investigating her.” Without another word, he shifted into his large black wolf and ran off toward the Alpha’s home.

Brenner snickered, watching Koril rub his leg. “So, Koril, did you—”

“Not one word, asshole,” Koril interrupted. “Let’s go.” He stalked off toward the Pack House, not even bothering to look and see if Brenner was following.

* * * *

“Hey, baby, what’s for dinner?” Remus walked up behind his mate and wrapped his arms tightly around her. Gently, he palmed the small mound that held their future pup while he nuzzled his lips against the side of her neck.

“Hmmm, that feels wonderful,” Maddie whispered. For a moment, she stood silently in his embrace, and then began to moan softly when he moved his hands up to cup her full breasts.

“I swear, Maddie, these babies get bigger every day. At this rate, I’m gonna be awfully jealous of our pup.”

Maddie giggled. “Don’t worry, wolf man. They’ll always be available to Daddy.”

Remus smiled and slid his hands up under Maddie’s blouse to open the front fastening of her bra. Lightly, he ran his fingertips over her swollen nipples and was pleased when she growled and pushed closer to his fingers. He’d just begun to pluck the sensitive nubs when there was a knock on the back door right before it opened, admitting his two brothers. Maddie squealed, the high pitch making him want to cover his ears, and pushed his wandering hands out from under her shirt. He stayed behind her, shielding her from his brothers' sight, while she refastened her bra.

"Oh, God, we're sorry, Maddie." Latan sounded embarrassed.

"Don't you knock?" Remus asked.

"We did knock. You just didn't hear us," Ethan argued.

"Just a little, quick tip, guys," Maddie growled. "When you knock at someone's door, the correct procedure is to wait until they say come in or they actually come and open the door."

"Wow," Ethan smirked. "Is that how it's done? Who would have thought? But here's a tip for you guys. Most people don't take their clothes off in the kitchen. Don't you guys ever use the bedroom for anything?"

"Sure," Maddie said saucily. "We sleep there every night." She walked over and hugged Ethan. "Don't knock the kitchen until you try it, little brother." She smiled and gave Latan an identical hug. "So what brings you guys here today? I miss seeing you every morning at the breakfast table."

Latan hugged her a little tighter. "We miss you, too, little mama wolf." He placed his hand on her growing mound. "How's our little niece or nephew doing?"

Remus spoke up before Maddie could answer. "Your future nephew is doing just fine."

Ethan laughed. "What makes you so sure it's a boy?"

Remus growled. "Everyone knows that an Alpha's firstborn is always male since he'll be in line to take over for me." He hadn't even considered the possibility of his firstborn not being a son.

Maddie snorted. "So, just maybe your precious pack will have to accept that their next Alpha will be female."

"Bite your tongue, woman," Remus teased.

She took a step back and looked at Ethan and Latan. "Wow, where're you headed all dressed up?"

Latan smiled. "We're taking the new teacher out to dinner tonight."

“Lucky girl,” Maddie replied with a wicked smile.

Remus didn’t like the idea of his brothers getting too involved with the young woman, at least until they knew more about her. But he knew they wouldn’t back off without a good reason. “Maddie, could you give us a minute alone? I need to have a private talk with my brothers.” He winced at the angry feelings that raced through their mating bond. Whenever wolves mate, their spirits blend together, allowing them to read each other’s thoughts and to speak to each other’s minds. He’d blocked his own thoughts from her, not wanting her to know how much of a threat Kaugh was, and she was furious. She knew he was hiding something.

“Fine.” Maddie gritted her teeth. “Then you and I are due for a little talk.” She stomped out of the kitchen without even saying goodbye to Ethan and Latan.

“Geez, Remus, what the hell is so important that you had to go and upset your pregnant mate?” Latan asked.

Chapter 2

"Sit down," Remus ordered, using his no-nonsense Alpha voice. Both of his brothers immediately took seats at the kitchen table. For the next few minutes, Remus told them everything that Koril and Brenner had learned about Kaugh and his associates. When he repeated what Brenner said about the scars on Sean Cross's face, both men growled loudly and leapt to their feet.

"What the hell are we waiting for, Remus?" Latan cried. "Why don't we just take these assholes out before they have a chance to do anything to any of our women?"

"Take your seats, now!" All wolves were protective of their females, and his brothers were no different. They weren't going to take the news about the new teacher very well. "There's more, and I need you to stay calm." When they both settled down, he joined them at the table. "This morning, Tania was observed spending time on Main Street gazing over at Kaugh's office."

"What are you trying to say?" Ethan asked with a deadly, flat voice.

"I'm not trying to say anything. I'm just giving you facts. After she left Michael's place, she stood beside her car and watched the front of Kaugh's office. She didn't make any personal contact, but it seemed a little strange to me that she would pick that office on the street to just watch. Hell, I don't even know why she was at Michael's. I wasn't aware that she even knew him, or Melissa."

"When we stopped by to give Melissa a message, Tania was there visiting with her." Latan spoke quietly. "The women seemed very friendly. She was still there when we left."

Remus sighed. "Look, guys, I'm not trying to upset you or run your life. I just think we need to show a little caution here. It seems pretty strange that she showed up right when Kaugh took up residence and that she has shown interest in his whereabouts. Were either of you aware she only asked for the position here on a temporary basis?" He could tell by the shocked looks on their faces this was the first they had heard this bit of information.

"Are you sure?" Ethan asked.

"Absolutely, she's only here for one, maybe two semesters."

"What do you want us to do, Remus?" Latan stared at his Alpha brother with sadness in his eyes.

"Just be extra careful, guys. Keep your eyes and ears open, and stay aware that things might not be as they seem. She may be a perfectly innocent party in all this, and if so, she needs our protection, too. Brenner said that Cross was showing a little too much interest in her when she was standing on the street."

"What?" Ethan bellowed.

"He watched her from Kaugh's office window. To quote Brenner, the man was drooling on the glass." Remus couldn't keep the disgust out of his voice. He watched his baby brothers for just a moment. "I need you with me on this, guys. She's a stranger to us. We don't really know anything about her yet. For all I know, she could be a plant put here by Kaugh. I just want you to be on your guard when you're around her. I'm trying to keep everyone in the pack safe, and most important, I'm trying to keep my mate and pup safe. I can't do it without you."

Ethan stood and walked over to Remus. He pulled him to his feet and gave him a bone-crushing hug. "We're with you, bro. We'll watch your back and protect your mate and pup with our lives if necessary."

Latan came up on Remus's other side and gripped his shoulders. "That goes for me, too, Remus."

"Thanks, guys. Your support means the world to me." He smiled. "Now, get the hell out of here. Go take your lady friend to dinner. I've got an angry mate that's just waiting to kick my ass."

His brothers were still laughing as they left through the back door.

* * * *

Maddie paced back and forth in their bedroom, muttering to herself. "He just thinks he can keep secrets from me." She snorted. "I'll show him secrets. I'll knock a secret out of him!" Her hand caressed the growing mound of her child. "I'm gonna practice blocking my thoughts, little one. Let's see how Daddy likes being shut out." She jumped when the door opened and then relaxed when Remus walked in.

"I'm pleased to find you waiting for me in here." He gave her a wicked grin and then turned and locked their bedroom door.

"Just what do you think you're doing?" she asked, with her hands on her hips.

Remus turned and held her gaze as he began to unbutton his shirt. "What does it look like?"

She swallowed hard, her hands gripping together tightly under her breasts. "It looks like you're gonna try and get out of telling me what all that was about in the kitchen."

"Baby, would I do that?" He smirked as he dropped his shirt on the floor and began stalking toward his mate.

Maddie bit her lip to keep from smiling. She could feel her hands tremble with the need to touch the hard, muscled chest he'd uncovered. *He always does this! He thinks he can make me forget he's hiding something.* She took a small step back. "You would do anything you could to distract me from asking questions that you don't want to answer, and we both know it." She took another step back. "Remus, I want to know what's going on, and I want to know right now!"

"Later," he whispered as he grabbed her shoulders and pulled her against his warm body. He bent his head and captured her lips with his before she could make any further protests.

Maddie felt a dampness trace along her bottom lip, tempting her to let it inside. It was a temptation she couldn't refuse. Her lips parted, and she savored the flavor of her mate. Unable to resist, she sucked gently on his invading tongue as her arms crept up, her hands linking behind his neck. After a few moments, Remus pulled from their kiss and buried his face in her hair. He nibbled his way down her neck while his hands glided down her back to rest on the swell of her butt. She gasped when he licked over her mating mark, the tingles traveling straight to the area between her thighs.

Remus gripped the bottom of her sweatshirt and pulled up steadily until she released her hold on his neck and raised her arms. It soon joined his shirt on the bedroom floor. He grasped the front fastener of her bra, growling impatiently when it proved to be difficult to open. Losing patience, he gripped the delicate material in his strong hands and ripped it open, allowing the swollen globes to tumble free. His warm hands cupped her breasts, squeezing gently, before thumbs began to rub back and forth across her aching nipples. A surprised look came over Remus's face when Maddie flinched. "Did I hurt you, baby?"

It surprised Maddie to feel herself blush. "No, not really. They're just a little tender these days." She smiled and then pressed her lips to his. "Tehran says it's perfectly normal. It's my body's way of preparing for me to nurse our baby." Tehran had been the pack's doctor for over twenty years.

"I'm sorry, baby, let me make it better," Remus crooned, right before he latched on to one of her swollen nipples and began to suckle. Maddie's back arched as he fueled the desire in her already aroused body. He raised his head and gazed into her eyes right before he lifted her and laid her on the bed.

Maddie blushed even more when she felt her jeans and panties being removed, knowing she couldn't hide the dampness between her thighs. Remus used his knee to shove her legs apart and then settled his hips in the space, bracing his weight on his arms.

* * * *

Remus looked down at his beautiful woman and wondered for the hundredth time what he'd done to deserve such a perfect life mate. Aroused, she was even more breathtaking. Her silky, smooth skin had a healthy, pink glow, with just a smattering of tiny brown freckles across her shoulders. His mother would have called them *angel's kisses*. Her breasts were full and rounded, tipped with nipples the color of dark red roses. As he watched, they hardened even more, almost seeming to reach up toward him, begging for attention.

He let his eyes wander down her length to the fine pelt of dark curls between her legs. His fingers sifted through the silky strands before stroking through her sleek, wet lips. He smiled when she groaned, and her legs came up to wrap around his hips. His thumb searched toward the top of her slit for the small bundle of nerves hidden there, and then began to make small circles to coax the little bud out of hiding.

Remus pushed back, causing Maddie's legs to fall back to the bed, and lowered his face to her feminine core. He inhaled the scent of her arousal deep into his lungs before allowing his tongue to trace from her clit down to her anus and back. Her sweet flavor burst inside his mouth. He draped her legs across his shoulders and then licked over her puffy lips before homing in on her clit. While he teased the tiny nub, his hand slipped into the crevice between the cheeks of her ass. As he continued to lick and suck her clit, his fingers brushed lightly over the delicate sphincter, causing her to gasp and the muscles of her pussy to clench. He pressed lightly against the puckered opening while nibbling on her sensitive skin. When Maddie cried out with her release, Remus swirled his tongue through her folds right up into her channel. Her heels dug into his back, while her fingers tangled in his hair.

He quickly rose up, aligning his throbbing cock with the entrance to her moist pussy. He gave a growl of satisfaction when he felt her dainty hand grip his hard shaft. She gently squeezed the base before guiding him inside her fiery warmth. Her arms wrapped around his neck, and she pressed her breasts against his chest as he began to pound vigorously toward his own pleasure. He was so aroused he knew it wouldn't take long. Grabbing her hips, he lifted to change the angle of his thrusts and began sliding against her clit with each downward stroke. In less than a minute, Maddie was crying out with a second release while Remus roared through his own climax.

Desperately trying to catch his breath, Remus slid from his mate, collapsed beside her on the bed, and pulled her firmly into his arms. Bending, he devoured her mouth with a kiss while he ran a hand tenderly over their growing child. "Are you okay?" he whispered. "We didn't hurt him, did we?"

Maddie giggled breathlessly. "No, we didn't hurt him." She grinned. "We didn't hurt her, either."

Remus scowled. "Woman, I've told you that it's part of our culture that says the Alpha always has a son born first. You can't buck tradition."

Maddie snorted. "Give me a break, Remus. I've bucked tradition so many times since we met, it's not funny. You're gonna have to accept that this baby just might be a girl."

"What does Tehran say?"

"Nothing, because I won't let him," Maddie replied.

"Huh?"

Maddie sighed. "I told him I don't want to know what the baby is before it's born, even if he knows for sure." She gave Remus a pleading look. "I've always dreamed of finding out the sex of my baby in the delivery room. I want the doctor to be able to look up and say, 'it's a girl', and me be surprised."

"All right, baby, have it your way. Just promise me you won't be disappointed when he says, 'it's a boy!'"

"I promise, just don't get your hopes up, either." She gave him a stern look. "Okay, you've delayed long enough. Now what was going on earlier with Latan and Ethan?"

Remus bent forward and licked her chin and then glanced down at her breasts. "Damn, baby, you've got whisker burns. I'm sorry. What can I do to make it better?" he said, trying to stall.

"Remus," Maddie growled.

He groaned softly. There was no way he was going to get out of telling her something. If he kept quiet, it would upset her, and she didn't need that in her condition. Maybe it would be better if she did know about the new threat. At least then he could count on her to be more careful, and maybe she would be willing to follow his orders without question. He nearly choked on his own thoughts. *My Maddie, following instructions without questioning them? That is so not going to happen.* Resigned to telling her everything, he laid his hand across their child in a comforting gesture. "I needed to talk to Latan and Ethan about—" His words cut off as a strange feeling shot up his arm.

"Oh, my God, Remus, did you feel that?" Maddie asked. Her hand joined his on the bump that signified her pregnancy.

"Was that what I think it was?" Remus asked in wonderment.

Maddie's eyes filled with tears. "The baby moved. It actually moved."

They stayed quiet, with their hands on Maddie's abdomen, for several minutes. "Do you think he's gonna move again?" Remus whispered. As if in answer to his question, Remus felt a soft, rolling quiver underneath his palm. From the look in Maddie's eyes, she felt the same thing. Suddenly, a horrifying thought froze Remus in place. "Maddie, are you all right? What have I done?"

"I'm fine, Remus," she said with a puzzled look. "It's just the baby moving around. Honey, that's not gonna hurt me."

"You should've warned me." Intellectually, Remus knew that the baby stayed well protected in his mother's womb, but visions of his dick pumping in and out toward his son, terrorizing him, while his weight pushed Maddie into the mattress, filled him with fear. "We could have squished him," he cried.

Maddie laid her head back on the pillow and laughed. "Oh, Remus, you're too much." She wrapped her arms around him and pulled him close.

Remus groaned and shook his head sadly. He just knew he wasn't going to be able to make love to his mate until after she gave birth. At least he could be happy that, in her excitement over the baby, Maddie appeared to have forgotten about him keeping secrets from her.

* * * *

Tania finished combing her hair and at the last minute decided to pull it back into a ponytail. She frowned as she stared at her reflection in the mirror. She'd always hated the color of her hair, not that it wasn't pretty, but it made it difficult for her to blend in with other people. There were times when it paid to be invisible in a crowd. She laughed as she tied the ribbon around the reddish-brown strands. Despite the fact it made her easily recognizable, she couldn't bring herself to cut, or color, it. Her bright green eyes gazed from the mirror. *Guess that makes me one extremely vain woman!* She turned toward the cabin door when she heard a faint knock and then turned back to her reflection. "Okay, Tania, this is it. Tonight's just for you. It's time to have a little fun and relieve a little stress with the good-time brothers." She laughed and then went to greet her dinner dates.

Tania threw open the door and had to bite her lip to keep from groaning out loud. Every time she saw these men, she had an overwhelming urge to strip them naked and lick them from head to toe. Both of them stood nearly six and a half feet tall, with brown hair and eyes. Broad shoulders and powerfully built chests topped their trim waists and curved butts. Thick, muscular legs were showcased in denim jeans so tight she could clearly see the outline of their erections. Tania swallowed hard and raised her eyes to meet the amusement in theirs. “Hey, guys, you’re right on time.” The eyes were the main difference between the two brothers. Latan had a serious, no-nonsense look in his, while Ethan’s appeared to be full of mischief. “Would you like to come in for a minute?” she asked as she stepped back to allow them to enter.

“Thanks,” Ethan replied.

“You look beautiful,” Latan added as both brothers walked into the small cabin.

Tania smiled and then frowned when she began to pick up strange feelings coming from them. “Uh, thanks, guys.” She pointed to the small couch that sat in front of the fireplace. “Please, have a seat. Can I get you something to drink?”

Ethan grinned at her. “No thanks, we’re fine.” He glanced around the room, and then at Latan, before returning his gaze to Tania. “Hey, where’s your cat?”

“Why would you want to know where my cat is?” Tania asked, puzzled and beginning to feel a little uncomfortable.

Ethan laughed, looking a little embarrassed. “I saw him in the window the day we brought you the wedding cake.” He shrugged. “I just thought he was cute, and I really like cats.”

She glanced over at Latan. “What about you? Do you like cats?”

Latan stared over at his brother, and then ran his eyes around the room. “Yeah, sure, I like cats.”

Tania cringed as she sensed the first outright lie of the evening. She almost choked when she felt the absolute loathing coming from Latan. There was no doubt in her mind. The man couldn’t stand cats! She briefly wondered what it would take to change his mind. “Well, my cat’s not here right now. She’s out playing in the woods.”

"She? Your cat's a girl?" Ethan asked.

"Don't you realize it's not safe for her to be outside around all these wolves?" Latan's voice clearly said he didn't really care if something happened to her beloved pet. As she watched, he walked over to her desk and raked his eyes over her exposed papers before sitting down in front of the computer.

"Yes, Kit's a girl, and she's perfectly capable of taking care of herself when she's outside. We've lived around wolves all our lives." Tania crossed to her desk and shut off her monitor. Glaring at Latan, she picked up her paperwork and shoved it in the desk drawer. "Sorry, this is a little personal. It's just some letters I'm writing to friends back in California."

"California, huh? Is that where your family is? Is that where you grew up?" Latan's face and tone of voice made his questions seem innocent, but there was something in the feelings he projected that she didn't like.

"Latan!" Ethan cried.

Understanding hit Tania, causing a pain to form around her heart. *They don't trust me now. I can sense a little bit of desire, but it's nearly overshadowed by their doubt. What the hell happened since this morning to make them feel this way?* Tania sighed, not really understanding why she felt hurt by the thought of them not trusting her. All of her relationships ended this way because she kept so many secrets, but she'd never had it happen so fast. Feeling resigned to a brief, unpleasant evening, she sent Ethan a smile she didn't feel. "You guys ready to go? I'm starving."

She didn't wait for their answer before she grabbed her purse and headed for the door. Her sigh of relief, when they got up to follow, seemed loud in the small room. *Get over it, Tania. It just wasn't meant to be. We'll just get through this dinner as quickly as possible, and then I can say goodbye. I can concentrate on getting this job done quickly, and then I'm out of here, and I won't ever have to lay eyes on them again.* For some unknown reason, the thoughts running through her mind failed to bring comfort.

* * * *

Mali felt Melissa tremble when he put his hand on her waist to guide her through the restaurant to one of the empty booths for dinner. His wolf prowled close to the surface, wanting to claim their mate right then and there. He struggled to keep the beast under control. He smiled and took her hand as shc scooted into the booth, and then watched her eyes widen when he slid in behind her, forcing her to the back corner.

"Wouldn't you be more comfortable sitting across from me? You would have plenty of room to stretch out then." Melissa tugged on her hand, looking uncomfortable, as a dull, red flush crept up her neck.

Mali had started to change seats to ease her embarrassment when he caught a whiff of arousal coming from his mate. His cock hardened painfully against the zipper of his jeans. He tightened his hold on her hand and leaned closer so he could gaze into her eyes. "No, it'll be better this way. This place gets pretty noisy during dinner, and this will make it easier to talk and look over those paint samples I brought with me."

Confusion clouded her eyes. "But you left them in the car."

He chuckled. "That insured us a pleasant dinner and time to get to know one another. I'll go get them when it's time for dessert."

"Why would you want to get to know me better?" she asked, still tugging lightly at her hand.

Mali frowned, not liking the uncertainty he heard in her voice. "Why wouldn't I, Melissa? You're beautiful, single, and fun to be around." Following her incredulous look, he moved closer and brought her hand to his lips, where he placed a gentle kiss on her fingers. "Woman, believe it or not, when I'm with you, I feel like sunshine is filling my soul. You make me want things I never thought

I could have. I wanna be close to you. I wanna know everything there is to know about you." He kissed her hand again. "Do you feel anything for me, anything at all?" He watched as her eyes sparkled and felt her fingers tighten against his own.

"Well, as I live and breathe, it's my good friend, Mali. Where've you been hiding yourself, honey? I haven't seen you around for a while."

Mali looked up at the young woman who'd been a waitress at the diner for the past few years and tried to control the anger he felt at her interruption. "I've been around, just don't eat out much."

She looked Melissa up and down with a smirk on her face. "Who's your friend?"

He felt Melissa tense and then watched as she shrank farther back into the corner of the booth before lowering her eyes to the table. A small growl escaped before he could contain it, causing Melissa to raise her eyes to his. She looked shocked. Mali threw an arm around her shoulders and pulled her tight against his body before he looked up at the annoying waitress. He didn't like the way she was looking at Melissa, and nobody was going to get away with making his mate feel uncomfortable. "This is Melissa Rogers, a very special friend of mine." To make his meaning clear, Mali tightened his arm and leaned over to place a light kiss on her lips. He smiled when he heard the waitress gasp. "Melissa, this is Linda." He glanced up at the young woman. "I'm sorry, but I don't know your last name." He wanted to make sure Melissa understood he only knew this woman in passing, and not very well.

"Mavers, Linda Mavers is my name," she said through gritted teeth.

"Pleased to meet you, Ms. Mavers," Melissa said politely.

Linda dropped two menus in front of Mali. "I'll be back in a minute to get your orders." Shaking her head, she quickly walked away.

"Okay, that was fun." Melissa looked up at Mali. "Not!"

Pleased to see her more relaxed, with her sense of humor restored, Mali ran his hand up and down her arm. “Are you okay, Sunshine?”

Melissa snorted. “Sunshine, right! Yeah, I’m just a ray of sunshine destined to bring happiness to everybody. I sure managed to brighten her day. What is she, your past coming back to bite you in the butt?”

Mali grimaced. “I swear, Sunshine, I’ve never dated her. Hell, I’ve never even seen her outside this diner.”

She gave him a shrewd look. “She tried to get you outside this diner, didn’t she?”

He could feel his ears beginning to burn. This evening wasn’t going anything like he’d planned. “Not just me. She pretty much goes after everybody.”

“Huh, I must not be everybody, or maybe I’m losing my touch. She didn’t invite me outside for a little rendezvous.”

Mali threw back his head and laughed. “I don’t think you have the right equipment to interest her, Sunshine.” His hand came up to caress her cheek. “I swear I never took her up on her invitations.”

Melissa grinned. “So, what’s good in this fine eating establishment?”

Unable to stop himself, Mali leaned forward and covered her lips with his own. His arm tightened around her when she tried to pull away, a small growl coming up from his chest. He let his tongue trace across her bottom lip before he took it between his teeth and nipped. When she opened her mouth to protest, he slipped inside, taking her taste and scent inside him. He felt like shouting his pleasure when he felt her tongue glide into his mouth. His hand was just beginning to slide toward her breast when he heard the clearing of a throat. He raised his head and glanced over his shoulder.

“Hey, guys, fancy seeing you here,” Ethan teased.

Mali glanced back down at Melissa and sighed. If the poor woman got any redder, she might just explode. “Did you want something, Ethan, or were just trying to ruin our evening?” He didn’t care if he sounded rude.

Ethan laughed. "We're just here to ruin your evening, Mali." He smiled at Melissa. "I'm sorry if we ruined yours as well, pretty lady."

"That's okay, Ethan," she replied. "Just keep in mind that payback can be a real bitch." Everyone laughed.

"Come on, guys, let's give them some privacy." Tania looked over at Melissa. "Sorry!"

"No problem, have a nice evening," Melissa responded. She watched as her three new friends walked over to a table and sat down, then turned her attention back to Mali.

He leaned down close and whispered. "Now, where were we?" He was just about to join their lips when the grating sound of the waitress's voice abraded his ears.

"Have you decided what you want yet?"

Mali growled, and Melissa giggled. He smiled and gazed into her fiery eyes. "Yeah, I know exactly what I want." He watched as color flooded her cheeks, and then turned to the impatient woman who'd interrupted them. "Just bring us both the special, and make it quick." He shook his head as she sauntered off. It was going to be a long, long evening.

* * * *

Tania sighed as Latan held her chair for her to sit. She'd been pleased to see Melissa having a romantic moment with a handsome man. The unhappiness had rolled off her in waves during the time they'd spent together. It made her happy to think that somebody's love life was working out, since her own definitely left a lot to be desired.

Ethan smiled at her. "We know you're from California, Tania. Are you from a large city or a small town?"

She laughed. "You couldn't get much smaller than my hometown. I'm from a little place called Sudden Falls."

"Never heard of it. What's it close to?" asked Latan.

Tania felt uncomfortable and wondered if this was the beginning of an interrogation. The feelings pouring off the two men proved they didn't trust her. "It's about as far south as you can get without speaking Spanish," she joked. She glanced down at her hands. "I would've thought that Alpha Remus would tell you that I grew up in one of the National Council's homes for orphans." She peeked at them through heavy lashes to gauge their reaction and knew immediately that Remus hadn't said anything to them.

"God, I'm so sorry, Tania. We'd no idea you had no family." Ethan couldn't hide the pity in his voice.

"Don't feel sorry for me," she replied sharply. "I don't need or want anyone's sympathy. My life hasn't been so bad, and it's just the way I want it now." She wondered if her statement sounded as false as it felt, but she couldn't stand it when people felt sorry for her.

Latan reached over and covered her hand with his. "It's not sympathy. It's sadness. We've always had our family and couldn't imagine life without each other to lean on."

Before Tania could respond, a glass of water slammed down on the table in front of her, causing her to jump.

"Hello, Linda," Ethan said before glancing over at Latan. "It's nice to see you again. How've you been?"

The young woman deposited a glass of water in front of each of the men and then began to hand out the menus. "I'm surprised you remember my name, considering how long it has been since you called me." She threw the menu down in front of Tania, hitting the small glass of water and knocking it toward her lap. Quick reflexes, and a desire not to ruin her new skirt, inspired her to propel backwards with her chair, allowing the water to run off in the floor.

"Oh, gee, I'm so sorry," the waitress said, sounding almost gleeful.

"Linda, that'll be quite enough," Latan growled. The tone of his voice should have stopped her cold, but Linda just smirked and ambled off toward the kitchen.

Both men grabbed napkins from the table dispenser and began mopping up the spilled water. They glanced at each other a couple of times, a grim look on their faces.

Tania scooted her chair back up to the table and sighed. She thought for a minute in silence and then shook her head and laughed. Both brothers looked at her a little strangely. She grinned at them. “Friend of yours?” she asked. She watched in amusement as both men flushed a slight rose color.

“Friend might be a strong word,” Latan responded.

“Look, Tania, we’re sorry for this.” Ethan gave Latan a look she couldn’t decipher. “I guess we should’ve considered what her reaction would be if we came in here with a woman, especially one she didn’t know.”

“It’s not like we had a relationship with her or anything serious,” Latan added. “We’ve spent some time with her, but we always made it clear up front that it was just fooling around, nothing serious.” He looked at Tania like he wanted her forgiveness.

“It’s okay, guys, I understand.” Tania wondered if the human waitress knew her former lovers were wolves. *Great, I’m out with the local playboy heartbreakers. It doesn’t matter anyway. I already know this will be the only date the three of us will ever have together.* She didn’t understand why that thought hurt so much. She felt a connection to these two wolves she couldn’t explain.

“Ethan and I are gonna have steak and baked potatoes. If that’s all right with you, I’ll go up and put in our order myself so she doesn’t have to come back to the table.” Latan smiled and looked at her expectantly.

She grinned back and handed him her menu. ‘Sure, steak is great. I like mine as rare as they’ll serve it, with butter and sour cream on my potato. Oh, and can I get a glass of iced tea?”

“No problem, I’ll be right back.” He winked and headed for the kitchen.

Tania smiled at Ethan. "Okay, you've asked me about my family and where I came from. Tell me about your family."

He laughed. "I'm not sure that's fair, considering you haven't really told us anything, but I'm willing to go first as long as you know I'm gonna keep trying to find out more about you."

She tried not to let his words make her nervous. He couldn't make her tell him anything, and he couldn't smell her deceit. One of the perks of her unusual heritage was the ability to mask her scent at all times. Most other shifters couldn't even tell her breed.

"You've met what's lcft of our family. There are only the three of us, with Remus being the oldest, me in the middle, and Latan the baby."

She laughed. "He's one big baby."

"You have no idea," he exclaimed. "Our mom died when I was six years old. She was shot by poachers in her wolf form."

"Oh, my God! How awful for you. That almost never happens anymore, with the more stringent game laws." She could feel the pain radiating from him as he thought about his mother, and she had an overwhelming urge to comfort him.

"Truthfully, I was so young I don't remember her very well. It was always just my dad and the three of us."

"He never took another mate?" she asked.

"No, I don't think he ever even considered it. He was hopelessly in love with her. His life was spent raising us and teaching us the family business."

"Construction, right?"

"Yeah, we own Wolf Construction. He made sure that all three of us were trained to handle some part of the company."

"Where is he now?" she asked. For a moment, she thought she could see tears gathering in the corners of his eyes.

"He died a couple of years ago. He pushed himself until Latan finished business school and then helped him learn the management of the company for two years. When we finally all had productive positions in the company, he went to bed one night and died in his sleep. We all believe he died of loneliness, heartsick over losing his own true mate. He just hung on until he knew we would be okay."

Latan returned, carrying a tray with three drinks. He carefully set them down and then discarded the tray onto a nearby empty table. He glanced over at Tania then back over to Ethan. "What the hell did you do, Ethan? I only left for ten minutes, and you've managed to put tears in her eyes!" Both Ethan and Tania laughed. "So," Latan continued, "you seem reluctant to answer questions about where you're from, so how about telling us where you went to college. We know you've got a teaching degree, so there must be some college stories in there somewhere." He smiled at her engagingly.

Tania shook her head, unable to resist the charm of the two brothers. She took a deep breath and then stopped cold. She was clearly sensing their arousal now, much stronger than their distrust. *It doesn't matter. I can still tell they don't really trust me. It's not like our relationship can go anywhere. They're both going to want to mate eventually, and I can't be anybody's mate.* With regrets, she proceeded to put them at ease by telling them amusing stories about her years at UCLA.

* * * *

Mali parked his truck in front of the Takoda Bed & Breakfast, cut off the engine, and then turned to face the beautiful woman sitting beside him. He could smell equal amounts of arousal and apprehension coming from her, and it was driving him crazy. His cock strained against his jeans, while his wolf hovered just beneath the surface of his humanity. *I'm a fool for spending so much time alone with her, knowing that Remus forbid me to mate with her yet.* Silently, he reached over and unbuckled her seatbelt.

"Um, I had a great time, Mali. I really appreciate dinner and a chance to pick out the colors for the office." She gave him a shy little smile and then yelped when he pulled her across the seat. "What are you doing?" she whispered. Her eyes got big as saucers when he easily lifted her onto his lap.

"I wanna kiss you, and I'm not doing it on somebody's front porch." He buried his nose in her hair and inhaled deeply. "I didn't figure you would be inviting me up to your room." He touched his lips to her forehead and then trailed feather-light kisses against her skin down her cheek.

"I, um, I uh, couldn't, I mean I, umph." Melissa's words cut off when Mali captured her lips with his. He licked across her bottom lip before sliding inside the silky warmth of her mouth. Mali could feel her hands fluttering against his shoulders, like she wasn't sure where to put them, as his tongue flicked against her own. She opened her lips wider, mating her tongue against his. The taste of his mate was addictive and sweet as honey.

Mali cupped the back of her head to hold her in place while he deepened the kiss. His hand slid down her side to her bottom and hauled her closer to him, anchoring her against his throbbing erection. He felt her hands gripping his shoulders hard and then groaned when they slid into the long strands of his hair. After lifting away from the kiss, he buried his lips in the curve of her neck and had to fight to keep his canines from dropping. He nibbled on her ear before trailing kisses down the silky skin and then ran his lips along her jaw down to the hollow of her throat. His hand cupped her breast and squeezed gently as he ground his erection against her ass.

"Whoa!" Melissa pulled back abruptly, placed both hands against his chest, and pushed. "Slow down there, big guy." Her cheeks were turning bright red, and she wouldn't meet his eyes. "I'm a little too old to be making out in a car."

"This is a truck," he stated, deadpan.

She brought her gaze up to his, and if looks could kill, he would be lying dead on the seat. "Are you serious?" she asked.

Mali laughed. “At least I got you to look at me again.” He placed a quick kiss on her lips. “Sunshine, I’ll never do anything to embarrass you. That’s a promise.”

Melissa snorted. “Your promise might hold more water if your hand wasn’t still on my ass.”

He laid his forehead against hers and laughed softly, before squeezing the soft cheek of her butt in his hand. “Nobody can see my hand on your ass, so you shouldn’t be embarrassed by it.” He leaned back to stare into her eyes. “Besides, you might as well get used to my hands being on your body. As far as I’m concerned, soon there won’t be a part of you that doesn’t have my fingerprints all over it.” He gave her a wicked grin. “And I’m hoping to have your fingerprints all over me.”

She swallowed hard and squirmed around on his lap. “I really need to get in now, Mali. It’s getting kind of late, and that poor woman will be waiting up for me.”

Mali sighed and took her face between his hands. “Okay, this time, you win. I can’t promise I’ll let you win every time, though.” He kissed her gently and then lifted her off his lap and placed her back on the seat. “Wait here,” he ordered. Her eyes remained on him as he got out of the truck, ran around to her side, and then opened the door to help her out. Holding her hand, he walked her up to the porch. Leaning down, he placed a soft kiss on her lips. “I’ll see you at the office tomorrow. I’ve really enjoyed spending this evening with you.”

Melissa grinned, stood on her tiptoes, and placed a quick kiss on his lips. “See ya tomorrow.” Before he could deepen the kiss, she’d pulled away, opened the door, and disappeared inside. He chuckled. *You won’t get away so easily next time!*

* * * *

Ethan glanced over at Latan as they walked Tania to her cabin. Their date had so many things go wrong it should be listed in the

Disastrous Dates Hall of Fame. He couldn't believe they hadn't anticipated Linda's reaction to them bringing a woman there. Hell, she'd been the reason he and Latan agreed to stick to strictly wolf shifters in the future. But even before her antics, he thought he'd sensed Tania pulling away from them. It was strange, but he couldn't sense her emotions like he could other shifters, and nothing about her scent was recognizable. He'd always been able to scent the wolf in the pack females.

Tania walked up onto the porch and turned and faced the two men. "Thank you for dinner. It was, um, interesting." She laughed lightly.

Latan took a step up onto the porch and smiled down at her. "It's still pretty early. Wouldn't you like to just relax, and maybe sit around and talk?" He lowered his voice suggestively.

She looked down at Ethan and then back up at Latan. Sighing, she straightened her back. "Look, guys, you're really sweet, and I've enjoyed our evening together, but I have to be honest with you." For a moment, a look of pain seemed to cross her face, and then it was gone. "I don't really see this relationship being able to go anywhere. Both of you are really great, but I don't even plan on staying in this area. I didn't sign a contract with the school board."

"Why didn't you?" Ethan asked.

She shrugged. "I didn't wanna tie myself down unless I was sure."

Ethan walked up onto the porch. "Sure about what, honey?"

Tania looked uncomfortable. "That I wanted to stay in this area. I've moved around a lot, trying different places out, trying to find one that felt like home."

"And this isn't it?" Latan asked with a touch of sadness in his voice.

She didn't meet their eyes. "No, I don't think so." Backing toward the door, she gave them a small smile. "I'll be leaving when this semester is over. I'm sorry, but I think it would be best to just cut things off before they go too far." Opening the door, she stepped inside. "Goodnight!"

Ethan watched the door close and turned to look at Latan. "Could anything else possibly go wrong tonight?"

Latan shook his head. "She was jumpy all evening, bro, even before the problems at the diner." He walked toward their parked car. "She's hiding something, Ethan. I can feel it."

"You can sense her feelings?" Ethan asked.

"No, I can't, and that's the problem. She shouldn't be able to mask her feelings, and that has to mean she's hiding something."

Ethan joined his brother in the car. "Do you think Remus is right? You think she's mixed up with Kaugh?"

"No, that's the one thing I'm sure of. I don't believe there's anything evil about her, but I sense she's sad and unhappy."

Ethan was quiet for a few minutes while Latan drove them home. "So, what do we do now?" He looked at his brother, feeling a little uncomfortable. "I can't just walk away, Latan. As strange as it may sound, I've got feelings for her. Feelings I've never had before."

"Shit, we may have an even bigger problem then."

"What are you talking about?"

Latan gave him an apologetic look. "I'm sorry, bro, but I've got feelings for her, too."

Ethan laughed. "Maddie always said that dating the same woman was gonna cause us big trouble someday." He looked over at his brother. "Let's go home and drink a couple of six packs of beer."

Latan laughed. "How the hell will that help?"

"It won't, but I'll need that extra fortification to tell Maddie she was right!"

"Can't beat that logic. Let's go."

* * * *

"Damn, Ethan, we would be laid out in a soft, comfortable bed with a naked Tania between us if we hadn't screwed up tonight." Latan put the beer can down on the porch and then leaned back in the rocker. "What color do you think her nipples are?" he asked, slurring his words just a little.

Ethan sighed. "You're drunk, little brother." They had gone through four beers a piece, but Latan had never been able to hold his liquor well.

"I'm not drunk enough. If I was, I wouldn't have the hard-on from hell." He got up and walked over to thc table to grab another beer.

"Don't you think you've had enough? We need to talk about how we're gonna help Remus nail Kaugh."

Latan looked at the beer in his hand and then sat it back down on the table. "You're right, as usual," he said, walking back to the rocker. He glared at Ethan. "I don't care what Remus said. There's no way that Tania's involved in that sick bastard's plans. I'm not gonna waste my time focusing on her."

Ethan leaned his head back and gazed up at the stars. "We're in agreement there. I don't think Remus would feel that way if he spent a little time with her and got to know her better."

"Holy shit!" Latan screamed.

Ethan jumped to his feet, ready to defend his brother, and then laughed when he got a good look at him. Tania's cat had apparently sneaked up on Latan and jumped into his lap. He was staring down at the tiny ball of fur like it was something dropped straight from the depths of hell. Laughing, almost uncontrollably, Ethan returned to the porch swing.

"Get the hell off of me," Latan cried. He roughly pushed the cat off his lap and onto the porch. Leaning over, he growled menacingly. Kit arched her back and hissed before running over and jumping into Ethan's lap.

"Doesn't seem like she's any more fond of you than you are of her, bro," Ethan said.

Latan stood up and walked over to his brother. He bent down close to the purring cat. "Aw, what's the matter? Is da wittle pussy cat mad at me?" he crooned. He jumped back, nearly tripping on his own feet, when Kit raised one paw and swiped at his face with her claws extended. "Damn, that cat's a menace." He returned to the rocker. "Why does the most beautiful woman I've ever known need to have a furball living with her?"

Ethan laughed and ran his fingers through the silky, black hair. Kit was rubbing her head all over his arm, while flexing her claws in and out on his jean-clad legs. Her purring was rhythmic and soothing. "If you ever expect to get anywhere with Tania, you're gonna have to develop some kind of friendly relationship with this cat."

Latan snorted. "You develop a relationship with the furry, little beast, and I'll work on figuring out a way to get back into Tania's good graces."

"I've got guards watching Kaugh's office until morning, but I promised we would take over for them fairly early." Ethan continued to rub Kit, occasionally scratching her behind the ears.

"Okay, but let's change tactics a little. Remus concentrated his investigation on Kaugh himself, and he's staying squeaky clean. I think it's safe to assume he's aware of being watched. We should take to the wooded area behind their office in our wolf forms and see what his associates are up to. The guys watching the office said that they've been checking out the countryside and even talking to a realtor. I wanna get really close and see what they're up to."

"Sounds like a plan to me," Ethan agreed. He stood up and placed the cat on the porch. "We'd better turn in since we need to be up and out so early." Using his foot, he gently pushed Kit toward the steps. "Go on home, kitty. It's not safe for you to be running around these woods."

"Oh, yeah," Latan laughed, "run on home through the woods, kitty. Maybe something big and hairy will have you for a midnight snack!"

Ethan shook his head. "I think the odds of you ever finding out the color of Tania's nipples are nonexistent!"

"Oh, man, if we just hadn't screwed up and subjected her to Linda, I would be between those creamy thighs even as we speak!"

"Don't say things like that," Ethan growled. "Now I'm never gonna be able to get to sleep with the pictures running through my mind." He continued to grumble under his breath as he made his way into the house.

* * * *

Latan looked over at his brother and growled. They'd been hiding in the trees behind Kaugh's Main Street office for over five hours with absolutely nothing to show for it. When they relieved the night watch, Connor told them the three human associates of Kaugh's had arrived an hour before they showed up. Since then, there hadn't been any sign of life inside the building. Tired of communicating telepathically with Ethan, Latan changed back into his human form and waited for his brother to follow.

"What's the matter with you? Are you trying to get us caught?" Ethan growled.

"Give me a break. Even in human form, we're more than adequately hidden here. I just couldn't stand lying in the leaves any longer and not being able to talk."

Ethan chuckled. "Your furry butt doesn't like lying in the leaves, but you don't mind your naked ass being attacked by mosquitoes? Bro, you are one sick puppy!"

"Very funny. I've been thinking."

"Wait, I'll alert the press," Ethan joked.

Latan glared at his brother. "I'm trying to be serious here, asshole. I think we should talk to Remus about Tania."

"What are we gonna tell him, because we really didn't learn anything new last night."

"We're gonna tell him what our instincts are telling us, that she's not guilty of anything. You and I both know he's nervous of anybody new because of what happened to Maddie. He trusts us, and I think he'll listen if we tell him that we trust her."

"He's not gonna settle for just our word."

"Then we make him spend some time with her. He can ask all the questions he wants." Latan gazed up into tree branches that were blowing slowly in the wind. "Man, I don't wanna let her go. She makes me feel protective and possessive all at the same time. I want her like I've never wanted another woman before, and I can sense you feel the same."

Ethan frowned and then sighed heavily. "Yeah, I know how you're feeling. What the hell are we gonna do? It's not like we can both mate her." He laughed, but there was no humor in the sound. "It doesn't even make any sense. She doesn't smell like she's my mate, but every feeling she brings out in me says she is."

"Exactly," Latan exclaimed. "Sometimes she doesn't even smell like a shifter, and I've never thought she smelled like a wolf. Did Remus tell you what she is?"

"No, he only said she was half-breed."

Latan watched his brother carefully. "So, are we in agreement then? We get Remus to spend some time with her so he'll lose any doubts he has, and then we make our move. We can forget the mating thing and just see what develops between the three of us."

Ethan grinned. "Little bro, that's the smartest thing you've said in the past five years." He ducked, laughing, when Latan threw a handful of leaves at him.

"Somebody's visiting," Latan said quietly. They'd chosen their hiding spot well. With Kaugh's office being on the corner, they'd managed to position themselves so they could watch the back windows and front door at the same time. Latan watched as a familiar looking woman exited her Jeep and walked into the office. "Who is that, Ethan?"

"Uh, Mitchell, her name's Mitchell. I think it's Arlene, no, wait, Alice. Her name's Alice Mitchell. She's the realtor from Kenyan that helped Michael rent the building for his new office."

"I don't remember—"

"Wait, she's coming out." As they watched, a tall man with dark, unkempt hair and a bushy beard got into the Jeep with Alice. "From Remus's description, that has to be Marty Dyer."

"We've got to follow them." Latan had barely finished his words before he shifted into his wolf and glanced over to make sure his brother was ready to follow. Together, they took off in the cover of the trees, keeping the four-wheel drive vehicle in sight.

* * * *

Tania watched as the two magnificent wolves ran off toward the road. Latan's wolf was the bigger of the two, solid gray in color, while Ethan's coat was a mixture of black and gray. They were beautiful and masculine at the same time. Her fingers fairly itched to slide through their shiny coats.

She'd been hiding in her spot even before the brothers showed up. The ability to mask her scent had kept them from spotting her. She smiled as she thought back to the conversation she'd overheard. *Remus is the one that has a problem with me. Latan and Ethan want me.* She felt a chill run over her body. *Oh, God, I want the two of them so badly. They're making me want things that just aren't possible.* She stared toward the running wolves. *No time to worry about it now.* Her eyes closed, and she took a deep breath and looked down at the ground. "I need you to help me out, Kit. You need to follow the guys and see what Kaugh's man is up to. Don't let me down. A lot of people are counting on you."

* * * *

Where the hell are they going? Latan sent his thoughts to Ethan as they stayed out of sight following the realtor and Kaugh's man. It hadn't been hard to keep them in sight. They'd been driving slowly. She'd turned off the main road early on then gone about two miles before turning onto this dirt lane. The dense forest made it easy to stay hidden. They'd been on this trail for a couple of miles now, and Latan could hear the sound of a nearby stream. He and Ethan came to a stop as they rounded the bend and spotted a cabin in a small clearing. As they watched, Alice stopped and parked in front, and then she and Marty got out. The two stood in front of the structure for a minute talking and then went inside.

We need to move closer so we can hear what they're saying. Ethan's words came through clearly in Latan's mind. Both wolves crawled closer to the small cabin, careful to stay hidden in the fallen brush. After about a twenty minute wait, the two people came back outside. Latan strained to hear their conversation.

Would you look at that? Ethan's words had Latan turning his head to see what had captured his brother's interest. He was shocked to see a small black cat crossing the dirt road, heading toward Alice and their quarry. *Is that Tania's cat?* Latan ignored his brother's question and looked around carefully to see if he could spot Tania. It didn't make sense for her cat to be this far out by itself. When he didn't see her anywhere, he turned his attention back to the small feline.

"Oh, look at that," Alice squealed. She bent down and held her fingers out toward Kit. "Come here, kitty." She looked up at Marty. "Do you think it's a stray?"

Marty bent down, and the cat immediately jumped into his arms. He chuckled and ran his hand over her back. "No, it's not a stray." He stood up, with Kit cuddled close to his chest. "She's too well fed to be a stray." His eyes narrowed as he stared at Alice. "Are you sure there aren't any other houses around here?"

"Absolutely not," she replied, shaking her head. "This lot includes seventy acres of surrounding forest, and I don't think there's anything closer than a few miles outside this property."

"That's good." Marty smiled as he continued stroking the cat.

Latan felt rage building in him at the sight of the large man's hands running over Kit. He turned and looked at Ethan when he heard a low-pitched growl coming from him. *What's wrong?*

He's got his hands all over her!

Latan turned his gaze back to the cat cuddled in Marty's arms. He felt shock when his wolf sent one word through his mind. *Mine!*

"So, did you like the cabin, Mr. Dyer?" Alice asked. "It's the only listing we have that even came close to your specifications."

"Yeah, I like it, but the price is way too high."

"Not if you compare it to other dwellings in this area with the same space. It has three thousand square feet, including the rooms underground."

"I didn't pay much attention when we were down there. Are all the rooms the same size?" he asked.

"Yes! They're the same size as the two bedrooms upstairs but without the closets."

"Why the hell did they build bedrooms underground?"

She laughed. "You would have needed to meet the former owner to understand. They aren't meant to be bedrooms, more like survival rooms, which is why it has that special little feature I showed you. The poor man was convinced the world was coming to an end, and he wanted a safe place for his family to go in case of disaster." She smirked. "He built this place himself but didn't think it through very carefully. There are no provisions for bathrooms or food storage in the survival rooms."

"What did you say the family wants for this place?"

"They have it listed at two hundred twenty thousand, and that includes the surrounding acreage."

Struggling to control his wolf's rage, Latan watched as Marty leaned down and rubbed his beard against Kit's head.

"Tell you what! You tell them I'm willing to pay one hundred seventy thousand, cash, but the offer's only good for the next twelve hours."

Alice looked at him for several moments and then smiled. "I'm sure they'll be willing to accept your offer, Mr. Dyer. I know they're anxious to finish settling their father's estate."

"Well, that's a good thing then." He raised Kit up and nuzzled his face against her nose. "I think I'll take this little lady home with me. What do say, kitty? Wanna come live with me? I think I'd like coming home to you every night." Suddenly, Kit stretched out and sank the claws from all four feet into his arm. "Shit," he screamed as he lost his grip on the tiny beast.

Latan could feel his wolf settle down as he watched Kit scamper across the road and disappear through the trees. He turned back and watched Marty shake his head, a sad look on his face, before getting into the Jeep with Alice and driving off.

Both brothers shifted as soon as the Jeep was out of sight. "What do you think Kaugh wants this place for?" asked Ethan.

"I don't know, but it's remote, easily guarded, with nobody around for miles. That can't be good for the wolves. We need to get back and let Remus know what's going on."

"Are we gonna tell him about Tania's cat being here?"

Latan looked thoughtful for a moment. "No, it would just make him even more suspicious of her." He gave his brother a grin. "What we're gonna do is pay little Ms. Schoolteacher a visit. I think it's about time she answered a few questions!"

Chapter 3

Mali pulled up and parked outside Michael's office. He sat there for a moment trying to get his wolf under control. Last night had been a struggle, keeping the beast from claiming its mate. He didn't know how he would get through the next few days working so closely with Melissa on this job. *I've gotta think of something really wicked to do to Remus as payback for making me wait like this.* He chuckled, took a deep breath, and then got out of his truck to head inside.

Walking into the nearly empty office, Mali glanced around, looking for Melissa. Her scent filled the air, bringing his wolf right back to the surface.

"Hello, I'll be right down," she called out from upstairs.

He groaned softly as he felt his cock begin to harden. Just the sound of her voice had his jeans feeling too tight. He watched as she came hurrying down the stairs, his breath stopping at the sight of the smile that came over her face when she saw it was him. *God, you're so beautiful!* "Hey, Sunshine, you're looking really pretty today." She was wearing a pastel pink, sleeveless summer dress with a scooped neckline that showed just a hint of the rounded tops of her breasts. His mouth began to water at the thought of what lay hidden beneath the dress.

"Thanks, Mali." Melissa lowered her eyes as a flush spread up her neck into her cheeks.

He smiled. "You ready for me to get started on the office?"

"Well, um." Melissa gripped her hands together in front of her and began to look very nervous. "There's a slight problem."

"Honey, what's wrong?" The anxiety was rolling off her in waves, and his wolf was pushing at him to do something to calm her down.

She sighed. "The movers got the dates mixed up, and they delivered my personal furniture this morning. I had to either let them bring it in or risk it being taken back to their warehouse and left until they had another delivery coming this way." She gave him an apologetic look. "I let them take it upstairs. I'm afraid it's gonna make it pretty difficult for you to get the work done."

Relieved it was nothing more serious, he shook his head and smiled. "Not a problem, we'll just find a way to work around it." He walked over and took her arm. "Let's go up so I can take a look and see what needs to be done." Without waiting for her to respond, Mali pulled on her arm, leading her up the stairs. When they reached the second floor, he looked around.

Melissa sighed. "See what I mean?"

Releasing her arm, Mali stepped forward to get a better idea of what all she had. There was a full-size bed with mattress and box springs already set up, but without any bedding, a dresser with mirror, and a small table and two chairs. "Sunshine, this won't be any problem at all. I can just move everything to one side of the room and cover it while I do the work on the other side. Is that okay with you?" He turned to get her response and found her staring at his ass.

"Oh, uh, sure, Mali, whatever you want."

He grinned, feeling very wicked. "Whatever I want?" His grin got even bigger when her face turned a dark shade of red. The smell of her arousal brought his wolf surging to the surface, demanding that they claim their mate. *To hell with it! Remus said I had to wait to mate her, not that we couldn't make love.* He held out his hand. "Come here, Sunshine." When she didn't move, he walked slowly toward her. He put his hands on her shoulders, pulled her close, and murmured her name against her lips. The scent of her arousal got stronger, nearly overwhelming him as it rose up around them. Flames of desire dancing in her eyes took his breath away. Taking a deep breath, he gave her one final chance to back away. “If the answer’s no, then say it now before it’s too late.”

Melissa looked up into his eyes and trembled. “No one ever made me feel the way you do, Mali. When we’re together, I feel beautiful and desired. You’re everything I’ve ever wanted in a man.” She blushed even more. “There’s no way I’ll ever tell you no.” She slid her hands up his arms and pressed her lips to his.

Mali growled and wrapped his arms around her. He licked at her lips, slipping his tongue inside when they opened. Her gasp of surprise allowed him to deepen thc kiss. When she groaned, he gently took her bottom lip between his teeth and nipped, then let his tongue glide along the sting to soothe it. Pulling away from their kiss, Mali trailed his lips down her chin and throat, his tongue tasting the silky flesh.

He let his hands drift down to the rounded curve of her ass and squeezed gently while his lips dipped below the neckline of her dress. He savored the taste of her milky white skin as he slowly explored her body. When her arms crept around his neck, his hands rose swiftly to the zipper behind her. He glanced down at the cleavage gradually being revealed against his chest and had to bite back a growl. He so wanted to taste every inch of his mate.

Melissa’s arms slid down to his chest as Mali pushed her away a couple of inches. He grabbed her loosened dress and pulled it off her shoulders and down her arms. It had just begun to pool around her feet when he yanked his own shirt over his head and tossed it to the floor. Mali cupped her ass and pulled her against his hard frame, his fingers digging into her hips hard enough to leave bruises.

Her hands tentatively settled on his shoulders and then moved down, tangling in the swirl of hair covering his chest. His breath caught when her fingers skimmed over his flat nipples and then exploded into a growl when she leaned forward and searched for the small brown disc with her tongue. “God, I want you,” he cried. Mali tangled his fingers in Melissa’s hair and pulled her head back.

Leaning forward, he slanted his mouth over hers, his tongue demanding entrance. While he ravaged her mouth, his hands peeled the lace cups away from her skin, tearing the delicate material impatiently.

Melissa hid her eyes against Mali's neck when he broke the kiss to stare down at the treasure he'd uncovered. Her bountiful breasts fell free from their prison, the skin pink and unblemished. The large, rose-colored tips beaded and pushed forward as if searching for something. His fingers reached out and trailed over one of them ever so lightly. "Your breasts are so beautiful, so full. They're begging for my lips." He leaned forward and pressed her hard nipples against his hairy chest. She cried out and undulated in his arms.

Mali bent down and took one large nipple into his mouth, tracing his tongue around the areola. He drew the tip between his teeth with an edge of roughness and was delighted to feel the sting of her bite against his arm in response. She arched her back, pushing her breast farther into his mouth as he let his hand slide down the soft skin of her stomach toward the silky panties covering her sex. Her knees buckled, and she began to slide to the floor when his fingers slipped beneath the elastic at her waist. Unable to go slowly, he ripped the underwear from her body before lifting her in his arms and depositing her on the bed. Reaching into his pocket, he pulled out a string of condoms, and then the remainder of his clothes quickly disappeared before he joined her on the naked mattress.

Lips pressed together in a gentle kiss as he gazed into her passion-filled eyes. "You're so beautiful. I've been looking for you for so long. I'd given up hope of ever finding my mate," he whispered.

"Your mate? I don't know what to say, Mali. Everything's happening so fast." Melissa closed her eyes and sighed. "I can't—"

"Shh." Mali quieted her. His tongue traced around her swollen lips while his hand traveled to her generous breast. Leaving her lips, he let his tongue glide over her chin, down her throat, and then across her chest, leaving a damp trail behind it. Her arms fluttered against his shoulders as he licked a trail around the fullness of her breast. Tightening his hand around the soft globe, he held it up and licked across the hardened tip before clamping his lips down and sucking strongly. He allowed his teeth to graze across the sensitive nub and then laved it thoroughly before moving to her other side. Her hands dug into his shoulders while he suckled at her breast.

Mali let his tongue slide from Melissa's nipple and roamed south along her rounded, soft abdomen, memorizing the taste of her skin along the way. His tongue stopped to dip into her dainty navel on its way to the curls covcring the entrance to her sex. Dragging his hand down, he searched between her legs to find her heat. Dipping two fingers inside, he opened her labia and watched as the cream flowed from her opening and slid down toward her ass. "You are so sexy, woman." He inhaled the scent of her arousal deep into his lungs. "You smell so good. You're mine, Sunshine, all mine." Leaning forward, he extended his tongue and lapped slowly. *Oh, God, my mate tastes like sweet nectar!*

Moving to lie between her spread thighs, Mali ran his tongue up and down her weeping slit before working to coax the center of her pleasure out of its hiding place. It wasn't long before her tiny clit was peeking out from its protective sheath. He took it gently between his lips and sucked while he continued to pump his fingers in and out of her pussy.

"Mali," she cried, her fingers tightening in his hair.

While his fingers played between her legs, and his lips teased her clit with gentle suction, Mali pressed his hand into the cleft of her buttock and slid his finger into a place he suspected no one had ever been before. Melissa cried out, her body shaking and thrashing beneath him. The fingers in her ass and pussy began to pump in rhythm while he nibbled on her swollen clit. Her slick channel began to contract around his fingers, and her legs came up to grip around his shoulders as her climax rolled over her.

"Mali," she cried out as she came.

"That's it, Sunshine, come for me, baby."

Not giving her time to catch her breath, Mali pulled his fingers from her body, grabbed her hand and placed it on his chest. "Touch me, Sunshine. I need to feel your hands on me." He moved up to lie beside her, encouraging her to explore his skin, and sighed when she laid her hands on his chest. The wolf howled in protest when he didn't immediately take possession of their mate, but Mali knew he needed time to cool down or he wouldn't be able to hold back.

Melissa took a deep breath and ran her hands down Mali's chest in a light caress, her fingers lightly teasing the hidden nipples. She jumped and seemed startled when he grabbed both her hands and pressed them hard against his muscled torso.

"Talk to me, Sunshine. Tell me what you see, what you feel when you touch me." He leaned down and licked his way into her mouth. "I need to hear you, darling," he whispered against her lips.

She swallowed hard and looked back at his chest. "I, uh, I see you're very muscular, and very hairy." She giggled, and then looked embarrassed.

"That's it, love, keep going," he encouraged.

Her fingers spread out. "You have all this thick hair that spreads across your chest." She let her hands slide down his stomach. "It narrows down past your belly button and then spreads out to form a kind of nest for your, uh, your…" She blushed furiously. "Your member?"

Mali had to bite his lip to keep from laughing and then groaned when she cupped his full length in her palm.

She sighed. "You're so hard, but it feels silky at the same time." Her eyes narrowed as she peered closer. "Criminy, you must be ten inches long." Eyes filled with worry gazed up at him. "I hope we're not being overly optimistic about us fitting together."

Mali couldn't hold back his laughter then. "Don't you worry, Sunshine. We'll fit just fine, no problems at all." He grinned when she rolled her eyes. To take some of her stress away, he lowered his hand between her thighs and began to tease her clit with soft touches.

"Oh, God," she groaned.

"Come on, don't stop now. Tell me what else you see."

She gave him a disbelieving look. "Uh, well, this is shaped like a mushroom." She ran her thumb across the head of his cock. "And it's leaking," she added. His groan morphed into a growl when she promptly sucked it into her mouth for a taste. "Hmm, you taste kind of salty, and bitter, but good." She smiled and stared up at him from beneath her lashes.

"Woman, you're teasing me," he cried.

Melissa laughed and scooted down in the bed. "It's only teasing if I'm not willing to carry through." She cupped his hairy sac, fondling gently, and then licked her way up his shaft and flicked her tongue over and around the head.

"Suck me, Sunshine. Open your mouth and suck my cock," he begged.

Gripping his shaft firmly, she opened her mouth and took him in as far as she could. She'd only managed to suck his length a couple of times before he reached down, grabbed her under the arms, and pulled her up until their faces were even. He kissed her deeply, almost savagely, as he slipped a hand between their bodies and traced the cleft of her sex, parting the flesh and dipping inside. Melissa rocked her hips, moving against his hand.

"I can't wait, baby, I need you now. I wanna come inside you this first time." His hands moved around to caress the cheeks of her ass before he gripped her firmly and rolled, ending up with him above her, lying in the cradle of her thighs. Bending down, he grabbed the condom package off the floor and tore it open with his teeth. After rolling the protective sheath on, he grasped his erection and pushed it inside his mate, watching as her flesh parted for him. A harsh breath released as he drove deeply, grinding his hips against her. He fought the wolf who wanted to place their mate on her hands and knees and claim her properly.

Mali withdrew and thrust deeply inside her again and again in a frenzy of deep thrusts. The wolf growled in pleasure when she locked her ankles behind his back and lifted her arms, looping them around his shoulders and threading her fingers through his hair. He could feel her legs quivering and her pussy clenching around his cock as he pounded into her soft, welcoming body. “Come for me, Sunshine, come for me again.”

Almost on cue, Melissa cried out with her release. “Mali!”

He came, his entire body jerking and rocking as his seed shot into the latex, pulse after pulse. Alarm settled in when he felt his canines drop in anticipation of claiming his mate, and he had to bury his face in her neck to hide until he could gain control. For long minutes, he lay still, buried within her warmth. When his razor sharp teeth finally receded, he slid free of her body, fell to the bed, and pulled her close into his arms. It pleased him and the wolf when she snuggled even closer and laid her face against his chest. “Are you all right, Sunshine?”

“Mmmm, perfect,” she groaned.

He chuckled. “That sounds like a compliment.”

“It is. You were wonderful.” She was quiet for a few minutes and then gazed up into his eyes. “What happens now, Mali? I mean, I uh, well, um, I’m not really into casual sex or just fooling around.”

Mali bent and kissed the top of her head and then closed his eyes. He couldn’t tell her what she wanted to hear. He knew Remus would allow the mating once she understood about the wolves, but he had no way of knowing what her reaction to any of it would be. *It’s not fair to promise you forever until I know you can love both me and my wolf.* He groaned and hugged her closer. He didn’t want to lose this special woman. “I’m not fooling around, Sunshine. I feel very strongly about you, and I would like for us to get to know each other a little better.” He tilted her chin up and brushed his lips against hers.

"Will you come home with me tonight? I want you to see my house, and I wanna spend the night holding you close in my arms. I wanna make love to you in my bed, with no interruptions. Will you do that?"

Melissa's eyes widened, and she swallowed hard. She nodded slowly. "Yeah, I'll come home with you."

"Hello, anybody here?" a loud, male voice called out from downstairs.

Melissa looked horrified. "We didn't lock the door before we came up here," she squealed.

Mali winced at the shrill tone of her voice and then watched in amazement as she jumped from the bed and proceeded to dress faster than anyone he'd ever seen. He chuckled. He had a feeling she was going to lay into him later about that unlocked door. Sighing, he rose and reached for his pants as she headed downstairs. It was then he remembered the used condom. Grimacing, he pulled it off and wondered what the hell he was going to do with the damn thing. He glanced around. *Hell, there isn't even any water up here.* He clenched his teeth and was just about to pull on his clothes anyway, when Melissa ran back up the stairs.

"It's the delivery guy from the hardware place bringing the paint and supplies. I'm gonna let him stack it down there. Here," she tossed him her purse, "I've got some wet wipes and tissues in there. It should be enough for you to clean up." Turning, she raced back downstairs.

Amazed, he looked down at the purse. She'd thought of his comfort even when she'd been embarrassed about almost getting caught. *I love her!* His thoughts didn't really surprise him. His heart had been involved since he'd first scented her at the wedding reception. Now he just had to convince her that living with a wolf was a good thing, and he had to do it before Michael got back from his honeymoon.

* * * *

Remus looked at Ethan and growled. "They bought a cabin?" he bellowed.

"No," Ethan replied, "he only made an offer. The realtor said she thought the family would probably take it, but it's not official yet." Ethan had never seen his Alpha brother lose his cool so completely before.

"How far away is it from pack holdings?" Remus asked.

"It's about twenty-five miles from here, which would make it about five miles outside our land," Latan answered.

Remus paced up and down his kitchen. "What's the place like? Hell, you remember the cabin Constantine held Maddie in, don't you? Bars on the windows, double locks on the doors, the damn place was set up like a prison, only with all his medical crap."

Ethan sighed, knowing that nothing he could say would calm his brother down. He'd been devastated when they'd rescued Maddie and he'd seen where they held her. Remus had ordered the small cabin leveled after they'd disposed of Constantine. "Right now, it's fairly normal. It sits in a small clearing, surrounded by heavy tree coverage on three sides and a stream on the fourth. We looked around the inside after they left, and it's got some peculiar features."

Remus narrowed his eyes. "What kind of *peculiar features*?"

Latan cleared his throat. "There are four rooms down in the cellar beneath the house, two large and two small. They're bare, with no windows. The upstairs has a couple of regular bedrooms, a living room, and a small kitchen. There's an outside door off the living room and the kitchen, along with four windows on the upper level. It has a generator in the basement that supplies electricity."

"Shit, it's a perfect prison," Remus whispered.

Ethan walked over and put his arm around his older brother. "It doesn't have to be a prison, Remus. I've left a full-time guard on it, so we'll know if anybody comes or goes from there. We're not gonna let anything happen to Maddie, bro, you have my word."

Remus turned and fully embraced his brother. "I know, Ethan, but I can't help but worry about what Kaugh's planning." He took a deep breath and stepped back. "Is there anything else?"

Ethan exchanged an uncomfortable look with Latan before attempting to answer Remus. He didn't want to tell him about seeing the cat, but it wasn't in his nature to hide things from his Alpha, or his brother, for that matter.

"Yeah, there was something else," Latan answered. "There was a black cat hanging around, one that looked an awful lot like Kit."

"Who the hell is Kit?" Remus asked.

"Sorry, that's the name of Tania's cat. Anyway, the cat just came walking out of the woods and kind of wandered over and jumped into Marty Dyer's arms."

Remus sat down at the table and ran his fingers through his hair. "So, let me get this straight. A cat, which looks like our new teacher's pet, came walking up to the enemy and just jumped into his arms."

Ethan shook his head. "Not exactly. She didn't jump into his arms, he picked her up." He laughed. "He thought she was a stray and was gonna take her with him when they left."

"What stopped him?" Remus sighed.

Latan smirked. "She sank all four sets of her claws in him and took off back into the woods. Believe me, that stopped him cold."

Remus glared at Ethan and Latan. "So we're just supposed to believe it's a coincidence that this cat just wandered into an area more than twenty miles from her owner's cabin and spent some time with one of Kaugh's men?" He shook his head angrily. "Not happening! You can bet if the cat was there, Tania was not far away. I'm telling you, there's something strange about that woman." He thought for a minute. "Koril still hasn't come up with anything on her background that's helpful. I want one or both of you to stick close to her for a few days. Since you've already been hanging around her, she shouldn't be suspicious of you like she would be of someone else. I want to know her every move until we know more about her or until we take Kaugh out."

Ethan looked at his brother. "Remus, do you know why she doesn't have a wolf scent?"

Remus growled softly. "No, but I know what you mean. I couldn't scent any animal on her when I met her. Vanard told me that she's a half-breed, but he couldn't, or wouldn't, say what breeds were involved. He said she's capable of shifting, but he didn't know anything more."

"All right, we'll keep an eye on her for you, but I gotta be honest with you, bro. Neither one of us believes she has anything to do with Kaugh. Just from the little time we've spent with her, we haven't sensed anything dishonest."

Remus gave him a stern look. "I respect your feelings, Ethan, I really do, but I need you to keep an open mind. This is the life of your Alpha Femm on the line here, not to mention all the other wolves on the mountain. Come on, man. Think with the big head and not the little one until all this is over."

Anger raced through Ethan as he stormed to his feet. "I've always been willing to give my life to protect my Alpha Femm, Alpha Remus, and you damn well know it. I'll keep my objectivity and keep my eye on Tania until you get all the information you need to take this man down. I guarantee you don't have to worry about my *little head* compromising your plans in any way." Without another word, he turned, threw open the back door, and left the house. He breathed a sigh of relief when he heard the door slam closed and felt Latan come walking up behind him. He turned and looked at his brother. "I'm sorry."

"Don't be." He snorted. "Remus had it coming. Don't worry, he'll get over his snit and probably apologize later."

"I don't want an apology. I want him to lay off Tania. You and I both know there's no way she's involved in any of this."

"I agree. That doesn't change the fact she's keeping secrets, though."

"No, you're right. It's definitely time to find out just what those secrets are. I vote we head over and pay a little impromptu visit to our new teach. What do you say?"

"Lead on, bro." Latan chuckled.

* * * *

Tania stared into the trees, waiting for Vanard to show himself. She'd been expecting him and had scented him on the wind while he was still a fair distance away. She narrowed her eyes as he came into view.

"Good evening, Kitania," he called out as he got closer.

"Hello, Vanard. What's so important that we needed to meet tonight?"

"No time for pleasant chit-chat, huh?" He smirked. "You're more like Remus than I realized."

"What the hell does that mean?" she asked angrily.

"Just that he never wastes time on pleasantries, either, always all business, just like you."

She sighed wearily. "Why are we here, Vanard?"

"I thought you would want to know that Remus has called a meeting of the Elders tomorrow night."

"What's the meeting about?" she asked curiously.

"I don't know. He wouldn't give any more information. I do know that he's getting increasingly suspicious of you, always asking me questions that I can't really answer. Today, I found out he has Koril doing an in-depth background check on you."

Tania laughed. "Let him check all he wants. He won't find anything. The National Council made sure of that."

Vanard gave her a strange look. "Where do you come from, Kitania? What's your background, and, more importantly, what's your purpose here?"

She shook her head slowly and gave him a feral grin, allowing her fangs to slip down and lie against her lip. "I could tell you all that, but then I would have to kill you." She laughed, quoting her favorite spy cartoon. To make her point, she let her eyes flash as she lowered her fangs even farther.

Vanard took a step back and glared at her. "I'm the head Elder of a wolf shifter pack. I have the right to know what's going on in my own territory. Maybe I'll just call a friend I have on the Council and find out what I wanna know."

She shrugged. "Go ahead, make your call. One less Elder isn't going to hurt this pack."

"I don't have to put up with your crap, young lady. I could just go to Remus and tell him what I do know. Believe me. He would be in your face so fast your head would spin."

She walked close and stared up into his eyes. "If you do anything to hinder my assignment, I'll personally see to it that the Council removes you from this mountain, and I won't care what they decide to do with you. I'm here to do a job for them, and not you or anybody else is gonna get in my way." Furious at her own loss of control, Tania turned and stalked off into the woods, leaving Vanard to think about his possible fate.

As she walked along the path that would take her back to her cabin, Tania wondered what the Council would say when she told them this was going to be her last job for them. For eight years, since she turned eighteen, she'd been on a quest to take Kaugh down. She'd been close several times, but not this close. He was going down this time, with the help of this pack, and then it would over.

The memories of her years in one of his testing labs still brought nightmares to her sleep now and then. She'd never known her mother or her father, only the cold, impersonal, and sometimes cruel treatment of the doctors and their staff. Kaugh hadn't been in charge then, merely an assistant to an equally evil and disturbed researcher. *Research, that's a laugh. How they could call the things they did to us "research" is beyond me.*

Her pain and misery ended when she was ten years old. Her guardian angel, a stranger by the name of Tocho, took out the facility that held her prisoner. He'd been filled with rage when he freed the shifters being held, but more so with her because she'd been the only child there. She'd seen him kill the doctor in charge, and then felt great sadncss when there was a price to pay for his bravery. Kaugh had managed to injure the brave man before escaping himself. As soon as she turned eighteen, Tania had sworn to find and kill the man that had brought pain to her savior.

She came out of the trees into the clearing that housed her cabin and stopped. Ethan and Latan were sitting on her back porch. Her steps slowed as she approached them warily. *What the hell are they doing here?*

"Hey, Tania," Ethan called out. "Hope you don't mind, but we wanted to talk to you for a minute."

"Hey," Latan added, "where you been?"

"Just taking a walk." She looked at them suspiciously, but only sensed curiosity and lust. "What's up?"

"Will you sit with us?" Ethan scooted over, making room for her to sit between them.

She frowned, but walked slowly over and sat down on the porch step. "Okay, I'm sitting, now talk."

Ethan chuckled and picked up one of her hands while Latan picked up the other one. "Don't look so worried, it's nothing bad."

"In fact," Latan added, "we're sort of hoping you'll think it's good."

Tania tried to tug her hands free, but they wouldn't let go. "Okay, if it's so good then spill."

"We want you to reconsider." Ethan smiled as he caressed her fingers with his thumb.

"Reconsider what?" she asked puzzled.

"We want to spend some time with you, get to know you a lot better," Latan said.

"We're attracted to you, Tania," Ethan added. "And we think you're attracted to us as well. Even if you're only here for a short time, we wanna see where the relationship could go."

"It can't go anywhere! The two of you are gonna want a mate and pups eventually, and I can't give you… I mean, I don't wanna be anybody's mate."

"Put the mate aspect behind us for now. Do you like us? Would you like to get to know us better, without any thoughts of the future?" Ethan asked.

She gazed into his eyes for a moment and then turned and did the same to Latan. She didn't sense any deception or ulterior motives, only pure, unfulfilled desire. *What can it hurt? I'm lonely, and they're really hot! If there's no danger of commitment then it should be perfectly safe.* She took a deep, shaky breath. "Would you like to come in and share a bottle of wine?"

Ethan glanced over at Latan, both men with large smiles on their faces. "Yeah, baby, that would be great." He glanced at Latan again. "How about we all take a run first, let our beasts out to play for a while?"

Tania tensed. She could sense curiosity mixed with their desire now. "No, that's okay, you two go ahead. I've already been for a run this evening," she lied.

"You sure?" Latan asked. "I'm not gonna lie to you, we're kind of curious about you 'cause you don't have a scent we recognize."

"Like I told Vanard, I'm a half-breed and only part wolf. I guess the combination doesn't leave room for much of a scent."

"What are you besides wolf?" Ethan looked at her with narrowed eyes.

She sighed. “It’s not something I’m really comfortable talking about.” She stood and walked over to the door. “You two, go ahead and run, and maybe I’ll see you later.”

“No way!” Latan jumped to his feet, followed quickly by Ethan. “There’s no way we’re gonna miss out on spending some time with you. We can run anytime, but you’re a hard one to pin down.” He smiled. “Now, I believe you said something about a bottle of wine?”

Tania snickered. They looked like two frisky pups about to get a treat. “Okay, but it’s getting a little chilly. Why doesn’t one of you get a fire going, and I’ll get the wine and pull together something to snack on.”

Ethan walked over and pressed his body against her back. His hands slid around her waist and pulled her back against his erection. “I definitely like the idea of starting a fire, baby.”

She giggled. “In the fireplace, Ethan. Get a fire going in the fireplace.” She pulled away, opened the door, and went inside, with the brothers following her.

“Fireplace, right,” Ethan mumbled.

Latan barked out a laugh as he followed his brother into the small cabin.

Tania watched as the two brothers went about starting a fire in the cozy room. She gripped her hands tightly together, trying to stop the trembling that had started when Ethan held her against his aroused body. Tania wasn’t a prude, and definitely not a virgin, but she’d never been with two men at the same time, and just the thought had her mouth dry and her thighs damp. *What have I gotten myself into?* Swallowing hard, she turned to the small kitchen area and pulled out the bottle of wine she’d bought recently. She smiled and laughed softly. She’d purchased it with the idea of having the brothers over for steaks, but put the bottle away in the cupboard after their disastrous dinner date. *Looks like they’re getting the wine, but not the steaks!*

“What’s so funny?” Latan asked, coming up behind her. His hands settled lightly on her waist.

Startled, Tania turned quickly and found herself held closely in Latan's arms. "Uh, nothing, really. I was just trying to figure out what to serve with the wine."

He smiled and reached for the bottle, keeping one arm around her waist, holding her close. "Petite Sirah, huh? Well," he glanced around the kitchen, "you've got a nice bowl of fresh fruit here, and what's this?" He pulled her over to the small table and picked up a brightly colored box. Grinning, he looked down at Tania. "Chocolate truffles?"

She felt her face flush. "Okay, so I've got a chocolate addiction. Sue me!" She stuck her tongue out playfully. Faster than she would have thought possible, Latan covered her mouth with his, taking advantage of her childish gesture by sucking her tongue into his mouth. The taste of him was intoxicating. Tania leaned closer and began to feel as if she could easily lose herself in the passion she sensed simmering inside him. Suddenly frightened, she pushed against his broad shoulders.

Latan released her mouth and leaned back, his arms still holding her close. "Too fast?"

Unable to speak, Tania simply nodded.

Sighing, Latan released her and stepped back. "Okay, pretty lady, we'll slow down." He grabbed the wine and searched through the cabinet for some glasses. When he found three, he handed the bottle to Ethan and followed him over to the rug in front of the fireplace. "Bring the fruit and chocolate and come join us, Tania."

She watched as the men settled on the floor with the pillows from the couch. "Do you guys like strawberries, grapes, and melons?" She blushed when they turned to stare at her. "I've got a bowl of mixed fruits in the fridge that I put together this morning for breakfast," she explained.

"Sounds great, honey. Grab the chocolates and the mixed fruit, leave the apples and oranges, and bring your sweet ass over here." Latan patted the pillow beside him.

Frowning at his demanding tone, Tania did as he asked. She handed Latan the bowl of fruit and started to join him on the rug.

"Ethan, would you go find us a corkscrew to open the wine?" Latan asked.

"I'll get it!" Tania stopped herself from sinking to the floor and started to turn toward the kitchen area. She wasn't prepared for Latan to grab her arm and pull her down into his lap.

"No, you don't." He laughed. "You're gonna sit here and relax, pretty lady, and let us take care of you for a while."

Shocked, she hesitated for just a moment and then scrambled off his lap, dropping onto the pillows piled beside him. She looked up into Ethan's grinning face. "Uh, you'll find it in the drawer beside the stove." She eyed Latan warily as Ethan went to look for the opener.

"Hey, you've got a CD player. Mind if I put on some music?" Ethan asked.

"No, that would be great." She was becoming very unnerved by the intense looks coming from Latan.

"Here, let me help you get more comfortable." Latan reached over and pulled her foot into his lap.

"Eeekk," Tania yelped.

Latan laughed. "Relax, honey, I'm only trying to help you feel better." He pulled her shoe and sock off and then began massaging her foot, allowing his hands to travel up under her jeans to the calf of her leg.

"Ahhh," she groaned, feeling herself practically melt at the touch of his hands. She didn't resist when he pulled her other foot close and gave it the same treatment. As she watched through lowered lashes, he pushed her jeans up and lightly caressed behind her knees. She was just about to object when Ethan's voice grabbed her attention.

"There we go!" He smiled and walked back over to the pillows strewn in front of the fireplace. He held his hand down to Tania as Percy Sledge's "When a Man Loves a Woman" began to play. "Dance with me?"

Hesitantly, she placed her hand in his, allowing him to pull her to her feet. Large, warm hands gripped her waist and pulled her forward until his erection pressed against her stomach. She could feel moisture flood her panties in response to his embrace. One of his hands moved around to the small of her back, while the other slid down over the curve of her ass. With nowhere else to go, her arms came up to circle his neck. Relaxing, she laid her cheek against his chest where she could hear the beat of his heart.

It wasn't long before she felt Latan moving in close behind her. His hands gripped low on her hips while he buried his mouth against her neck, licking and sucking. Tania felt a hard ridge press against her back and stomach as the three of them swayed to the beat of the music. She was fast approaching the point of no return and knew she had to say something soon or it would be too late.

Tania leaned her head back against Latan's chest and gazed up at Ethan. Her breath caught at the hunger shining in his eyes. Before she could collect her thoughts, Latan's hands cupped the weight of her breasts, his thumbs snaking out to flick lightly back and forth across the nipples. "Oh, God, I've never..."

"Shh," Latan whispered against her ear. "We won't hurt you."

She watched as Ethan's lips came closer and then stopped just before they made contact. She moaned, the moist heat from her mouth mixing with his as Latan plucked gently at her throbbing breasts. Passion, and a desperate need for the two men, took the place of her fear as Ethan claimed her lips. She opened, allowing his tongue to explore her mouth as if they'd been lovers forever. Her mind ceased to function, not knowing where to concentrate her feelings as she felt Latan lick his way up her neck.

Ethan ended the kiss and glanced behind her at his brother. "I think it's time to get a little more comfortable, don't you?" He took a step back, pulled his shirt over his head, and then tossed it in the direction of the couch. Smiling, he moved close enough for her to reach up and touch his hard shoulders. Her fingers traced up his neck and across his chin. Lips, soft as silk, nipped at her fingers as they traced across his smile.

Latan's hands gripped the bottom of her shirt and began inching it up. Wanting to feel their skin against her own, Tania lifted her arms to make it easier and soon found herself standing in only her bra and jeans. Warm skin cocooned her, filling her with an internal fire that threatened to consume her very soul. *Why does it feel so right to be here, between them?*

Without warning, Tania was turned around, her back firmly against Ethan's warm chest. Latan bent and nibbled lightly at the corner of her mouth then traced her lips with the tip of his tongue. Ethan pushed her hair aside and bit the back of her neck before trailing his lips down the middle of her back. His hands squeezed the cheeks of her ass before coming around to caress her mound through the stiff denim.

Her eyes closed as Latan pulled down the lacy cup of her bra and captured the taut nipple between his fingers, rolling the tip. A whimper of pleasure escaped her when his mouth moved down and covered the aching crest of one breast. Ethan's hands smoothed across her naked back after he released the hooks of her bra and pushed it down her shoulders. Latan's lips kept it from falling to the floor.

Arms slid around her hips, fingers opening the fastening of her jeans and tunneling underneath her silk panties. It felt so wicked to have a pair of hands searching between her legs while another tortured her breasts. Tania decided she'd been a bystander too long. It was time for her to do some exploring of her own.

Smiling, she pushed Latan away and let her bra drop to the floor. His eyes lit with a whole new interest. Ethan pulled free of her jeans and then grabbed the waist and peeled them, along with her panties, down her body. He encouraged her to step out of them and then allowed his hands to move slowly up her thighs. Gripping her hips tightly, he traced his tongue from the back of her knee up to the curve of her ass. Nuzzling between the round globes, he licked a line straight down, stopping to tease the tiny, puckered opening. Tania tensed and clenched the muscles tight.

Ethan chuckled. “That won’t stop me, honey. Nobody ever play around back here before?”

Tania gulped and had trouble answering. Latan had discovered the silky hair covering her sex. “No, never,” she managed to groan.

“That’s okay, we’ll take it slow. I promise, if you don’t like it, we’ll stop.” He went back to caressing the virgin territory, leaving goose bumps along her skin.

Latan abandoned her breast and dropped his hand to the area between her legs. His fingers trailed leisurely through the trimmed hair and then traced around her labia, causing Tania to go up on her toes. “What’s wrong, baby?” He laughed.

She decided it was time to make these macho men squirm just a little. Latan’s chest was broad and very muscular, with just a smidgen of hair trailing down the middle. She reached out and flicked the tip of her tongue back and forth across one male nipple a couple of times, delighting in the sound of his gasping breath. Ethan came to his feet behind her. She could only guess he was envious of the touches she lavished on his brother.

Her fingers delved beneath Latan’s jeans, her fingers curling around his hardened flesh. He stepped up close to her caressing hand when she reached between their bodies to tear open his fly. Tania’s eyes widened when his cock jumped out eagerly as his zipper lowered. He hadn’t bothered to wear underwear under his jeans. He was huge, at least nine inches, and fully aroused. *There’s no way I can even get my hand around that monster.*

She turned her head when she felt movement and heard the rustle of clothing behind her. Ethan pushed his jeans to the floor, quickly stepping out and kicking them away. He was nude, his thick cock rising up from a nest of black curls. He wasn’t quite as thick as Latan, but she would be willing to bet he was a little longer. Tania licked her lips and reached out to cup his sac while stroking her hand firmly up and down Latan's cock. Both men growled, their eyes closed, their heads thrown back.

Leaning over, she licked across the head of Ethan's twitching cock. He growled loudly, reached out, and hauled Tania clear off the floor, plastering her against his chest. His lips ravished hers almost brutally.

"On the pillows, Ethan, now." Latan groaned as he discarded his own jeans.

Tania felt herself lowered to the floor and then sank into the softness of the pillows. It had grown dark outside, and the firelight made dancing patterns across the muscular bodies of the two brothers as they dropped to lie on each side of her. Latan's hand caressed across her chest, his palm filling with her breast as she pushed into his touch. She groaned as he massaged, plucking gently, rhythmically, at the nipple.

Ethan's fingers played across her other breast, right before his tongue flattened over the rigid tip. He licked and sucked at the tiny nub before moving to her mouth. Fingers threaded through her hair as he captured her lips in a hot kiss, sucking steadily on her tongue, filling her with his taste. Her tongue twined with his, teasing it back into her own mouth, where he explored, finding all her sensitive spots.

Latan released her nipple, slipping his hand down her belly to rake his thick index finger along her cleft. He plucked and teased her clit before slipping his finger inside her slit, moving it slowly in and out before tracing her cleft again.

Tania looked down as they each grabbed a thigh, coaxing her legs apart. She could see Ethan's very large cock bob up and down in his excitement. She swallowed hard and wondered if it would hurt. She'd never been with anyone that large before. Ethan began to suckle her breast, while Latan ran his fingers through the hair guarding her pussy.

"This is so sexy, the way you trim here." Ethan leaned down and inhaled deeply. "I can smell the cream that's collecting between your legs." His finger ran up her slit gathering the proof of her desire. While he held her gaze, his finger plunged between his lips. "God, you taste good, baby." Moving to lie between her spread thighs, Ethan lowered his face to her pussy and inhaled deeply once more. "I feel like I could take you inside me and hold you forever." His shoulders pushed her legs wider. "I'm gonna bury myself in your velvet wetness, Tania, and I may never come out."

Latan alternated between sucking and flicking her nipple with his tongue, before transferring to the other side. He gently closed his teeth over the turgid nipple, dragging them to the tip, while continuing to tug and pinch the neglected side. Tania lost control, groaning, nearly purring at the exquisite pleasure. Latan bit harder and then soothed the sting with his tongue.

Ethan's fingers stroked her labia and opened her wide to his gaze. His tongue licked the length of her slit, laving the pulsing bundle of nerves hidden in the folds. He gently pushed two fingers into her channel, causing her to squeeze her thighs together, trapping his hand inside. She clenched her pussy around his fingers in an effort to get the friction she so desired. He ran his tongue up the slit of her wet pussy, feasting on her juices. "She's delicious, bro," he cried. His teeth captured her clit and tugged, while his fingers began pumping in and out.

"Ethan," she moaned as she felt her pussy flood with cream so fast it trickled down her thighs. She felt herself reaching, yearning for the fulfillment that only these two men could give her. Her words cut off as Latan covered her lips, plunging his tongue deep at the same time Ethan drilled his tongue deep into her pussy. Ethan pressed down on her clit at the same time Latan pinched her nipple hard, and Tania flew over the edge. She screamed as her orgasm hit with a kaleidoscope of colors, stealing her breath away, and making her wish it could go on forever.

When she was able to focus on her surroundings again, Tania found her legs thrown wide, her arms above her head with her hands gripping the pillows securely, and two sets of male eyes trained on her body. She could feel the blush moving up her chest as she slowly lowered her arms.

Ethan surged forward, grabbed both her arms, and held them down by her head. "Don't be embarrassed, you're so beautiful when you come." He prodded her opening with his erection while he gazed into her eyes. "I wanna bury myself in your sweet pussy," he whispered, and then waited as if he wanted her permission. She nodded once and then moved toward him eagerly, aiding his descent. She cried out as he thrust, filling her almost painfully, and then relaxed when his body stilled. "Relax, baby, we'll take it slow and easy. I don't wanna hurt you."

Latan leaned down and sucked a nipple into his mouth, teasing the hardened tip with his tongue. "You're so beautiful, Tania."

She gasped. "Wait, stop."

Ethan froze. "What's wrong, baby?"

"Condom," she groaned, "we forgot condoms!" Tania felt like crying. Never before had she gotten so carried away that she forgot about protecting herself. It was doubly important for her since she would never risk getting pregnant.

Ethan leaned forward and pressed a tender kiss against her lips. "Shh, baby, it's okay. We took care of it."

"You did?" She glanced down to where their bodies joined.

He chuckled. "Well, you can't see mine, but look over at Latan."

She looked and felt relief when she saw the latex covering his cock. She turned back to Ethan. "Sorry, I didn't see you put them on, and I was..."

"Shhh, it's okay. We would never do anything to hurt or endanger you, baby, I promise." He thrust his hips a few more times and then abruptly pulled out. He grinned down at her with a wicked glint in his eye. "Turn over and get on your hands and knees, baby. We both wanna play."

* * * *

"Take off the condom, Latan. I want to taste you."

Ethan watched as Tania slowly turned over and got up on her hands and knees. He'd been perfectly content with her on her back, but Latan had sent him a message through their link threatening to kick his ass if he didn't let him play, too.

He watched his brother approach Tania's face and then focused his attention on the gorgeous rear end in front of him. His hands tightened on her buttocks, his thumb tracing the lower crease of her ass. A single finger pressed against her anus, followed immediately by her groan and the clenching of her butt cheeks. Ethan chuckled. "Relax, baby. I'm not gonna do anything you don't want. I'm just playing around right now, I promise." He curved his hand over her bare flesh, stroking the fleshy globes again and again until she relaxed. He pushed with the tip of one finger until it slipped past the outer ring of muscle into the heat of the dark, forbidden entrance. "You're so tight. It's gonna be a little piece of heaven in here." Ethan sighed, slapped her hard on one of her cheeks, and then laughed when she growled. "You've got a beautiful ass, baby, and I'm gonna fuck it someday." He leaned down close to her ear. "Count on it!" He grinned when she mumbled, because her mouth was stuffed full of Latan's cock.

Ethan aligned his erection with her pussy and thrust upward into her fiery warmth. He groaned when she squeezed his shaft with her inner walls and then slapped her ass again when he heard her muffled giggle. In one smooth move, he was buried balls deep. Grabbing her hips, he rode her hard, pumping back and forth. He pushed deeply, grinding his hips against her clit and then retreating in rough, jerky movements. Reaching below her, he grabbed her breast and began pinching and tugging on her nipple. She urged him on, pushing her hips back to meet his thrusts.

Tania pulled her mouth from Latan's erection, her breath coming in shallow pants. "Harder, oh, please, fuck me harder, Ethan," she cried before sucking Latan back inside.

Ethan responded by pounding into her like a freight train. "I'm not gonna last long," he cried. His balls drew up tight against his body when he felt her muscles contract around his cock as she climaxed. He shuddered and thrashed as he came, shooting pulse after pulse of his semen into the latex protection. Spent, he fell forward onto the smooth skin of her back, listening as Latan growled out his own release. He couldn't understand the feelings he had for this woman. Even sharing her with Latan, he felt as if they belonged together. Her scent didn't identify her as his mate, but everything in his head and heart told him that they were meant to be together. *What the hell is wrong with me? We've shared lots of women, and I've never felt like this before. I want something more with her, something more than sharing her with Latan.* He glanced at his brother. *What's he gonna say when he finds out? Will she come between us?*

Tania looked over her shoulder and grinned. "Okay, big guy. You're a little heavy for me to support for too much longer."

"God, I'm sorry, baby." Ethan pulled away and froze at the voice sounding clearly in his head. It wasn't his brother. It was his wolf! *Mine!*

* * * *

Latan breathed a sigh of relief as Ethan encouraged Tania to turn over. He thought he might explode if he didn't feel the damp heat of her mouth soon. He'd nearly exploded when she said she wanted to taste him. He scooted over to kneel in front of her, his cock jutting up toward her face. She looked up at him with a wicked grin, reached out and ran her finger over the head of his cock, and then sucked the finger into her mouth.

"Hmmm, good," she moaned.

He shook his head, smiling. "You are wicked, woman." His hands pushed back her beautiful reddish hair so he could gaze into her bright, green eyes. He'd thought her beautiful, but the firelight made her positively glow. Latan leaned down and licked her lips, memorizing their taste and texture. "I wanna feel your lips around my cock," he whispered. "Take me in your mouth. Will you do that, honey? Will you take me in and suck me dry?" He felt her body shudder and watched as her head descended to his shaft.

Tania flicked her tongue out and then dragged it slowly over the mushroom-shaped head of his cock, licking in a circle around the slit. A drop of pre-cum formed on the tip, quickly disappearing when she ran her tongue down in the slit with a teasing look in her eyes.

"Tease," he whispered.

Tania winked up at him, the firelight reflected in those amazing green eyes. She opened her mouth and wrapped her lips around him, sucking the head of his cock and then running her tongue around the sensitive ridge at its base. Her body jolted back and forth from the force of Ethan's thrusts when she suddenly pulled her mouth away from his throbbing erection and glanced back over her shoulder. "Harder, oh, please, fuck me harder, Ethan," she cried.

Latan rubbed her cheek with the head of his cock, leaving behind a damp trail. "Suck me, Tania, please, honey," he begged.

Gripping her fingers as far around the base of his erection as they would go, Tania leaned over, took him all the way to the back of her throat, and began sucking in earnest.

Latan threw back his head and closed his eyes. "I fucking love your mouth," he groaned.

Tania sucked him deep while she reached out to fondle his balls. Her dainty hand squeezed gently, making his eyes roll back in his head.

"That's it, honey, take me deep," he cried. He grabbed the sides of her head and held her in place as he slid in and out of her mouth, matching the steady rhythm of Ethan as he thrust into her pussy harder and faster.

He came with a growl, his cock jerking in her mouth as his orgasm tore through his body like an explosion. His hips jerked, spurting thick ropes of semen over her tongue and down the back of her throat. He struggled to catch his breath as he watched her lick him clean and then chuckled when she looked over her shoulder and told Ethan to move.

Sated, Latan fell down beside her, cuddling up to her warm body. *Shit, this feels so perfect. Like it's where I'm meant to be. By now, Ethan and I are usually seeing who can get out the door first. So why is it I don't wanna leave?* He looked over at his brother. *What would Ethan say if I asked him to step back and give me some time alone with Tania? I don't wanna hurt him, but I'm beginning to think she just might be my mate!*

"Hey, we never got to the wine," Ethan exclaimed.

Tania giggled. "I don't think I'm up for any wine now, guys. I'm wasted!"

Latan leaned down and nuzzled her neck. "Wasted, huh? Sounds like a pretty apt description to me."

"You know," Ethan continued, "as much as I love a romantic fire and all these cushy pillows, this floor is hard on the ass!"

Tania leaned up and looked down at the ass in question and smirked. "Well, we can't be damaging anything as fine as those cheeks of yours. It just so happens, I have a nice, soft, warm bed not twenty feet away from here."

"Sounds good to me," Latan said as he jumped to his feet, pulling Tania up behind him.

"You guys lock up for me while I take a minute to clean up, and then I'll join you in the bed." She walked into the bathroom, closing the door behind her.

Ethan walked into the kitchen, pulled off his condom, and then ran some water on a paper towel to clean up. "Bro, I don't wanna hurt you, but I'm developing some pretty strong feelings for Tania."

Latan looked at his brother in amazement. "This can't be good then because I have feelings for her, too! In fact, I think she may be my mate." He watched his brother closely for his reaction.

Ethan frowned. "That doesn't make any sense because my wolf's telling me to claim her. He should know if she's his mate or not."

"What are we gonna do? Because I'm not backing off. I know I'm meant to be with her." Latan looked at his brother for several long minutes. "Do you think that's why we've always wanted to share our women? Were we meant to share a mate as well?"

"I never heard of two wolves mating the same female, have you?"

"No, but that doesn't mean it can't happen. Maybe we should talk to Remus."

"Right, tell our Alpha, who already distrusts Tania, that we both want to mate her and bring her into the family." He gave Latan a shrewd look. "You get right on that and get back to me with what he says!"

"All right, you've made your point. So, what do we do?" Latan asked.

Ethan crossed over to the bed and lay down on the far side. "We wait and see if our feelings get stronger, and we wait until this business with Kaugh is settled. At least then, Remus will know that she's not involved in any of it."

Latan climbed onto the other side of the bed, leaving the middle for Tania. "Sounds like a plan, bro!" He glanced around the room. "Hey, where do you think her cat is?"

Ethan leaned up on his elbow. "I don't know, and it's weird. Look around. There aren't any food or water bowls here."

Latan looked around the room. "Okay, so what does that mean?"

"It means that something's not right with her precious cat, and I mean to find out what it is."

Chapter 4

Vincent Kaugh stopped in front of the small cottage and looked out at the woods surrounding the clearing. The early morning sounds of the forest coming to life were soothing. The rise of excitement in him was getting harder and harder to contain as he moved closer to achieving his life's goal. He glanced over to where his three associates waited beside the front door.

"So, what do you think, boss?" asked Marty.

"It's perfect, Marty, absolutely perfect. Plenty of cover. Well isolated, and easy to defend. Absolutely perfect. Is the paperwork all done?" Kaugh was anxious to move forward with his project.

"It will be as soon as I deliver a cashier's check for the full amount. The realtor called last night and said she would have everything ready after lunch today," Marty answered.

Kaugh felt a rush of satisfaction. "We'll go by the bank as soon as they open. I want you at her office by noon. The sooner we can move in, the better." He turned his attention to Calvin Ames. "When we get back to town, I want you call the lab in California. Tell them I want my equipment packed up. Ask for David, he'll know what I need. I want it here within the next two days, no excuses." He took a couple of steps toward the house and turned back. "Tell him I want at least twenty vials of the Catalyn Inhibitor and two surgical setups."

Stepping carefully through the weeds, Kaugh went and stood in front of the nearest window. "Sean, put bars on all the windows, and reinforce the doors on all the rooms upstairs and downstairs. I want double locks on both of the larger basement rooms and the bedroom that faces the creek. Get me some type of metal cots or hospital beds.

I want two in each room downstairs and one in the back bedroom upstairs." He gave the man a shrewd look. "I want them bolted to the floor, and they should be fitted with heavy, leather restraints. And, Sean, I want it done by Friday morning, no excuses."

Sean grinned. "Any chance we'll be entertaining that hot little redhead hanging around that architect's office?"

"For God's sake, Sean, keep it in your pants. Haven't you learned your lesson yet?" Calvin asked. He looked over at Kaugh. "If you don't mind me asking, how did you get started with these animal people?"

"Animal people." Kaugh laughed. "I guess that's as good a description as any. I was fresh out of college when I met Mark Landry. He ran the California lab until he was killed in a raid about sixteen years ago." He walked over and sat down on the porch. "He was a fucking genius in so many ways, but an idiot when it came to security. He never told me how he first became aware of shape-shifters, but I strongly suspect it had something to do with his government funding. He was trying to mix the species together."

"What the hell for?" asked Sean.

Kaugh shrugged. "My guess is that it was the government's idea. They were looking to create a new breed, answerable only to them. Landry tried to combine the most fearsome of the shifters we knew about, to form one new species that had all the traits of both. The theory being it would be practically unstoppable, and at the beck and call of the US Government." He laughed. "It didn't work out that way, though."

"What happened?" Marty asked.

"His first success at mixing the DNA of two shifters resulted in a less than fearsome creature." He chuckled. "His disappointment is what got him killed. He got lax in his security, and one of the male test subjects escaped. I tried to get him to move our operations to a secure location, but he refused. He said the animal would be so grateful to finally be free it would run and never look back."

"Okay, so it came back?" Marty crouched down and gazed into the doctor's eyes.

"Oh, yeah, he came back all right," Kaugh answered. "He came back and brought quite a few of his friends with him. They stormed the lab, freed all the subjects, and killed Landry. I barely escaped with my life." He thought for a moment. "It was strange. He came back with friends, but not all the same species. The original escapee was Felidae, *Puma concolor*, otherwise known as a cougar or mountain lion. When he returned, he was accompanied by Canidae, *Canis lupus*." He looked at his three associates. "In other words, gentlemen, wolves!"

"So how did you escape?" Calvin asked.

"Easily, my friend. I like to think I'm smarter than the average animal, even if that animal has a human side."

"You think the bars and restraints can keep them from escaping this time?" Sean was beginning to look a little nervous.

"It's not a problem anymore. I perfected a formula several years ago that, once injected, will keep the creatures from shifting. It can go either way, keep them from shifting into their animals, or keep the animals from shifting back to human."

"Permanently?" asked Calvin.

"No, it'll last about forty-eight hours without a second injection. It's my practice to inject every twenty-four hours to keep them in whatever state I want." He got to his feet. "Okay, we've wasted enough time here. Is everyone clear on what their jobs are for the next two days?" When everyone nodded, Kaugh headed for the car. "Well then, gentlemen, let's go hunting!"

* * * *

Tania slowly became aware of the sun shining through the cabin window. She stretched lazily and then froze when her arm encountered warm skin. In a flash, the events of the night before flashed across her mind's eye. *Oh, God, they're still here! What am I gonna do? I never should have let this happen. They make me feel things and want things that can't be. Why couldn't they have left while I was still sleeping?* She almost snorted. *Because, you dolt, you told them to stay, even invited them into your bed. What the hell were you thinking?* She felt her beast stir close to the surface. She was sending her thoughts to Tania's conscious mind. *Oh, no, not now, you little traitor!* Great, her animal half wanted to keep the big, bad wolves!

A large, calloused hand trailed down her arm. "I know you're awake, baby," Ethan whispered.

Tania yelped and jumped clear out of the bed. Her eyes narrowed when Ethan laughed. "You startled me." She pulled the blanket off the bed, wrapped it around her nude body, and then glanced toward the open bathroom door. "Where's Latan?"

Ethan shrugged and sat up. The covers drifted down to his lap, revealing his broad chest and the light sprinkling of hair tapering down and disappearing beneath the covers. "He got paged on his cell about an hour ago and had to take off." He grinned wickedly. "I told him I would stay here and keep you company."

She was shaking her head before he even finished his statement. "No, you can't stay."

"Why not?" he asked with a grin, and started scooting toward the side of the bed.

"I mean it, Ethan, you have to go now. Last night was nice, but it was a mistake. I'm still not gonna be here for very long, and this relationship doesn't have anywhere to go." She looked away as he got to his feet, afraid of being tempted.

"Last night was more than just *nice*, and this relationship can go anywhere we want it to. You just have to believe."

"I *believe* that last night should never have happened. No matter what kind of person you believe me to be, I can't just be a plaything for the Alpha's brothers." Her voice rose as she fought her own desire and that of her inner beast. *I have to get him to leave before I do something stupid, like knock him back into the bed!*

"Plaything for the Alpha's brothers," he bellowed. Ethan rushed forward and grabbed Tania and then slung her over his shoulder as she squealed. He walked back to the bed, her ass thrust high in the air.

"Put me down, you big oaf," she yelled, kicking her feet and pounding on his back. One stinging slap to the back of her thigh had her quieting down. "You hit me," she said through gritted teeth.

"Damn right I did, and I'm about to hit you several more times. You're gonna get your butt spanked for even thinking that we consider you a plaything."

"You better not lay one hand on me, Ethan Wind River, or I'll make you sorry you were ever born."

"I'll take my chances, baby." He set her on her feet beside the bed and yanked away her blanket protection. Before she could form a protest, he sat down and pulled her over his lap.

"Ethan, I mean it, let me up." The blood rushed to her head, partially from gravity, but mostly from the embarrassment of her naked ass exposed across his lap.

"No can do, baby. It's time for your spanking. By the time I'm through, you're gonna admit that we're all more than just playmates."

Tania felt his hard hand rub across her butt in a gentle caress. Then cool air kissed her clenching skin right before a slap on her rump had her squealing and trying to jerk away. "That hurt, you overgrown ass," she cried.

"It's supposed to hurt, woman." He ran his hand gently over the stinging flesh before giving the other cheek an equally hard blow. Ethan balanced her on one knee and hooked his other leg over hers, effectively holding her still for his punishment. Again and again, his broad hand smacked against the tender cheeks of her ass. After several blows to each side, he slipped his hand between her legs and found her clit with his fingers.

Tania's ass was on fire, the heat going straight to her pussy. She groaned at the feel of his fingers and raised her hips to give him more room to play. "Please," she whispered when he pinched the little bundle of nerves.

Ethan released her legs, stood up with her in his arms, and tossed her onto the bed. Quickly, he crawled up her body, pressing his hardness against her. "You're so much more than a plaything, Tania," he whispered. "Latan and I both have feelings for you, real feelings that we don't wanna let go of. I'm asking you to give us a chance."

Tania gazed into his eyes and reached out with her feelings. She couldn't sense anything but sincerity, lust, and some confusing fear. She sighed. *I am so screwed!* "You're squishing me, big man," she taunted.

Ethan tightened his arms around her and rolled, leaving her sprawled across his chest. "Is that better?" he asked with a smirk.

"Oh, yeah." She grinned. She reached down and licked his neck, then watched the flare of heat in his eyes. Ignoring the hands trailing down her back, she attacked his lips, tracing them with her tongue before licking them open. His hands cupped the back of her head, fingers threading through her hair, as he took control of their kiss. He bit at her lip, his mouth hard and unyielding as he nibbled. His taste flooded her senses and left her inner beast begging for more. She swept the inside of his mouth with her tongue and brushed her breasts against his chest. His moan broke the silence of the cabin.

Tania broke from the kiss and ran her lips down his throat as she slid down his muscular length. Her hands slid through the sparse hair covering to the brown, flat nipples. Leaning closer, she pressed her lips against his chest and then sucked one of the small nubs between her teeth.

"Tania." He hissed. "You're killing me, baby!"

Ignoring him, she dragged her tongue across his chest and gave the other nipple the same attention. Giving one final nip, she trailed a line of wet kisses down the middle of his chest. Scooting down farther, she got a close-up look at his cock, rock hard and lying against his stomach. Her fingers closed around the base as she bent and placed a kiss, then a lick, across the tip. Ethan's hips jerked, his shaft twitching in her hand.

She cupped his hairy balls and squeezed, just enough to make him moan, while she licked away the pre-cum forming on the plum-colored head.

Ethan's hands tightened on her shoulders. "Baby, please, I can't take much more."

She looked up and saw a face flushed with desire, all that desire aimed only at her. He took her by the shoulders and urged her up, his hands sliding down, rubbing and kneading her back. Her hands slid over the taut muscles of his thighs as she pushed herself up. The need was building inside her, and she knew she couldn't wait much longer.

She placed a soft, seductive kiss against his stomach and another against his neck before claiming his lips for herself. Her tongue swirled inside, flicking against his teeth and across the roof of his mouth before retreating. "We need a condom," she gasped.

He nodded toward the table beside the bed. "Right there."

Looking over, she grabbed the foil pack and opened it, then reached for his cock with her trembling hand. Carefully, she rolled the latex over his length. Inching down, she placed the tip at the entrance of her pussy, anchored her hands on his chest, and impaled herself slowly. He groaned, the muscles in his chest quivering.

"Oh, baby, I love how you feel. I'll never get enough of you," he moaned.

Tania dug her fingernails into his shoulders and squeezed his shaft with her inner muscles. His hands moved to her hips, then cupped her bottom and raised and lowered her on his cock. His hips flexed, letting him sink just a little deeper inside her. She held on to his shoulders and rocked her hips, then sat up and started to ride him faster, her orgasm getting closer and closer.

Ethan began thrusting his hips up, matching her strokes. "I'm not gonna last long, baby," he mumbled. His hand reached between her legs. When his finger touched her clit, she groaned and tried to open her legs wider. Ethan left his finger pressed against the tiny bundle of nerves, and every time she sank down on his cock, it rubbed back and forth across the center of her heat.

She felt her release building deep inside her body. As she strained toward a peak, Ethan rammed up into her, stroking her clit one final time. Her scream echoed through the cabin as she came, the walls of her pussy gripping his cock tightly. It was enough to send him over the edge, growling out his own release. She could feel the pulsing of his climax as he came inside her. Exhausted, she collapsed against his chest and tried to catch her breath.

Ethan's arms came up and tightened around her waist. He nuzzled his face into her hair. "I'm falling in love with you, Tania. I don't wanna lose you," he whispered.

Tania froze, and then looked up to meet his gaze. Before she could say anything, his lips covered hers, his tongue plunging deep. Her inner beast screamed inside her head. *Yes, mine!*

Ethan freed her lips and nibbled his way into the crease of her neck. "It's still pretty early, how about a little more sleep, and then I'll take you to breakfast."

Tania snorted. "I prefer to eat my food, not wear it. You think your ex is up to serving me breakfast?"

His face red, Ethan groaned. "Okay, what if I promise to make you breakfast?"

She laughed. "Sounds better." Slowly, she raised her hips, gritting her teeth as their bodies pulled apart. Sighing, she dropped down on the bed beside him.

He leaned over and gave her a brief kiss. "I'll be right back." As she watched, Ethan left the bed and went into the bathroom, shutting the door behind him.

Tania rolled over onto her back. *What am I gonna do now? I need to get out of here and finish this job so I can disappear. They're getting to me. He's making me think of homes and pups and...* Tania wiped at the tears that escaped from her eyes. It didn't matter what she wanted, she knew what she could never have.

* * * *

Tania watched the sleeping man beside her and sighed quietly. She'd pretended to fall asleep about an hour ago and waited patiently for him to succumb to slumber himself. Feeling like the time was right, she slowly began to inch off the wide bed. After several minutes, she finally found herself standing on the floor gazing down at the man who'd professed to be falling in love with her.

Love, is that really what I'm feeling? She walked toward the door, her beast furious at being led away from its mate.

My mate? He's my mate?

The answer came swiftly from the beast within. *They both are!*

Tania had never heard the words *I love you* spoken to her, much less said them to anyone. And now she faced the prospect of having to walk away from the two men who might have been able to love her. Quietly, she walked over to the back door, turning one last time to gaze at the man in her bed. "I love you, you and Latan," she whispered.

At least I got to say it once in my life.

Opening the door, she slipped outside and immediately shifted into her beast. Raising her face to the wind, she growled, then took off running through the trees.

* * * *

Melissa snuggled up against the warm, male body behind her and smiled. For the past two nights, she'd awakened in exactly the same spot, safe and cozy in Mali's house, in Mali's bed. She'd never been so happy and so scared, all at the same time.

She couldn't believe this handsome man was so taken with her. He treated her like a queen, and she'd never felt so beautiful and desirable in her life. She knew without a doubt that she loved him, and it would break her heart when she had to walk away. A man like him was bound to move on sooner or later in search of new conquests, so she'd made up her mind to enjoy him for as long as she could.

Her eyes closed in delight when she felt warm, soft lips against the curve of her neck. "Hmmm," she moaned.

"Good morning, Sunshine," Mali crooned.

Melissa turned over in his arms and smiled up at his handsome face. "Good morning to you, too. Did you sleep well?"

His arms tightened, pulling her closer. "I always sleep well with you in the bed beside me." He leaned over and pressed a light kiss against her lips. "You taste so good in the morning." He moved in closer, his gaze on her lips, and growled softly when Melissa put a hand on his chest and pushed him away.

She giggled. "What is it with you and growling?" "Why did you push me away?" he asked, his voice sounding hurt.

"Sorry, but I need to talk to you, and if you start the kissing, then I'll forget everything I needed to say."

He laughed. "Okay, Sunshine, we'll postpone the kissing temporarily. What's on your mind?"

"I'm leaving today," she said, and then winced when he growled once more.

"What the hell does that mean, you're leaving?"

She started, surprised at how angry he sounded. "Don't get all bent out of shape. It's only for a couple of days. I got a really good offer on my house, and now, I have to go back for the closing."

He narrowed his eyes. "And you're just now telling me?"

She gave a very unladylike snort. "Well, yeah, I only got the call yesterday from the realtor. The offer's really good, but they want to close right away since the house is vacant. I came over last night to let you know." She glared at him. "You never gave me a chance to say anything. I walked in the door, and you jumped my bones. We made love for hours, and you drove it right out of my head. I've been lying here waiting for you to wake up so I could tell you my news."

Mali stared at her for a minute, a frown on his face. "I don't like it, not one bit. Nope, sorry, you can't go alone."

"Excuse me?" she said quietly.

"You heard me, you can't go alone. It's not safe. Call her back, and tell her it'll have to be next week."

"And just why would it be safer next week?" she asked, trying to calm her temper.

"Because I can get away then and come with you. I'll be able to handle things for you."

* * * *

Mali watched as his mate sat up in the bed, her face so red he worried for her health. *Uh-oh, I guess I've put my foot in it now!* He ran his hand up the smooth skin of her back. "Sunshine, don't be mad. I just wanna keep you safe."

"You overbearing, pompous bag of hot air! I've been taking care of myself pretty much for the last ten years, and I see no reason why I can't go on doing it for the next ten. I'm not some silly little twit that needs a man to take care of every little thing. I'm a businesswoman, a full partner in Michael's new firm, and I think I'm perfectly capable of traveling to Houston to sign a stack of papers to sell my house."

Mali winced, and then sighed as his mate's tirade went on and on. He'd obviously taken the wrong approach. He needed to do something to make things right before she got up out of the bed and left. *Things would be so much simpler if I could just put my mark on you to claim you. The mating fever would keep you close to me no matter what.*

"Are you listening to me?" she yelled.

Making a quick decision, Mali pounced. He tackled her down to the bed and then covered her body with his.

"Get off of me," she cried, pushing at his shoulders.

"Never," he whispered. "I need you, Sunshine. I want you in my life. I'm falling in love with you, and I have this insatiable need to keep you safe."

"You're falling in love with me," she said, her voice hesitant, her hands relaxing against his chest as he rolled them to their sides.

He smiled down at her. "I'm more than halfway there, Sunshine." Mali nuzzled his face against her cheek and traced the softness of her lips with his finger. "I want you, Melissa," he whispered against her soft skin. She closed her eyes when he kissed her eyelids softly, her lips parting on a sigh. His tongue dipped into her ear before licking a trail down the side of her neck. The wolf had to be restrained when her head fell back, exposing her throat, Mali's canines lengthening in anticipation of the mating.

"Tell me this isn't a dream," she whispered.

Mali cupped her face in his hands and brought his lips down to hers. He captured her mouth in a deep kiss, tongues tangling together, their breath mingling, while his hand slipped along her shoulder and down to her waist. His groan vibrated against her lips as she pressed closer, rubbing her taut nipples against his chest. Reaching up, he cupped the rose-tipped mounds.

Grinding his throbbing arousal against her belly, Mali began licking his way down to her breasts. Gently, he thumbed one nipple, then leisurely drew circles around the tip with his tongue while his other hand continued to mold and squeeze. Melissa moaned softly as he rolled her nipple under his thumb, teasing the sensitive flesh. Capturing the tip between his thumb and fingers, he tugged, and then ran his tongue over the hardened nub.

Sliding down her trembling body, Mali let his hand skim down her back, tightening briefly on her buttocks, before moving down to her dainty ankles. He took one of her feet in his hands and began to suck her toes one at a time, chuckling when she squirmed, and tried to pull away.

"Are you crazy?" she cried. "Stop that, I'm ticklish!"

Licking the bottom of her foot one last time, his hand caressed up her shin and over her knee, where he allowed his knuckles to brush against the inside of her thigh as he urged her over onto her back.

"Oh, Mali," she groaned.

"Shh, Sunshine, let me love you," he whispered. His hand brushed against the curly patch of damp hair over her mound, his fingers slipping into her folds, probing her moist heat. His thumb stroked her wet pussy before he nudged her legs apart and settled between her thighs. Her slit was slick with juices when his finger stroked inside her molten core. In and out of her hot sheath he stroked as he leaned forward and breathed in the scent of his mate's arousal.

Melissa's harsh groan sounded loud in the quiet room when his fingers spread open her labia and pushed back the hood covering her clit. He leaned forward and licked at the tiny bundle of nerves while his fingers continued thrusting inside her warmth. His thumb rubbed at the swollen nub before taking it between his fingers and tugging, her hot juices pouring over his hand. A taste better than sweet candy flooded his mouth as he licked her from anus to clit, flicked the little bud with the tip of his tongue, and then closed his lips around it and sucked. Her legs trembled, her inner muscles clenching around his invading fingers, when he blew softly against the center of her pleasure.

"Come for me, Sunshine. Come on my tongue."

Melissa's hips jerked, and she cried out as she came, fresh, hot cream flooding her pussy. Mali lapped and sucked until her tremors began to slow down, then he got slowly to his knees, his cock jutting out from a nest of black curls at the juncture of his thighs. Melissa licked her lips, her eyes glued to his erection, as he lowered himself to lie on the bed beside her.

Taking her hand, Mali led it down to his straining shaft. "Touch me," he moaned raggedly. Pleasure made his balls tingle as she began stroking up and down his throbbing cock. A soft moan escaped his lips at the feel of her cool fingers against his warm skin, and he buried his face in the crook of her neck when she ran her thumb across the sensitive tip. He trembled at the feel of her tongue as it swept across the broad head before sliding up and down the hard length. The hot suction of her mouth was like heaven and hell as it caressed his aching dick. He started when her hand caressed his sac and then growled loudly when he felt something warm and wet slide across his balls.

He couldn't wait any longer. Glancing down, he eased his rock-hard cock into her welcoming mouth, his hips pushing forward as if they had a mind of their own. Several times, he pumped in and out while she hollowed out her cheeks and sucked strongly, then suddenly pulled free of her hold and sprang up to his knees.

Melissa gazed up at him, a question in her eyes. "What's wrong?"

Mali smiled and reached toward the bedside table and grabbed a small foil packet. "Nothing's wrong, Sunshine. I just don't wanna come in your mouth, at least not this time." He ripped open the package and rolled the latex protection over his erection. "If you're going away, I'm gonna fuck you so hard you'll feel it for a week!" One knee moved between her thighs, parting them, followed quickly by the other, his body pushing her back against the pillows. His cock slipped between her spread thighs, probing her fiery entrance and rubbing in her slick folds. He slid in with a powerful thrust, her legs wrapping around his hips, her nails dragging down his back. He pushed his cock deeper until his balls bounced against her ass and then began pumping in and out. Her inner muscles clamped down, making him lose his rhythm for a moment. Cupping her bottom in his hands, he lifted her ass, changing his angle so he rubbed against her clit as he pounded into her wet sheath.

"I need to…please, Mali, I need to come."

Mali hammered into her several more times, then bent forward and roughly took her nipple between his teeth and tugged. "Come for me," he groaned.

Melissa stiffened in his arms and then shuddered. Arching upward, she let out a cry as she came, her walls convulsing around his shaft. Her body went limp as he surged into her harder and faster, his balls drawing up in preparation for his own release. Then, he grunted in pleasure, his cock jerking as it exploded deep inside her. For several minutes, he lay connected to his mate, memorizing the feel of her body and the scent of her skin, and then withdrew and collapsed to the bed, pulling her tightly into his arms.

Mali rubbed his cheek along the top of her head, spreading his scent as much as he could. *Damn, I hate letting you go without a mating mark. Anything could happen to you, and I wouldn't be there to protect you.*

"Mali, I know you're not happy about my trip, but you're gonna have to get over it. I'll only be gone a couple of days, and then I'll be back for good. Don't you trust me?"

He sighed heavily. "Sunshine, it's not about trust. I trust you explicitly. It's everyone else I have problems with." He cupped her cheek and turned her face up. "I'm old-fashioned, brought up to believe a man protects his mate at all times."

"Mate?" she squeaked.

He coughed and pressed her face against his chest. "You know what I mean. You're my woman, and I don't like the idea of you traveling alone."

"Get over it," she said, her voice muffled, her head held tightly against him.

"Not likely," he snorted, and then held her even tighter when she tried to get up. "Settle down, Sunshine. I said I didn't like it, I didn't say I wasn't gonna respect it." His lips buried in the curls at the top of her head. "I'm not gonna try and stop you from going, but I am gonna count the minutes until you're back."

She pulled back and gazed up into his eyes. “Thank you.” Her hand caressed along the side of his face. “Why don’t you concentrate on finishing my apartment while I’m gone so I have a place of my own when I get back?”

“When’s Michael due back from his honeymoon?” he asked. He didn’t bother telling her he had no intention of finishing the apartment. He firmly expected to move his mate into his own house after she learned about the wolves. Michael could do whatever he wanted with the apartment upstairs from his office, but Melissa would live in it over his dead body.

“They’ll be back this Friday.” She lay back against the pillows. “That’s why it’ll be good for you to have a few uninterrupted days to finish. I know he’s gonna want to jump into work when he gets back, and it’ll be easier if I’m living upstairs.”

Mali grunted. “Yeah, okay, I’ll get everything done that needs to be done before he gets home Friday.” To take her mind off his vague promise, he changed the subject. “Where are Michael and Ariane gonna live while their house is being built?”

“Michael said Remus and Maddie offered to put them up for a while. Maddie said their house is big enough they could be there for weeks without ever seeing one another.” She laughed.

Mali grinned at the sound of her laughter. “Are you gonna be a good girl and let me take you to the airport?”

“You don’t have to do that, I can—”

“Sunshine,” he growled.

She looked up at him, bared her teeth, and growled back, causing Mali to throw back his head and laugh. “All right, Mr. Growly, I’ll give in this once and let you drive me. You do realize that means you’ll have to pick me up when I fly home, don’t you?”

“I’m glad to hear you call this home. I’ll happily drive to the airport to bring you back here.” Bending his head, he closed his lips over hers, his tongue sliding deep, licking and exploring. After several minutes, Melissa placed her hands against his chest and pushed. Mali leaned back and stared at her flushed face.

"Don't start something I don't have time to finish, big man. I need to get a shower and get back to the bed and breakfast to pack a bag."

For just a moment, his arms tightened, his wolf not wanting to let her go any more than he did, and then he sighed and released her from his hold. "All right, Sunshine, we'll do it your way this time, but things are gonna change when you come home."

Melissa gave him a puzzled look, shrugged, and rolled out of the bed. She headed toward the door and then glanced back over her shoulder, a wicked grin on her face. "I still have a little time. Last one in the shower has to get on their knees."

Melissa yelped and ran for the bathroom when Mali jumped from the bed. He chuckled at her disappearing back. "Not much incentive there, Sunshine. I win either way." Grinning, he stalked toward his escaping mate, visions of her standing naked, water sliding down between her thighs, filling his head.

* * * *

Latan's footsteps quickened as he neared the small cottage where Tania was staying. He'd received a call before sunrise from one of the wolves keeping tabs on Kaugh. When he'd heard Kaugh, and all three of his men, were at the remote house they were trying to buy, Latan had shifted and quickly gone to check things out for himself. Hauling himself out of Tania's warm bed had been the hardest thing he'd ever done.

He didn't understand the feelings he had for this woman, feelings that he'd never had before. *I'm gonna have to sit down and talk to Ethan soon. I've got to find a way to make him understand that it's different for me this time. I need her in my life.* He looked up as the cabin came into view. *I don't hear anything. Maybe they're still asleep.* He shifted and walked up to the cabin door, careful not to make any noise. The thought of sneaking in and crawling up beside a naked Tania had his cock standing at attention in record-breaking speed.

Easing the door open, he stopped to listen. *It doesn't sound like they're up. Wait, what is that?* He stepped through the door and glanced around. *Oh, for crying out loud! Ethan, you sound like a damn chain saw!* Stepping farther into the darkened room, he was dismayed to see his brother spread eagle on the large bed, snoring loud enough to wake the dead, and all alone. Latan checked the bathroom, hoping to find the woman of his dreams, and came up empty handed. He took a moment to grab his clothes and redress. Fuming, he stalked over to the bed.

"Ethan," he called out. His anger climbed another notch when his brother continued sleeping. "Ethan, damn it," he yelled a little louder. This time, he got a snort and the shaking of a hand for his trouble. Exasperated, he picked up a pillow and brought it crashing down on Ethan's chest. "Ethan, wake the hell up!"

"Hey," Ethan growled as he sprung up in the bed.

Latan shook his head as he stared at his brother. Ethan crouched in the center of the firm mattress in a fighting stance, naked, with a morning erection. "Where the hell is Tania?"

Ethan growled again. "What the hell did you do that for?" He glanced around. "Where's Tania?"

"I asked you first, asshole. I left her here, against my better judgment, curled up next to you. How the hell did you lose her?"

Ethan looked around in confusion. "She's not in the bathroom?"

"No, she isn't," Latan said through gritted teeth. "What happened after I left?"

"We made love and then went back to sleep." Ethan climbed off the bed and reached for his pants. "She was all cuddled up next to me when I fell asleep." He laughed. "You really missed it, little bro."

"Missed what?" he asked suspiciously.

"Our little lady has a slightly kinky side. I spanked her naked ass, and she really got off on it."

In spite of his annoyance with his brother, Latan felt his cock begin to harden. "She liked it, huh? Damn, I wish I could've been here for that." He looked at Ethan through narrowed eyes. "You're sure she liked it? Something made her run off while you were snoring away."

"Trust me, she liked it. She sure as hell didn't fake that wet pussy." He eyed his brother for a moment. "I really like her, bro. She's something special."

Latan walked over and looked out the window. "Yeah, she's definitely something else." He didn't want to have this conversation with Ethan, yet. He needed more time to figure out how to ask his brother to back off.

"Keep a watch for her. I'm gonna look around some."

Latan turned and looked at his brother. "Look around for what?"

"Remus is so convinced she's up to something, we should see if we can prove him wrong." He walked over to the dresser and began opening drawers. A couple of minutes later, he let out a long, low whistle. "Holy shit," he groaned.

"What is it?" Latan asked. He turned and saw Ethan holding up something red. He looked closer and saw it was a red, lacy thong. "Have we really stooped so low you're fingering her underwear now?"

Shooting Latan an evil glare, Ethan dropped the feminine garment and slammed the drawer shut. "We both know she's keeping secrets, and we both wanna know what those secrets are." He walked over to her desk and began rifling through her papers. "Since I don't think she's just gonna up and tell us what we wanna know, I don't see any other options but to snoop."

Latan shrugged and returned his gaze to the outside clearing. He hated to admit it, but Ethan was right. They needed to find out what Tania was hiding. He couldn't shake the feeling that some type of danger stalked her. The sound of kitchen cabinets closing caught his attention. "Nothing?" he asked.

"No, there's nothing that's even remotely suspicious." He walked back over to the couch and grabbed his shirt. He'd just put one arm in a sleeve when he froze and glanced around the room. "Where's the cat?"

"Huh?" Latan looked up.

"The cat, where's the damn cat?" Ethan asked.

Latan looked around. "I don't know, maybe she went out with Tania."

"Maybe," Ethan replied. "But where's the litter box, the cat toys. Hell, where's the cat's food and water." He surveyed the room. "There's nothing here that even suggests a cat lives here."

"Okay, so what're you saying?" Latan asked, clearly puzzled.

Ethan sighed. "I'm not sure, but something's not right. I just haven't figured out what yet." He dropped his shirt and headed for the bathroom. "I'm gonna take a shower."

"We're not leaving?"

"Not me," he called over his shoulder. "I wanna be here when our vanishing princess returns."

Latan shrugged and began peeling off his own shirt. "Don't use all the hot water," he yelled out. No way would he leave Ethan here alone with the woman he wanted to mate. *Holy shit! I really do want to take her as my mate!* He glanced toward the bathroom when he heard the sound of water running. *Shit, what am I gonna do? It doesn't feel right to cut him out.* "I'm gonna have to talk to Remus and get his advice," he whispered. Sighing, he flopped down on the bed and grabbed up a pillow. The smell of her perfume seeped into his skin. *Why is it we only smell your perfume and not your beast?*

* * * *

Remus looked around the room and sighed. He'd called this meeting with the Elders to update them on the surveillance of Dr. Kaugh, and now, he regretted involving them. He knew the National Council had told Vanard they wanted the Wind River Pack to back off. Apparently, they had their own plan for dealing with the deadly doctor and didn't want interference from the local wolves. That would have been fine with Remus if his own mate wasn't in danger from the doctor's research. Kaugh's history with Dr. Constantine made it impossible for Remus to step back.

"You're wasting all this manpower on watching Kaugh and his men. Have you actually learned anything?" Vanard asked.

"We've learned plenty," Remus argued. "This so-called doctor, who has access now to all of Constantine's research, just bought a secluded house only five miles away from our territory. Early this morning, he gave orders to have his equipment moved here from California."

"You're sure about that?" Lanicor asked.

"Yes," Remus said. "Sortee, the guard Latan left watching the house, overheard everything. They're also doing a little remodeling on the place. The kind of remodeling that involves bars on the windows and double locks on the doors."

"I understand your concern, Alpha, but you're walking a fine legal line here. You're already bordering on stalking this man. When, in actuality, he hasn't made any threats to the local population."

Remus grimaced. He hated lawyers with a passion, even those devoted to the pack. "Trust me, Lanicor. I'm not in the least worried about being charged with stalking."

"What's the plan, now that you have his location?" Vanard asked. "You know the Council wants us to take a step back and only observe."

"I don't give a damn what they want. I'm not gonna sit back and do nothing when the life of my mate, or, hell, the lives of all the wolves on the mountain, is in danger." He glanced around at the other

Elders. "I want a clean operation. We're watching them all carefully. Once his equipment, and all the research, is at the house, we'll take them out permanently."

"What can I do to help?" offered Koril.

Remus smiled gratefully at one half of his security team. "Right now, just make yourself available at a moment's notice. There's no way of knowing when this will go down, so I need everyone on standby."

Koril gazed over at his partner, Brenner, and nodded. "We'll be with you, Alpha," he promised.

Remus felt relief. "Thanks, guys, I want you to—"

"What the hell," Taynor yelled.

Remus looked to the back of the room. Taynor was kneeling down, struggling with something under the table. When he finally stood, a very familiar black cat thrashed about trying to escape his hands.

"Son of a bitch," Remus roared as he stormed toward the back of the room. "Well, well, well, I believe your name must be Kit." He glared down into the eyes of the struggling cat, trying to control the anger that was driving his wolf to the surface. "Koril, Brenner, search the building and the surrounding woods for our new schoolteacher. I'm willing to bet if her damn cat's here, she's not far behind." He reached out and grabbed Kit by the scruff of the neck, pulling her from Taynor's hands. Holding the tiny animal up so their eyes were even, Remus grinned. "I'm gonna find your owner, and when I do, I'm gonna make her extremely sorry for spying on us."

"You're making a fool of yourself," Vanard scolded. "What the hell's threatening a cat going to accomplish?"

Remus looked at his head Elder and gave a tiny growl and then looked back at the struggling feline and growled louder. Kit responded by hissing, then swinging her legs around and digging all her claws into Remus's unprotected arm.

"Shit," Remus yelped, and promptly lost his hold on her. She ran toward the door and then stopped and ran full speed back toward Remus. Her right front claws swiped toward his leg, her teeth bared, hair standing on end. "Hey," Remus yelled out as he jumped back to avoid further injury. "Grab that damn cat! I'm gonna lock her furry butt up for her own good!" He watched as the Elders scrambled, each of them trying to grab the crazed, little beast. Holding his stinging, bleeding arm, Remus watched incredulously as the small bundle of black fur sailed out the open window next to Vanard. "How the hell did that window get open?" he growled.

"Sorry, Remus." Vanard shrugged. "I opened it when I got here because it was so stuffy in here." He looked embarrassed. "I guess I forgot to close it."

Koril and Brenner came walking through the door before Remus could say anything to the older man. "Well, did you find anything?" he asked the two men.

"Sorry, Alpha," Brenner replied. "There's nobody in the building or anywhere within a half-mile radius of here that didn't belong. We never saw or smelled the teacher."

"Damn it." Remus kicked a chair out of his way as he headed out the door. "What the hell is going on?"

* * * *

Tania ran along the riverbank in her beast's form, enjoying the night sky and the soothing sound of the flowing water. Her thoughts centered on the two men who'd shared her bed the night before. *I've got to stay focused. I can't afford to have any distractions right now.* She stopped and gazed out over the water. Memories of the passion they'd shared flooded her mind. *Oh, God, how am I gonna walk away when this is over? I don't even know how to tell them what I am.* Despondent, she turned and headed for her temporary home.

As soon as the cabin came into sight, Tania let herself shift back into her human form. For several minutes, she stood and looked at the small structure she'd found such happiness in. Goose bumps spread over her naked skin as she cooled in the gentle night breeze. Thinking back on her day, she hung her head in shame. For the first time since she began working for the National Council, she'd failed to perform her duties. She'd been so caught up in thoughts of Ethan and Latan, she hadn't spent one minute on keeping track of Kaugh. Revenge for Tocho and justice for herself and the others had been her sole purpose for living as far back as she could remember. To think that the passion the brothers infused in her made her forget her whole purpose for being on the mountain was disgraceful. With a heavy sigh, she climbed the steps, opened the door, and stepped into the warm room.

Too late, she realized the room was too warm, a fire burning brightly in the fireplace that should be cold. She scented the male wolf just seconds before steely arms closed around her, binding her arms tightly to her sides. Fear surged for a moment, and then recognition of his scent filled her with longing. "Latan," she whispered. Ethan came walking out of the shadows, his expression one she couldn't read. As he came into the firelight, she gasped. He was naked, his cock fully erect, long and thick. At the same time, she became aware of a hardness pressing against the lower part of her back. She tried to pull away but was unable to break Latan's hold.

Ethan continued walking forward until a mere inch separated their skin. His hands slipped into her hair, his fingers curling into it. Moaning, he pressed a soft kiss against her mouth. His tongue skimmed across her lips, and she opened and touched the tip of hers to it. He caught and sucked, teeth nipping at the tender skin, before plunging inside to tease the roof of her mouth.

Latan trailed his lips up her throat, his tongue touching the tingling flesh. He paused to lick the inside of her ear before closing his teeth around the fleshy lobe. His warm breath cascaded over her as he leaned in to whisper, "You've been a very bad girl, Tania."

"Bad girl?" she asked shakily.

"Oh, yeah," Ethan replied silkily. "You left our bed this morning without permission." He stepped closer, their bodies touching, and nodded to Latan.

"Permission," she fumed. "I don't need permi—" Ethan claimed her mouth in a rough kiss.

Latan's arms released her, his hands coming up to cup her breasts. "You don't have permission to talk right now, pretty lady."

Tania groaned as Ethan's tongue filled her with his taste. Her hands flattened on his broad, muscular shoulders, his skin smooth and hot. She could feel Latan's lips against the side of her neck, his fingers plucking at her nipples, when she pulled from Ethan's kiss. Dampness trickled from between her legs, slicking the inside of her thighs.

Ethan's hands settled on her waist. "If you disobey, I'll have to punish you again," he teased.

Thoughts of the spanking she'd endured by his hand brought her nipples to painful points under Latan's fingers. Wanting Ethan to feel out of control, she leaned forward and licked a path down his chest, breathing in his scent, her nails digging into his shoulders. Her hands slid slowly over the hair-roughened skin, stopping to circle, then tweak the small, brown nipples. Taking the swollen bud between her teeth, she tugged gently, relishing the vibrations of his growl against her lips.

Latan's hands left her breasts, caressed across her shoulders, and massaged down her back, stopping at the curve of her ass. He clasped the rounded globes in his palms and squeezed then trailed a single finger up the cleft between the cheeks.

Tania lowered her hand and feathered her fingers along Ethan's bobbing shaft, stopping to tease the leaking tip. Bending, she closed her wet mouth over the head, her tongue flicking in circles like it was an ice cream cone. She could feel Latan's finger stroking over her anus.

"Baby, wait," Ethan cried. He grabbed her shoulders and pulled her up, her puckered nipples brushing against his chest. His cock felt long and hard against her stomach, his scent filling her senses. He stepped closer, his chest crushing her breasts, pushing her back against his brother.

Latan's erection nudged her buttocks, his hands clutching her waist. Fingers drifted down her hips then curled over to the tangle of hair between her thighs, tugging playfully. She felt his tongue sweep damply up the back of her neck.

Ethan held her gaze while his brother played between her legs, a devilish half smile curving his lip. He looked up at Latan. "We need to be somewhere more comfortable." Latan pulled his fingers away just seconds before Ethan bent, pressed his shoulder to her stomach, and lifted her in a fireman's carry.

Tania yelped and grabbed on to his back for support. "Ethan, what the hell are you doing?" She squealed loudly when his hand connected firmly with the flesh of her ass. "What was that for?" she cried.

"Silence, woman," Ethan ordered, right before he dumped her unceremoniously onto the mattress. He fell down on the bed beside her and grabbed both her hands, easily holding them in his large palm above her head. He licked her lips and gazed into her eyes. "If you don't do what we say, we're gonna spank you, hard!" When he leaned forward, she parted her lips to allow his tongue to explore her mouth, their kiss going deeper than any she'd ever had. Drawing her lip between his teeth, he nipped before pulling away and burying his face in her neck.

Latan crawled up her body. One knee planted on either side of her calves, he leaned in to lick her chin. "I need to taste you, pretty lady." A wet tongue traced along her neck before his gaze dropped to her breasts, and he scooted down to the foot of the bed. Warm hands gripped her ankles, pulling her legs apart, allowing him to lie between her thighs.

Ethan's tongue brushed along her shoulder and then trailed down her chest. Tania trembled when his hand cupped the underside of one breast and squeezed before tracing the softness and teasing the hardened tip. His mouth opened, sucking the nipple deep inside, his tongue swirling over the tight bud. Sucking and tugging with his lips, he tortured them into tighter and tighter peaks. "Baby, you're so beautiful," he moaned against her breast.

Tania's body was already on fire when she felt Latan's hot breath on her skin as he settled in the valley between her legs. The men were driving her crazy with their dual assault on her senses.

"Your pussy glistens, it's so moist and hot," Latan purred. He ran his finger down between her pussy lips before leaning forward and tracing her slit with his tongue. "Pretty lady, you taste so good," he moaned.

Tania gasped when Ethan's hand joined Latan's, rubbing tiny circles around her clit. Someone's finger rubbed over the tiny nub, while another pushed inside her core. Latan dipped inside, lapping at her juices with the flat of his tongue.

Ethan's mouth engulfed her breast, drawing hard on the throbbing bud. The pleasure seemed to streak straight down to the ache Latan was feeding in her feminine center. Her hips began to buck, one hand gripping in Ethan's hair, the other in Latan's. Lips closed around her aching clit and sucked gently, while fingers pumped in and out of her pussy. She strained to clamp down on them with her inner walls.

"Come for us, baby. Give Latan your cream, come all over his hand," Ethan crooned.

Tania felt her thighs tremble. She was breathing faster and faster when, suddenly, her body stiffened as she reached her summit. Bright colored lights swirled behind her closed eyelids as the pleasure washed over her. She didn't know how long it was before she realized both men were watching her closely. She could feel the burn of embarrassment flooding her cheeks.

"God, baby, you're so beautiful when you come," Ethan declared.

Latan ran his finger from the top of her slit, down to her anus, grazing the puckered opening. He grinned up at her. "I want this perfect, round ass of yours, pretty lady." He nodded his head. "I want you to turn over and ride Ethan so I can fuck this tight hole."

Tania stared at him, doubt and a little bit of fear coursing through her thoughts. "Look, guys, I've never done that before, and both of you are awfully big."

Latan laughed and pulled her into a sitting position, while Ethan smoothed the hair away from her face. "You don't have anything to worry about."

"I promise you, baby, it'll fit just fine. There's no way we'll do anything to hurt you." Ethan pressed a kiss to her shoulder.

She sighed and moved over in the bed. "Just be sure and use plenty of lubrication," she said, trying to keep the tremble out of her voice. A hand skated along the skin of her back.

"Don't you worry none, pretty lady. We brought a tube with us. All you have to do is say stop if you don't like it," Latan soothed.

Tania watched as both men sheathed themselves in latex, Latan liberally coating his in a clear liquid he squirted out of a small tube. She felt a hand on her arm and turned around to look at Ethan.

"Come here, baby," he urged. "You don't have to be afraid. I promise we won't hurt you." He tugged her closer then steadied her with his hands as she threw her leg over his waist and settled on top of his stomach. His erection pressed against the small of her back. Large hands came up and caressed her breasts, thumbs teasing the sensitive nipples.

Latan trailed kisses along her thigh, massaging and kneading the cheeks of her ass. Leaning forward, he licked her crease, sliding his tongue around the puckered skin. Tania froze, her ass clenching, when a scorching heat brushed across the forbidden opening.

"Relax, Tania, this ass was made for my cock. It's perfect." Latan punctuated his words with a sharp nip to her fleshy globe.

Ethan reached between her legs, flicking her clit with the tip of his finger, while he continued to pinch and tug the tips of her breasts. She could feel the moisture leaking out onto her thighs. "We're gonna get you situated on me first, baby," Ethan said right before he grasped her by the waist. He lifted her as if she weighed nothing, placing his cock at the entrance of her dripping pussy, and then slowly pushed down, impaling her onto his erect shaft. "Oh, God, you feel so good," he moaned.

Tania felt the head of his thick cock push past the opening of her body, stretching and filling her to capacity. A hand at her back pushed her steadily forward until she lay across Ethan, her breasts crushed against his muscled chest, her long hair falling forward, forming a curtain around the two of them. She gazed into his passion-filled eyes and swallowed hard. She didn't understand why it felt so right to be with both men. The way they made her feel frightened her.

Latan ran his finger down the cleft of her buttocks and then followed with a swipe of his tongue, teasing the hole. She glanced back when he pulled away and watched as he coated his fingers in more of the cream from the tube.

"Tania," Ethan whispered.

She turned back around and pressed her lips against his chest, using her tongue to make tight circles around his nipples. His hands came up, shoving her hair behind her shoulders and bringing her face close for a kiss.

Something cold and wet dropped between the cheeks of her ass, with Latan's finger immediately spreading it around the tight, puckered opening. She tensed when she felt something hard and cold against her anus and then squealed when the cold spread rapidly inside her rectum. She turned to glare over her shoulder at him.

He laughed at her reaction. "Relax, pretty lady, it's only lube. I squirted some inside you to make things easier. I don't wanna hurt you."

She moaned when he probed her butt, automatically tightening the muscles in her ass.

"Relax your bottom, Tania," Latan said. "There's gonna be a little bit of a burn while we stretch you out, and then everything will get better, but you gotta let me in."

"Push out for him, baby. It'll make it easier for both of you," Ethan suggested.

Tania took a deep breath and pushed out against the invading finger. She felt a brief moment of pain, and then the finger surged past the ring of muscle in her rectum and settled inside. *This isn't so bad. It doesn't really hurt.* A second finger joined the first, and the burn began to be more noticeable. "Oh, crap," she cried out. "You weren't just whistling Dixie about the burn, were you?"

"Come on, pretty lady, take a deep breath. It'll get better in a minute," Latan assured her. "I'm gonna start scissoring my fingers back and forth to stretch you even more. We need to get at least three fingers in her before I can fuck this sweet ass."

"Three," she groaned as the fingers began moving inside her. After a moment, the pain died away, and something, she couldn't put a name to it, took its place. It wasn't exactly pleasure or pain, but something she wanted to learn a little more about. She raised her butt and pushed upward, moaning as his fingers pressed deeper.

"That's it, baby," Ethan murmured.

The pain had receded well into the background when Latan introduced the third finger. She didn't really experience more pain, more like a full, uncomfortable feeling. For several minutes, she breathed deeply while his fingers moved back and forth, stretching the tiny hole for his entrance. She jerked when his fingers suddenly pulled out.

"Okay, pretty lady, are you ready?" he asked.

Chapter 5

Tania swallowed hard and just barely managed to nod in consent. Large hands pulled apart the cheeks of her ass. She froze, automatically clenching her muscles when she felt something thick and hard prod against her opening. A hard slap against her thigh had her grunting in shock.

"Open up, Tania, let me in honey, please," Latan begged.

She took a deep breath and forced her muscles to relax. A burning feeling gripped her as he forced the head of his shaft into her body. Sweat beaded on her forehead while he slowly worked his way into her ass, a burning pain tearing through her at the invasion. She moaned, feeling his cock stretching her, filling her from behind. For just a moment, she thought she would have to ask him to stop, and then the pain eased up, and a new feeling rolled over her. It wasn't pleasure or pain, but something in between the two.

"Okay, it's getting better, isn't it, love?" Latan gasped out. "I can feel you relaxing around me. God, you're so damn tight." He pulled out, almost all the way, leaving just the tip of his cock inside her body. "Ethan, I won't last long. She's squeezing the life out of me," he groaned as he slid slowly back in. She could feel his balls press against her pussy.

"Let's get this show moving then. I'm about to come myself just from her wiggling around while you took your damn time," Ethan complained. His hands pushed her hair out of her eyes. "Baby, in this sandwich, Latan does all the work, we just have to hold on and enjoy." His hands gripped her hips, and he nodded at his brother over her shoulder.

Latan pulled her hips up slightly, and she felt Ethan's hips move back and forth, his cock sliding in and out of her pussy. Pleasure rocked her body as his thrusts kept him in constant contact with her sensitive clit. The brothers began to thrust in and out, almost in slow motion, in a coordinated rhythm, convincing her that they'd definitely done this before. Latan began to move faster, working his thrusts against Ethan's movements, sweat dripping off his body onto her shoulders.

She groaned loudly as they increased their speed, Latan literally pounding her ass as she rode Ethan harder. Familiar tingles tightened low in her belly, signaling her coming release. Both men were gripping her tightly, muttering words she couldn't understand under their breath.

"God, Ethan, I'm coming," Latan cried out.

"I'm with you, bro," Ethan growled.

Tania came with a cry, muscles tensing, head falling back. Ethan and Latan roared out their release almost simultaneously and then leaned in close to their lover. Ethan sunk his canines into the fleshy junction of her neck, while Latan sunk his into the back of her shoulder on the other side. The feel of their teeth, followed by the injection of their mating enzymes, had Tania screaming and convulsing into another orgasm. Exhausted, she collapsed on top of Ethan.

For several long minutes, the three lovers fought to catch their breaths, and then Latan withdrew from her ass and pulled her away from Ethan. Tania looked at Ethan and then turned her gaze to Latan. She struggled to understand what had just happened.

"Are you all right?" Ethan asked quietly.

Her hand came up to touch the mark on her shoulder, while her other raced to the one on her neck. "What the hell have you done?" she whispered.

Latan looked over at Ethan and then reached an arm out toward Tania. He seemed surprised when she jumped off the bed. He sighed and looked at her pleadingly. "Tania, you have to believe me, I didn't plan to do this." He shrugged. "It just seemed so right. Deep down, I know you're my mate, and so does my wolf. He just kind of took over at the last minute and claimed you."

She glared at Ethan. "What about you?"

Ethan shot a look at Latan she didn't understand and then slid over to sit on the side of the bed. "I didn't plan it either, baby. I've felt like you're my mate since the night we took you to dinner. Tonight seemed perfect and natural between us. I just couldn't stop myself." He glanced at Latan again. "I didn't know Latan felt the same way, I mean, we didn't discuss it beforehand."

Furious, Tania began to pace beside the bed, ignoring the fact she didn't have any clothes on. "I'm not your mate, either of you." She stopped to face the two men. "I can't be mate to a wolf, or anyone else for that matter, and certainly not to two wolves." She raised her arms in frustration and began pacing again. "What were you thinking? Wolves don't share mates," she stated emphatically.

"That's not some law engraved in stone," Ethan stated. "It can be done if all parties are willing." He took a step closer and frowned when she backed away. "Please, just calm down. We need to go and talk with Remus, or the Elders. They'll be able to advise us, and they should know if there are any other cases like this where both wolves insist the female is their mate."

Tania shook her head and took a step back. "Both of you need to leave, now."

"No," Latan yelled, "you're not just gonna toss us out."

Angry with everything so far out of her control, Tania growled and moved closer to the door. She couldn't help thinking the two brothers were going to be her downfall. They affected her in ways that made her forget everything. She hadn't even scented them in her house when she returned from her run, and now, they'd managed to mark her as a mate. She was just about to order them out when she felt a strange feeling nudge at the corner of her brain. Puzzled, she thought for a moment and then froze as she remembered the mating link. They were trying to link with her mind, and that was something she couldn't allow. "No," she screamed, and then bolted out the door, calling on her beast as she cleared the porch.

* * * *

Latan was closest to the door, and although fast, he didn't make it in time to catch a glimpse of their mate before she disappeared into the darkness. "Son of a bitch," he yelled, then slammed the door hard enough to rattle the windowpanes. He shot an angry look at his brother. "What the hell were you thinking?"

"Me? What the hell were you thinking? Why didn't you tell me you wanted her for a mate?"

"Probably for the same reason you didn't tell me. Neither of us wanted the other to interfere." Latan grabbed up his jeans and pulled them on. "Question is, now what are we gonna do?"

Ethan pulled on his own pants and sat down on the bed. "I don't know what to do. I only know I don't wanna lose her." He looked up at Latan. "Are you willing to back off?"

"Hell, no. I can't even imagine life without her now." He looked down at his hands, his grip on the back of the chair so tight his knuckles had turned white. "Are you willing to share?"

Rising abruptly, Ethan crossed to Latan and gave him a hug. "It would be my honor to share a mate with you, bro. But I don't think it's gonna be that easy."

"Yeah, I know what you mean," Latan groaned. "She may not be willing to take either of us now."

"Won't the mating fever force her to stay close?" Ethan asked.

"No way to tell since she's not full-blooded wolf. Hell, we don't even know what her other part is. The fever may not affect her at all."

"If that's our only problem, I'll be a happy man," he said dryly. "Unfortunately, I think we've got more trouble coming. Do you know what I mean?"

"She's keeping secrets, and she's in some kind of trouble. I can feel it." Latan walked over and started adding small pieces of wood to the fireplace. "The mating bonds had begun to form when she slammed shields into place, kicking me out of her head."

Running a hand through his hair, Ethan grimaced. "Shit, same here." He gave Latan a grin. "I was in there long enough to know she has feelings for both of us, and I don't believe she has anything to do with Kaugh in a bad way."

"Well, hell, I didn't think she was working with him before we mated her. She—" The ringing of his cell phone interrupted Latan's thoughts. "Where the hell did I leave my phone," he mumbled.

"Here." Ethan grabbed it off the table and handed it to him.

"Hello," he barked into the small phone. He listened for several long minutes and then glanced at his brother. "It's Brenner," he whispered, before returning his attention to the call. "No, Ethan and I are at the teacher's cabin, and she's not here. Come on by and give me what you have." He closed the phone and smiled. "Brenner did a background check on Tania for Remus. He said he didn't find much, but he did come up with a little something. Remus isn't home, and Brenner needs to leave, so he's coming by here to fill us in so we can pass it on to Remus."

Ethan laughed. "Isn't that convenient?"

"I'll say. He called from the car after he left Remus's house, so he should be here any minute."

"Couldn't be too soon for me," Ethan declared.

* * * *

"You did well, Marty. Everything's perfect!" Kaugh walked around the small house, testing the strength of the bars on the windows. He glanced outside and frowned. "The clearing's too dark at night. Get some floodlights put up on the corners of the house. I want this place lit up like it's the middle of the day."

"Sure thing, boss. Do you want motion detector lights?" Marty asked.

"No, I want us to be able to see everything all the time, not just when something comes close enough to set off the sensors. Once we bring the wolves here, we're gonna have to be extra careful. We may need to bring in some more men to double up on guard duty." He walked down the steps leading to the underground rooms. "Did you find out when the equipment will be here from California?"

"Yes, sir, it'll be here first thing in the morning. Do you want us to supervise the delivery?"

"No, I'll be here to do it. I want to make sure everything is just right before we collect our specimen." Entering the smaller of the two rooms, he gazed at the pair of small beds. More like army cots, he nodded in approval when he saw the large bolts fastening all four of their legs to the concrete floor. "Excellent," he murmured. Walking over, he pulled on one of the leather straps hanging from the metal frame. Each bed had three straps spaced so one could be fastened across the chest, one across the waist, and the last one across the legs. They were merely a precaution. He had every intention of keeping his subjects sedated as much as possible.

"What's so special about this female you're so anxious to get your hands on?" Marty walked over and sat on one of the beds.

"Truthfully, there's really not anything special about her. Her biggest draw is she'll save me years on my research."

"I don't understand."

"Constantine had her as a patient for years. She's not a pure specimen. Her grandmother was a full-blooded shifter, her father a half-breed. According to Constantine, Maddie never found her own wolf. He experimented over the years with various ways to try and bring it out but never succeeded. She's also telekinetic, either born that way or she developed the ability after a traumatic accident when she was a child."

Marty frowned, clearly confused. "If she never found her wolf, what good is she to your research?"

"Constantine's last entries in his journal indicated that Maddie had recently mated a full-blooded wolf shifter, the Alpha of the pack here. He felt, with the addition of the wolf's DNA, and the mating enzyme, some of his older formulas might just work."

"And if they don't?"

"Then his research will still save me countless years on my own. I have the physical data and her responses to every experiment he ever ran. I'll be able to try out all of the new formulas I'm working on, already having a baseline of the subject's reactions."

"What about the telekinesis? Won't it be a problem?" Marty had just a tinge of fear lacing his voice.

"No, the injection I have that prevents shifting should also disable any type of telekinetic activity."

Marty grinned. "Sounds like you've got everything under control."

"I certainly hope so, Marty." He narrowed his eyes. "Did you get the locks for both sides of the tunnel doors that I requested?"

"Yes, sir. The door at the end of this hall and the one at the end of the tunnel have double bolt locks on both sides of the doors. I am curious why you wanted locks on both sides."

"Simple, my friend. The locks will be thrown on the inside of the doors to keep anyone from gaining entrance from the creek tunnel." He gave a sly grin. "Should we be raided for any reason, we'll be able to escape through the tunnel, locking the doors with the bolts from the opposite side, slowing down anyone chasing after us. That reminds me, I want you to leave a car at the far end of the tunnel. Hide it in the brush where it's not easily seen, and leave the keys under the driver's seat."

"Wow, you really think of everything, don't you?"

"I try, Marty, I try. It's what kept me alive when they raided the facility sixteen years ago. Some lessons you learn the hard way." He strode toward the door. "Everything's fine here. Let's get back to town and get some dinner. I plan to be here bright and early in the morning, and I want to be well rested before we pick up our subject."

* * * *

Latan yanked open the door almost before the sound of the knock had faded. "Come on in, Brenner."

Brenner nodded and glanced around the room. "Hey, Ethan."

"Brenner," Ethan greeted him. "What've you got for us?"

He snorted. "Not a hell of a lot." Dropping down on the sofa, he sighed. "She's more than just an ordinary teacher, I can tell you that."

"What makes you say that?" Latan growled.

Brenner looked startled for a moment and then visibly recovered. "Her past is hidden better than some government types I've known. I have a friend, who would prefer to remain nameless, that works in the main office of the National Council. I've had him searching for anything he could find on her background, and, my friends, even he was surprised at how little there was."

"So what did he find?" Ethan asked impatiently.

"She came into the Council's custody sixteen years ago. She was ten years old then. She'd been rescued in a government funded raid on a secret research facility run by one Dr. Mark Landry."

"Never heard of him, have you?" Latan eyed his brother.

"No, what else did he tell you?"

"Landry actually worked for the government but had gone rogue with his own research. He was killed in that raid, but his research lived on in the possession of his assistant, Dr. Vincent Kaugh."

"Son of a bitch," Ethan exploded. "You're telling us Tania is involved with Kaugh."

"No, that's not what I'm saying. They rescued her from the lab, Ethan. She was in a damn cage, like a lab rat."

Latan felt physically sick. "Dear God, what did they do to her?" He glanced at Ethan and realized his brother was in shock.

Brenner sighed. "My friend couldn't find any details about what went on at the lab. They either don't know, or somebody went to a lot of trouble to cover it up. He couldn't confirm it, but he thinks she was born in the facility."

"What?" Latan cried.

"Her file indicates she was born in the California facility while it was under the control of Dr. Landry."

"Did it say who her parents are?" Ethan whispered.

"No, the file on her says *parents unknown*." He stood up and walked over to the door and then turned and faced Latan, a puzzled look on his face. "There was one other strange thing, but it's more a rumor than a fact in a file."

"What is it?" Latan demanded.

"They say her name was given to her by the doctors at the facility."

"So, what's so strange about that?" Ethan asked.

"The rumor says the name was meant to be a joke."

"A joke?" Latan laughed. "If it's a joke, I don't get it."

"No, I didn't either. I know it's an unusual name that I've never heard before, but I haven't had time to research it for a meaning." He opened the door and stepped out onto the porch. "I have to run, guys. Let Remus know what I found out, and tell him I'll be back in a couple of days, hopefully with a little more information for him."

"Thanks, Brenner. Be careful, man." Latan watched as he hurried out to his car then turned and looked at Ethan. "So, what do you make of all that?"

Ethan shook his head and groaned. "I have no idea. How the hell could somebody's name be a joke?" He thought for a moment and then looked over at the desk in the corner, her computer taking up most of the surface space. In a flash, he was on his feet, heading for the rolling office chair.

"What are you doing?" Latan asked, walking to stand behind his brother.

"I'm gonna see if I can find out what her name means." The two men watched as the computer booted up.

Latan searched around the desk. "How's she hooked to the Internet? I don't see any cables."

"There's a satellite hookup here on the mountain. How do you think we have Internet access?"

Latan shrugged. "I don't know. Guess I never thought about it. Hey, maybe we should check her e-mail. It might give us an idea of what she's up to."

Ethan clicked on the icon and then shook his head. "Nope, it's password protected." Clicking another icon, he grinned when Explorer came right up. "At least her mail's the only thing protected." He started typing. "Now, Google, tell us what you know about Tania."

Latan peered over Ethan's shoulder while the two of them read the search engine's results. After a moment, he stepped back and stared into Ethan's amused eyes. Before he could think of anything to say, Ethan threw back his head and laughed heartily.

"Oh, my God," Ethan snorted, "did you see what it says?"

"Yeah," Latan sighed. "The word's Australian, and it means 'fairy queen,' 'long awaited,' or 'kitten.'" He shook his head, watching his brother nearly fall to the floor, tears of laughter streaming from his eyes.

"All this time, and we never knew." Ethan dissolved in an undignified fit of giggles again. "No wonder she doesn't have any cat food or cat toys. She is the damn cat!"

"Oh, no," Latan groaned.

Ethan grinned up at him. "You are such dead meat, bro." He snickered. "You think she'll remember all the times you said you hated cats, or when you told Taynor she'd make a tasty snack? Or, hey, how about when you growled at her, trying to scare her away on our back deck." Again, he doubled over with laughter.

Latan scowled and began to pace back and forth. "What the hell are we gonna do now?"

After a moment, Ethan pulled himself together enough to answer him. "We find our mate, that's what we do now."

"You still wanna share her with me?"

"Of course," Ethan assured him. "I love her, you love her, and I sense that she loves us, too. I don't care that she turns into a cat, do you?"

"Of course not, I'm worried that she's in some kind of trouble, and somehow, Kaugh's involved."

"So, we find her, make her tell us everything, and then we protect her."

"Simple as that, huh?" Latan smiled.

"She's our mate. The whole pack will back us up." Ethan looked thoughtful for a moment. "How do you feel about pups? Will it bother you if we can't carry on the pure Alpha line?"

"No," Latan snorted, "let Remus carry on the line. Hell, even his children won't be full-blooded." He sighed, and stared off into space. "I don't care if we have wolf pups that purr and have retractable claws or kittens that growl with fangs. I just wanna spend my life with Tania. I wanna grow old with her and fill up our house with a happy family."

Ethan smiled. "I couldn't have said it better, bro. Okay, first things first. We need to find her, make her tell us what she's keeping secret, and we need a plan in place to protect her." He thought for a moment. "We're gonna need help."

Latan grinned. "What are Alphas for?"

* * * *

"You did what?" Remus growled.

Ethan glanced at Latan and then back to his Alpha. "We mated Tania last night."

"Both of you, together?" Remus asked incredulously.

Latan sighed. "Yes, you heard right, together. But there's a problem, and we need your help."

Remus snorted. "There's more than one damn problem, little brother. Three wolves cannot mate together."

"And exactly where is that written, oh, great Alpha?" Ethan sounded disgusted.

"Well, it's, uh, it's…"

"Hey, guys, what's going on?" Maddie padded into the kitchen, her brow wrinkled in concern.

"It's nothing, baby," Remus replied before his brothers could say anything. "Just some pack business I need to handle with Ethan and Latan."

"Okay," she smiled, "what business?"

"Don't worry about it, baby. I don't want you upset. It wouldn't be good for you in your condition." Remus cringed when he saw the fire of anger flash in her eyes.

"My *condition* is just fine and will stay that way as long as certain people stop trying to hide things from me. I'm the Alpha Femm of the Wind River Pack, and I demand to know what's going on," she growled.

Remus sighed and then glared at his brothers. He rolled his eyes and then waved his arm, giving them his permission to tell her their news.

"Ethan and I mated with Tania last night," Latan stated.

"Ahhh," she screeched, and then hurried over to hug both their necks. "That's so great! I really like her. It'll be great having her in the family."

"Are you crazy?" Remus asked through gritted teeth.

Maddie laughed. “No, I’m not, so lighten up, Alpha. It’s great news, for everyone. The pack could use a little shake-up every once in a while, and a ménage marriage between two wolves and a cat ought to do the trick.”

“What?” Remus cried.

“How the hell did you know she’s a cat?” Ethan asked.

“You mean it’s true?” Remus felt like his world was spinning out of control. His gaze shot to Ethan.

“Yeah, it’s true. We just found out tonight.” He turned to Maddie. “How did you know she isn’t a wolf?”

She wrinkled her nose. “Actually, I think she’s both. My sense of smell is a lot more sensitive since I got pregnant. I can scent both wolf and cat on her, but the cat is quite a bit stronger.” She looked up into Ethan’s eyes. “Do you love her?”

“Absolutely,” Ethan replied without hesitation.

“Do you?” Maddie repeated her question to Latan.

“With all my heart,” he vowed.

She gazed into Latan’s eyes for a full minute then turned and repeated the process with Ethan. Apparently pleased with what she saw, she smiled, and stepped back. “Okay, what can we do to help?”

For the next half hour, Remus and Maddie listened as Latan and Ethan filled them in on everything they’d learned from Brenner.

“So, we need help to protect our mate. We both know, from the mating bond, that she’s not connected to Kaugh in a bad way, but we also both believe he’s the reason she’s in danger,” Latan explained.

“So,” Ethan asked, “will you help us?”

Even though he wasn’t convinced in Tania’s total innocence, Remus’s answer was immediate. “Of course I’ll help you, we’re family, and that’s what families do.” He smiled at his beaming mate and then returned his gaze to his brothers. “Go back to her cabin and wait for her. She’s bound to turn up there, sooner rather than later. Don’t let her get away again. Bring her here so we can question her together and find out what’s going on. If she needs protection, it would be better to keep her and Maddie together and focus our manpower."

Ethan nodded, and turned his attention to Latan. "Let's get going, bro. She could be back any minute."

"Thanks, Remus," Latan added. "We're grateful for you help." He walked over and kissed Maddie on the cheek. "Take care, little momma-to-be."

Ethan grinned and kissed her other cheek. "Thanks for sticking up for us, little sister."

"You guys," Maddie sniffed, "you're gonna make me cry. Get your furry butts out of here."

Remus laughed when the boys saluted then rushed out the back door, leaving it open on their way out. He walked over and shut the door, wondering what kind of trouble Tania would bring into their home. He glanced over at his mate.

"You're wrong," she stated.

It always unnerved him when she read his mind. He used to be able to shield his thoughts from her all the time, but her abilities had sharpened since the onset of the pregnancy. "We'll see," was his only reply.

Maddie walked over, pushed him down into a kitchen chair, and then climbed into his lap. Her arms draped across his shoulders, and she placed a light kiss on his lips. "Tania's good, Remus, I feel it in my heart. She's your brothers' mate, and you know they have good judgment when it comes to character. Can't you give her the benefit of the doubt? Let her be innocent until proven guilty?"

Remus smiled, knowing he'd never been able to say no to his beautiful, sexy mate. "All right, baby, I'll give her a chance."

"Mmmm," Maddie groaned. "I knew you could be reasonable." Her arms slid up over his shoulders, her fingers gliding through his hair. Her mouth settled against the side of his neck, her lips sucking gently. "I want you, Remus." His hands tightened around her waist, his head turning, searching for her lips. He nipped playfully at her chin and then ran his tongue up her cheek. She turned her face to his, and their baby kicked firmly under his clasped hands. Remus froze as visions of his son beaten about the head and shoulders by an engorged cock filled his mind. He groaned in frustration.

Maddie raised her head and gazed into his eyes. “Not again,” she moaned. “Remus, Tehran says the baby’s fine, and there’s no reason why we can’t continue marital relations right up until I deliver.”

Remus sighed. “Intellectually, I understand that, Maddie. It’s psychologically I have a problem with it, and unfortunately, the psychological aspect can play hell with my libido.”

“Great, am I just supposed to remain a frustrated bitch until after the baby’s born?”

Remus thought for a moment, then tightened his arm around her shoulders, and thrust the other one under her knees. Standing, he held her close against his chest, ignoring the startled yelp escaping from her mouth, and then strode quickly toward the living room. Carefully, he laid his precious bundle down on the sofa. Holding her gaze, he peeled his shirt away and watched as her glance raked over his naked chest. Smiling, she crooked her finger, beckoning him closer.

He lay down beside her on the soft cushions, wrapping his arms around her tightly. His smile widened when she snuggled closer into his embrace. Warm fingers reached up to stroke across his cheek and jaw before dropping to trail through the heavy mat of hair covering his chest. Inhaling deeply, Remus buried his nose in her fragrant hair and then kissed his way down her neck. “You smell good,” he crooned.

A guttural groan escaped his lips when one of Maddie’s hands drifted down and massaged him through his jeans. He let the hands he held at her waist run up her torso to the outside of her breasts and then back down in a sweeping caress. Her skin felt fiery against his fingers when he moved his hand up under her shirt. Her back arched sensuously when he rubbed the tips of her breasts through the lace bra.

"Remus," she whispered.

Needing to feel the core of her heat, he guided his hand beneath the elastic band of her maternity pants and stroked her over her soaked panties, pleased when her hips lifted into his touch. Quickly, he slid his hands around to the back of her silky garment and began to slip them down past her hips.

Remus swirled his tongue inside her belly button as he tugged her panties down, lingering to massage and knead the fleshy globes of her butt. "Oh, baby, the skin on your ass is smoother than silk." The stretchy pants and panties found themselves swiftly relegated to the floor before Remus surged upward. He took her earlobe between his teeth and gave it a small tug, a surge of arousal flowing through him when she shuddered in response. His lips teased, nibbled, and played their way across her cheek.

Maddie growled softly when his tongue ran across her plump lips and then slid along her own when her mouth opened on a sigh. Moving lower, he licked and sucked along her neck, working his way down her body as she squirmed in obvious pleasure, her fingers tunneling in the long strands of his hair.

An impatient tug opened the front fastener of her bra, allowing his fingers to trace the tips of her breasts. Calloused thumbs circled her nipples, torturing them into hard nubs, while she strained toward his caresses, purring like a contented kitten. He bowed his head to one breast and laved the nipple hungrily with his tongue, while kneading the other one between his fingers. Hands clutched at his shoulders when he sucked the tiny bud into his mouth, grazing it with his teeth.

Giving her breast a final lick, Remus kissed a trail down her smooth, rounded stomach. Placing his hands on her bare thighs, he spread her legs and placed his knees inside of hers. His fingers sifted through the soft curls at the top of her mound before he penetrated her with one long finger. Feminine knees came up, gripping him tightly on each side of his hips. "Relax, baby, let me love you. I just want you to feel pleasure."

Leaning forward, he pressed a kiss to the top of her slit, rubbing his nose in the dark curls. Her cream poured over his invading finger as she cried out in pleasure, her hips thrashing against his lips. His hand came down gently across her abdomen to hold her still. A second finger joined the first as he licked back and forth across her little clit.

"Remus," she cried out, her inner walls clutching at his fingers as she came.

"That's it, baby. Come for me." He continued stroking for a few moments longer, and then Remus stripped off the remainder of his clothing and prowled up her nude form. His lips captured hers as he feathered tiny circles on her sensitive inner thigh. Fiery sensations whipped through his body when her hands ran over his back and buttocks, her nails biting into the fleshy cheeks of his ass. Slender, smooth legs rose up to grip around his waist as he continued to ravage her lips. Maddie groaned slightly, whimpering, and then began thrusting her hips when he lowered his hand and rubbed against her swollen clit.

He placed the head of his cock at her entrance and slowly sank down into her molten depths, careful to keep his weight off the swollen evidence of their coming child. Remus inhaled, filling his lungs with the scent of his mate, and began sliding in and out of her pussy in a slow, steady rhythm. Maddie moaned softly and closed her eyes, kissing his throat and then gliding her lips to his shoulder. She trailed her fingers across his chest, tweaking his nipple between her thumb and forefinger.

Remus groaned and began to thrust faster, snaking his hand down to tease the little bud between her thighs. Suddenly, Maddie cried out, writhing in pleasure, the walls of her cunt convulsing around his throbbing erection. He thrust three more times before his climax burst inside his body, his seed pulsing into the depths of his mate. Remus leaned forward and sank his canines into the mating mark on Maddie's shoulder, throwing her from one orgasm into another. His head swung sharply to the left when the clock on the wall flew across the room.

"Well, baby," he chuckled, "I see I haven't lost my touch."

"Damn," she groaned. "I thought I finally had that under control."

Remus kissed her lips tenderly. "I love you, Maddie. Baby, I hope you never learn to control that. I like knowing that I can make you lose control so completely."

She giggled. "Just promise me you won't ever try to make me lose control in the kitchen. That could be downright painful." She smiled up at him. "I love you, too, wolf man. You're everything I ever dreamed of wanting, Remus."

Grimacing, he separated slowly from his mate and laid his hand across their future child. "Do you think he's all right? I never felt him move."

Maddie's hand covered his. "He's fine, Daddy, he's just sleeping."

"How can you tell?" He felt carefully around her swollen abdomen.

She groaned. "Because the little devil likes to sleep during the day when I'm up and moving around and play touch football during the night when I'm trying to sleep."

He stared at her in shock. "Why didn't you say something sooner?"

"What for? It wasn't as if you could do anything about it. I figured one of us deserved to get a little rest."

Remus snuggled her closer and pulled the throw off the back of the couch over their nude bodies. "Well, he's quiet now, so we can take a nap together." He felt Maddie rub her cheek back and forth against his chest and then heard the unmistakable sound of her little snores. He shook his head and managed to hold in his laugh. His mate could fall asleep faster than anyone he ever knew. He tightened his arms around her. *I've got to figure out a way to keep you safe, Maddie. I'm not gonna let Kaugh get his hands on you and our child.*

* * * *

Ethan watched as Latan paced back and forth in front of the fireplace. They'd been waiting for Tania to show up for over two hours, and he knew his brother had just about reached the limit of his patience. "Why don't you just sit down and try to relax?"

Latan stopped and glared at him. "I am relaxed," he grunted through gritted teeth.

"Right," drawled Ethan. "You know, we could—"

"Shh, listen," Latan whispered.

Ethan turned his head toward the open window and heard something like leaves rustling outside. He stood, motioned for Latan to move closer to the window, and then took up a position at the foot of the bed. For several long, frustrating minutes, he heard nothing, and then a weak feline cry pierced the air, followed by a small black cat sailing in from outside and landing on the chair sitting beneath the window.

Breathing a sigh of relief, Ethan watched as the cat froze when it saw the two men. For a moment, he worried that she would turn and race back out the way she came. He nearly laughed out loud when she threw her head back, gave them a disdainful look, and then jumped down to walk across the floor nonchalantly. "Well, look here, Latan. It's the pretty little kitty." Ethan walked over and picked Tania up, sending up a prayer of thanks when she didn't automatically bite him.

Latan quietly slid the window down and gave his brother a wide grin. "Yeah, she sure is a pretty little thing."

Ethan cuddled the cat close against his chest, his fingers running back and forth in the silky hair, the constant purring vibrating along his arms. Lowering his head, he buried his nose in the black strands and inhaled deeply, needing to imprint the scent of his mate in his mind.

Latan's fingers joined his in stroking the firm body of their feline mate. "She's so soft, Ethan, so beautiful."

As the minutes went by, Ethan watched his mate get more and more relaxed, her contented purring becoming louder and louder. She laid her small head on his arm, rubbing her cheek and whiskers across his skin. He glanced over at Latan, whose hand caressed right alongside his, with a question in his eyes. "Now?" he asked. His arms tightened when the cat stopped purring at the sound of his voice.

"Yeah, it's time." Latan nodded.

Ethan rubbed the furry head twice more and then leaned in to whisper near her ear. "We've got you, baby, and you're safe." He rubbed his nose along her head. "We're always gonna love you, Tania!"

* * * *

Tania froze for just a moment, hardly able to believe her ears, and then struggled to free herself from Ethan's hold. She stretched out her claws when she felt his arms tighten around her body and was preparing to sink them into his skin when his voice compelled her to draw them back in.

"Woman, if you scratch or bite either one of us, I will turn that sweet ass of yours so red, you won't be able to sit down for a week." Ethan threw back his head and sighed. "Damn it, you're our mate, and you're gonna sit down and talk to us." He bent over and placed her on the floor. "Shift, right now!"

Tania shifted, glared at the two men, and then walked over to the closet and pulled out a pair of jeans and a T-shirt. Quickly, she pulled the clothes over her naked body. She couldn't decide if anger or embarrassment had made her cheeks feel so fiery hot. "Let me make something perfectly clear, Ethan." She turned and narrowed her eyes at him. "You will not hit me in anger. No one will ever hit me in anger again."

"Who hit you?" Latan demanded to know.

When she realized what she'd revealed, Tania cringed and changed the subject. "How did you figure out it was me?"

Ethan frowned at his brother and then returned his gaze to Tania and smiled. "It doesn't really matter how. But I will tell you this, your name has a beautiful meaning." His grin widened. "I like that pretty blush on your face, too."

"My red cheeks are from anger, nothing else. My name isn't beautiful. It was a joke, a humiliation to remind me that I didn't measure up to expectations."

"Enough with all the cryptic comments," Latan growled. "Don't you think it's time to tell your mates who you really are?"

She snorted. "That was a mistake, and we all know it. Neither of you meant for the other to bite me too."

"That may be true," Ethan replied, "but it doesn't change the fact that we did mate you, together."

"Three people cannot mate," she stated angrily.

"Why not?" Latan asked, his innocent look a little too innocent to suit her tastes.

Growling, she threw up her hands. "Everyone knows wolves don't share their mates. They're very territorial!"

"Well, baby," Ethan laughed, "we're wolves, and we're perfectly happy sharing you."

"Besides," Latan added, "our Alpha and Alpha Femm gave us permission. They said it was perfectly acceptable as long as it's what we all want."

"You told Remus about it?"

"Of course, he's our brother, and we value his advice." Ethan walked over and sat down on the couch, then patted the seat beside him.

"What about children? Don't you wanna be able to carry on your family name?" Tania asked, ignoring Ethan's obvious invitation.

"Remus already has that covered with the pup they're expecting." Latan gave her a puzzled frown. "Are you saying you can't have kids?"

Shifting her feet, Tania refused to meet his eyes. "No, I think I can have them. I'm just not real sure what they would be if I do."

"Baby, who cares? Pups, kits, we'll love them no matter what they are. Hell, we'll start a whole new branch for the family." Ethan patted the couch again, smiling.

Tears welled in her eyes, and for a moment, love and hope filled her heart. Then, memories of her past came crashing down around her. "I can't."

"Come on, pretty lady." Latan took her by the arm and guided her over to the couch. Gently, he placed his hands on her shoulders and pushed her down onto the cushions next to Ethan and then curled up on the floor at her feet. "It's time for you to tell us all about yourself, why you're here, and what you're afraid of. Will you do that for us?" He ran his hand soothingly up and down her leg.

Her eyes closed for a moment while she considered what they asked her to do. *Can I tell them everything? Should I tell them?* She sighed and gazed into Latan's warm, brown eyes. *I have to tell them. They have the right to know why I can't stay here.* Taking a deep breath, she stared into the fire. "Okay, I'll tell you everything." Her eyes cut over to Ethan. "You must already know some of it or you couldn't have figured out I'm the cat."

"We know you came to live at the Council's home when you were ten years old after being rescued from a lab, and we were told you were born in the lab."

She laughed humorlessly. "You've been busy snooping around in my past. I'm not sure born is the right word, hatched might be a better choice." Blinking back her tears, Tania stared defiantly at the two brothers. "I'm a product of an experiment, a failed experiment." She decided to ignore their shocked looks and continue with her saga. "Dear, departed Dr. Landry was trying to create perfect, strong, ferocious warriors for your government. Unfortunately for him, he created me."

Latan looked over to Ethan and scowled. "I don't understand, Tania. How could he create you?"

"The brilliant, and slightly twisted, doctor tried to merge the DNA of a wolf with a cougar. The idea was to create a shifter that had the cunning and speed of the wild cat and the bulk, brute strength, and viciousness of the timber wolf." She paused and glanced toward the kitchen. "Can I have some water?"

Latan jumped up, walked over to the fridge, and brought back a bottle of water. "Here you go, love."

"Thanks." She smiled up at him. Turning the bottle up, she drank about half the water before going on with her story. "Landry impregnated a female wolf shifter with semen from a male cougar, and I was the result." She laughed bitterly. "You can imagine his dismay when I shifted on my sixth birthday into a tiny kitten." She raised her bottle of water as if toasting them. "And that, gentlemen, is how I got my name."

"Wait, what was your name before you shifted?" Ethan asked.

This time, she couldn't stop the tear from escaping her eye. "Subject A112," she replied.

Latan exploded. "Son of a bitch." And then quieted when Ethan laid a hand on his shoulder. "Sorry," he said. "Go on with what you were saying."

She gave him a small smile and ran her hand along his cheek before leaning back against the cushions. "Since I didn't turn out the way they wanted, I was relegated to being a subject for a few of their experiments. Mostly, they used me to test samples of a serum they were trying to develop that would inhibit a shifter's ability to change. I don't think he perfected it before he was killed."

Ethan ran his hand across her shoulders and pulled her close to the warmth of his body. "Tell us about your rescue, Tania."

For the first time since coming back to the cabin, she felt a genuine smile spread across her face. "I'd given up hope of ever leaving the cage they kept me in." She looked up when she heard a low growl coming from Latan. "There'd been rumors that some of the shifters had escaped, but I didn't know for sure until years later. That morning, everything was going along like it usually did, and then there was a loud explosion somewhere in the building. Landry's people were terrified and running for their lives, not really giving a damn whether we lived or died. Then, suddenly, the door flew open, and my savior came barreling through."

"Who was your savior, baby?" Ethan asked.

"His name's Tocho, and he's a feline shifter." She looked up into Ethan's eyes. "He freed me and the others, killed Landry, and then received an almost fatal wound from Landry's chief aide."

"Let me guess," Latan added. "His chief aide was Vincent Kaugh."

She smiled. "You got it! My soul purpose in life, since being freed from that hell, is getting vengeance for the pain my hero suffered. When Kaugh chose to continue Landry's work, the National Council decided something needed to be done. They sent me here to take him down."

Latan looked shocked. "Why you?" he demanded.

Swallowing hard, she stared into the fire. "I've been working for them as an agent for the past five years, since I turned twenty-one, taking on assignments just like this one. Basically, I'm the one they send to do their dirty work." She winced when she saw the shocked looks on their faces. "It's not so bad, guys. I'm really very good at what I do."

"Was it your idea, or theirs, to make you into an agent?" Ethan growled.

Now she understood their anger. "It was strictly mine, Ethan. I had to practically beg to get them to agree." She grinned. "After I proved myself on my first two missions, they stopped giving me any grief."

Ethan shifted on the couch to face her. "We didn't find any records of your parents, baby. Do you know where they are?"

She sighed. "I don't even know who they were, Ethan. Landry said the previous experiments didn't work because the host subject rejected the DNA of the male. To bring me to term, he used what he called *special drugs* to keep the problem from happening again. According to him, the female subject didn't survive the birth." Tania finished the water from her bottle. "He never said what happened to the sperm donor."

Latan rose up on his knees and took her face between his hands. Leaning in, he placed a light kiss against her lips. "Earlier, you said no one would ever hit you in anger again." He raised her chin, forcing her to look into his eyes. "Who hit you, pretty lady?"

"It would be easier to say who didn't," she said wryly. "Anytime I acted less than cooperative with their experiments, someone reminded me who was in charge."

"Oh, baby, come here." Ethan picked her up and sat her on his lap, then scooted over a little so Latan could join them, her legs lying across his thighs. Tucking her head underneath his chin, he rocked her back and forth in a comforting rhythm.

"Tania," Latan whispered, "I want you to let your shields down for us. We're mated now, and we need to firm up the bond." He took her hand and pressed a kiss against her knuckles. "I want you to look into my thoughts and see how I feel about you, pretty lady, please."

Tania pulled back and looked for a similar need in Ethan. Satisfied with what she saw in his sparkling, cocoa brown eyes, she slowly lowered her mental shields. Gasping, the cascade of emotions, memories, and feelings coming across the link momentarily overwhelmed her. Then, one by one, the feelings became easier to define until two stood clearly out from the rest. She locked her tear-filled eyes on Ethan and then turned to take in Latan's smile. "You both love me," she said in wonder, right before a flood of tears streamed down her cheeks.

"Oh, God, what's wrong, baby?" Ethan groaned.

"Nothing," she cried. "I'm just really happy." She reached out and tugged his T-shirt out of his jeans, her fingers sliding up his chest.

"Wait. Let me take it off for you." Swiftly, Ethan yanked his shirt over his head and tossed it on the floor.

Reaching out, Tania tugged Latan closer and licked along his chin while she pulled on his sleeve. "Now you, lover."

Latan complied with her demand then stood up and lifted her from Ethan's arms. "We want you, mate, right now, naked on that bed." He glanced down at Ethan. "Isn't that right, bro?"

Ethan grinned and ran his hands along her hips. "Oh, yeah, we definitely want her naked on that bed." For a moment, he looked uncomfortable. "Latan, do you want me to give you some time alone with our mate? I mean, I already spent one morning with her, and it doesn't seem quite fair that you don't get the same chance."

"Absolutely not. I don't want you to go anywhere but over to turn down the covers on the bed." He sighed heavily. "We're all mates, and that makes us a family. I don't wanna think of it as you getting your time and me getting equal time. It's our time, always. Sure, you'll be alone with her occasionally and the same for me, but I don't ever want either of us to worry whether we're infringing on each other. Does that make any sense?"

"Yeah, it does, and thanks, bro." Ethan stood and clasped him on the shoulder.

Tania pulled Latan's head around and kissed him passionately. "It makes perfect sense to me, too, and it makes me love both of you even more. You might not realize it, but you just told me that the two of you aren't really sharing me at all. We're really just one big, happy trio."

Latan locked his arms around Tania and nudged her forward. "Come on, mate, on the bed, naked, now!"

She stumbled over to the bed and found herself sandwiched between two very sexy male bodies. She melted with a sigh when she felt Latan's lips and tongue against her neck, licking, sucking, and gently biting.

Ethan leaned forward and nuzzled her cheek before lowering his head and sucking her nipple through the cotton of her T-shirt. She groaned and then plunged her fingers into the fine strands of his hair and pulled sharply. Chuckling, he abandoned her breast and whipped the T-shirt over her head. His mouth smoothed over hers, sucking first her upper, then lower lip. Plunging his tongue inside, he took their kiss deep.

Latan stroked his hand down her back to her bottom and then hooked his fingers under the waistband of her jeans and pulled down carefully. He lifted each foot, placing a soft kiss on the heel of each one, and kicked the discarded clothing aside. Warm, calloused hands traveled up the outside of her legs as he stood, making a brief detour around her hips to brush through the curls between her thighs before continuing their upward journey. Tania could feel her pulse racing a mile a minute when he buried his face against her neck, his lips nibbling at her throat.

"Eeekk," she squealed when Latan swatted her rump with his open palm. "What was that for?" she complained halfheartedly.

"You, pretty lady, are much too tense." His hands closed on her shoulders. "We need to do something to relax these muscles."

"Agreed," Ethan added. "On the bed, baby, on your stomach. Latan, on the shelf in the bathroom."

"Yep, I'm on it, bro." He kissed the side of her neck lightly and then disappeared through the bathroom door.

Tania climbed onto the bed and lay down on her stomach, her arms folded under her head. As she watched, Latan returned, holding a small bottle in his hands. When he got closer, she recognized the strawberry lotion she used on her legs. He got on the bed, straddling her legs, and bent forward to press a slow kiss between her shoulder blades. Strong hands came up to massage her back, working in the lotion, relaxing her muscles.

Ethan placed himself at the headboard, letting his legs fall to each side of her prone body. He pulled her arms from under her head and stretched them across his thighs. Warm, slick fingers began kneading from her elbows down to the tips of her fingers. A lusty groan rent the air when he leaned in and began to nuzzle the back of her throat. Soft lips teased, nibbled, and played with her flesh.

The muscles of her ass clenched when Latan's hands slid to her bared buttocks. Tania began shivering and moving on the bed sensuously when she felt the slippery caress in the cleft between her cheeks. *I want you, Tania.* She glanced over her shoulder when she heard Latan's thoughts through their mate bond. Dark eyes, nearly black in his passion, looked down, drawing attention to the hard shaft pressing into Tania's thigh.

Feeling a sudden need to give these men something of herself, she pulled her hands from Ethan's clasp and attempted to turn over on her side. Catching Latan by surprise, he growled as she tumbled him off her legs.

"What's wrong, did I hurt you?" he asked hesitantly.

She grinned and got up on her knees. "No way, love. I just think it's my turn to play." She reached out and trailed a finger down both of their chests. "Are you men game for a little fun?"

Chapter 6

Tania took a moment to enjoy the shocked looks on the faces of her mates and then calmly pushed Latan over onto his back. Moving quickly, she crawled up his body and straddled his thighs, her nipples skimming over his abdomen as she straightened. Glancing over to where Ethan rested on his side, she let her foot slide up the inside of his thighs and pressed lightly against his balls. He groaned loudly when she wiggled them slightly, giving him an erotic massage.

She ran her hand along Latan's hard shaft and watched it jerk, then tightened her grip and ran her thumb across the slit in the top. Fingers from her other hand brushed softly over his furry sac as he whispered her name in a ragged voice.

Ethan grabbed the foot that was torturing his balls and brought it to his mouth, sucking each toe in turn and running his tongue down to the heel. She squirmed to pull away, her feet the most ticklish part of her body. With a final nip on her ankle, Ethan moved to kneel behind her on the bed, putting his knees between Latan's spread legs.

Tania began to move down in the bed, sliding her body across Latan's muscular legs. Ethan squeezed her shoulders and then let his hands glide down the middle of her back until they rested on her ass. He moved her hair to the side and bit lightly at the back of her neck, then ran his warm, wet tongue down the middle of her spine. She trembled when he spread her cheeks apart, guiding his damp caress over the sensitive, puckered hole.

Rubbing the side of her face against Latan's erection, she marveled at the velvety smoothness of the skin. She licked in lazy circles down and then up the shaft, swirling her tongue around the crown before licking back down to take one of his balls into her mouth. Carefully, she rolled the firm sac on her tongue, his pubic hairs tickling the skin of her nose.

"Finish him," Ethan whispered. "When you're done, I'm gonna run my tongue along this pretty, pink slit and lap up every bit of your cream. Then, I'm gonna fuck your pussy while Latan reams your ass, and we're gonna claim you all over again." He nudged her forward. "Go on, now. I wanna see your beautiful lips around his cock."

Tania shuddered as his erotic words formed pictures in her mind's eye. She placed her lips around the solid length in her hand and sucked, the cock pulsing with the caress. He began thrusting into her mouth when she fondled his tightly drawn up sac.

"Your mouth's so hot, so wet. Suck me, Tania, suck me dry," Latan whimpered.

Encouraged by the sounds of his pleasure, Tania increased her efforts, taking more and more of his length until he was hitting the back of her throat. Swallowing with each stroke, she bobbed her head up and down and then squeezed the base firmly. Latan groaned, halfway sitting up as he spurted into her mouth. His seed poured down her throat, the taste exploding on her tongue. She swallowed repeatedly, sucking and licking the pulsing length as Latan continued slow, shallow thrusts into her mouth. When he relaxed back against the bed with a sigh, Tania licked him clean and smiled then squealed when Ethan pulled her off his brother and tossed her onto her back.

* * * *

Unable to wait any longer, Ethan pulled Tania from between Ethan's legs and rolled her onto her back, immediately covering her body with his own. His hands roamed over her nude form, delighting in the different textures of her silky, smooth skin. He began sliding down her body, pausing to lick the dusky nipples that had already hardened into tight little points. Fondling her breasts, he slowly stroked, his thumbs running over the hardened tips. His mouth fastened on to the rounded globe, latching on to her nipple and flicking his tongue back and forth. She cried out when Latan took possession of her other side, her hands going to both their heads, fingers tangling in their hair.

Ethan rubbed circles on her belly before his fingers sought the moist heat of her clit. Slipping a finger down her drenched slit, he spread her pussy lips apart and delved his tongue inside, probing her folds. He looked up when she called out his name and saw Latan licking and tweaking her nipples, his hands wandering over her supple form.

Opening her folds with his fingers, Ethan began to lick her clit. He rolled the hard nub between his thumb and forefinger, sliding one finger in and out of her tight center. Her entire body shivered in response, her breathing labored.

"Please," Tania begged as she pulled strongly on his hair. "Please, Ethan, come inside me. I'm so hungry for you, for you and Latan."

Shivers of delight raced up Ethan's spine at her words. Gripping her hips almost bruisingly, he sucked hard on her clit. "Tell me where you want my cock, baby. I wanna make you come. I wanna feel you against me."

"I want you up here, inside me," she gasped, "with Latan in my ass."

Ethan smacked her lightly on the thigh. "Spread your legs more, baby." When she followed his directions, he slid up between her creamy thighs. She made a hissing sound when the tip of his erection grazed her slick opening. With no warning, he thrust deep, the feel of her warm wetness around his thickness making him want to growl. Dainty hands squeezed his ass, her legs wrapping around his waist as she drew him inside her.

"Make those thighs hold me tight." Ethan rolled to his side, taking her with him. He focused on Latan over her shoulder and watched as he coated his cock with lubricant. When he moved up close to Tania's back, Ethan pulled her leg higher on his hip to open her up wider for his brother. Her nails dug into Ethan's shoulders as Latan made several firm pushes as he slid into her luscious ass.

Hot inner walls tightened around Ethan's cock as he bent his head and sucked a nipple into his mouth. Latan bit lightly onto her shoulder and ran his hand around to pinch and tug on the other side.

"Come on, guys, move," she demanded. Tania began moving her hips, like she was trying her best to ride the cocks buried so deeply inside her.

"Patience, baby," Ethan scolded. He rocked their lower bodies together in a rhythmic wave, coordinating with Latan's thrusts, keeping the pace slow and steady. He felt the muscles in his thighs clench when she ground her hips against him.

Gradually, he and Latan increased the pace until they were both pounding into her burning depths. Ethan let his hand slip between their bodies, his fingers brushing against her clit. Her breathing quickened, and her body stiffened as she cried out her release, her pussy convulsing repeatedly against his throbbing cock.

"That's it, baby. Come all over my cock." Ethan tightened his grip on her waist when he felt a twinge in his balls and then threw back his head. With a wailing cry, he came, pumping his seed into their mate. Needing to solidify his claim, Ethan let his canines sink into the mating mark he'd left on her neck. At the same time, he heard Latan calling out his release. Shivering, he slumped over and rested his head on Tania's shoulder, listening to the fast rhythm of her breathing. His legs twined through hers in an effort to keep her from moving away. Peering at Latan through his lowered lashes, he saw his brother licking across his own mating mark on her other side.

"I love you, Ethan," she whispered.

Before Ethan could raise his head to express the joy her words had brought to his heart, he felt the sharp sting of her teeth as she sank them into his neck, claiming him for all time. Buried deep inside her heat, his cock hardened almost painfully. Forcing his hips to still, he felt the swipe of her tongue across the bite and then watched as Latan leaned forward so she could vow her love to him before claiming him with a mating bite.

Together, the brothers began to pound into her relentlessly. Knowing he wouldn't last long, Ethan pinched her clit lightly and rubbed the tiny, hard nub. Still sensitized from her earlier orgasm, Tania tightened her legs around his waist, threw back her head, and screamed. A throbbing began in his balls, his hips thrusting like crazy as he drove toward his own release. Finally, his body stiffened, and his cock erupted as the world around him exploded.

For several minutes, Ethan cuddled his mate close to his chest, while Latan snuggled up to her back. Feeling happier than he ever remembered feeling before, Ethan pressed a kiss to Tania's head. He looked over at his brother. "You ready, bro?"

"Yeah," Latan groaned.

Ethan held their mate tightly while Latan slowly slid from her ass, then allowed his own body to slip free of his woman. He gently rolled her to her back so both brothers could nestle close. His hand smoothed up her side to cup a breast, while Latan toyed with the nipple on the other side.

She sighed when Ethan nuzzled her cheek. "Do you really think we can make this work?"

"Absolutely," he insisted.

"No doubt about it," Latan declared.

She giggled. "You have to know there're gonna be problems."

"Sure, baby, every relationship has problems, no matter how many people are in it." Ethan leaned over and pressed a kiss to her lips.

"What's the biggest problem you see us having?" Latan asked.

She looked uncomfortable for a moment and then wouldn't meet their eyes.

Ethan leaned up on his elbow and gazed down into her worried face. "Come on, baby, tell us what worries you the most."

Tania sighed. “This hasn’t changed anything. I still have a job to do for the Council, and I’m not gonna walk away from it.”

Latan glanced at Ethan. “Nobody’s asking you to walk away, but things have definitely changed.”

“What’s changed?” She frowned.

Ethan took her chin between his fingers and turned her to face him. “Now, you don’t have to do the job alone, and you don’t have to hide what you’re doing from us.”

“But I can’t—”

“Yes, you can, and you will, let us help,” Latan argued.

“Tomorrow, we’ll go explain everything to Remus and come up with a plan that works for everyone.” Ethan wanted to take the fear out of her eyes but didn’t know how.

“And you think he’ll be okay with all this, helping me, and accepting our mating?”

“Oh, yeah.” Ethan grinned. “If he doesn’t, he’ll have to answer to our Alpha Femm.”

“And she’ll kick his furry butt,” Latan added, laughing. “She said it would be great to have you in the family when we told her about mating you.”

Tania looked surprised. “She really said that?”

“Absolutely,” Ethan confirmed. “In fact, she said this pack could use some shaking up, and a ménage mating between two wolves and a cat just might do the trick.”

“Oh, my God.” Tania laughed. “How did they react when you told them I shift into a cat?”

“Remus was shocked, and a little annoyed he didn’t already know about it.” Ethan smirked. “But we didn’t tell Maddie. She already knew.”

“How? I mean, that’s not possible.”

“She said she scented both cat and wolf on you, with the cat being stronger,” Latan explained.

“That’s weird. She shouldn’t be able to scent me at all.”

"Why's that, baby?" Ethan asked.

"They manipulated the DNA to make sure I don't have a scent."

"Why the hell would they do that?" Latan asked.

"They were making government agents, soldiers, if you will. We would be able to slip in and out unnoticed if there wasn't any type of scent trail." She gave them a look of embarrassment. "I should probably tell you I don't have fingerprints either."

Sensing Tania's discomfort, Ethan leaned forward and captured her lips in a tender kiss. Pulling back, he watched as Latan kissed her lips lingeringly. "I love you, Tania, with all my heart. You're my mate, and I'll do everything in my power to make you happy and keep you safe."

"I love you, too, pretty lady, more than you'll ever know." Latan kissed her hand.

"It's late, and we're all gonna have a busy day tomorrow. Early, we're gonna go talk to Remus and fill him in on everything. But for now, can we just hold each other, enjoy the feel of being mated, and get some sleep?" Ethan looked at her pleadingly.

Tania smiled, her face glowing with happiness. "Yes, we can get some sleep, if I can cuddle up to the two of you."

Latan grinned and pulled her against his chest. She snuggled up close and then wiggled her butt back toward Ethan.

Laughing, Ethan reached over and turned off the bedside light. Moving close to his mate, he curled around her back, her ass cradled against his groin. Ignoring his filling cock, he kissed her soft cheek and settled back against the pillows. For a long time, he listened to her breathing, slow and steady as she dropped off into sleep. He felt like they'd passed one huge hurdle. Now, all they had to do was figure out a way to keep her safe and out of the way while they took care of Kaugh. He looked down at his sleeping mate, feeling slightly remorseful. She hadn't realized he'd failed to use a condom. If they were lucky, they'd impregnated her tonight. *I hope to hell you realize you're about to turn in your resignation to the Council, effective immediately.*

* * * *

Remus walked into the kitchen and stopped short at the sight of his expectant mate cheerfully humming, apparently cooking breakfast. Maddie had never been a morning person, usually dragging around for a couple of hours before she even bothered getting dressed, let alone making breakfast for anyone. Mornings had become even worse for her since giving up coffee for the baby. He approached her cautiously. "Good morning, baby. Are you feeling okay this morning?"

Maddie whirled around from her position at the stove and smiled brightly. "Hey there, sleepyhead. I didn't wake you, did I?"

"Uh, no, I'm always up this early." Remus slid his arms around her waist and kissed her cheek. "What're you doing up, little mamma-to-be."

"What does it look like I'm doing, wolf man?" She snorted.

"Well, it looks a lot like you're scrambling eggs," he said, peering into the skillet. "But, since I know for a fact you haven't been able to stomach the smell of food before noon in weeks, my eyes must be playing tricks on me." He laughed and dodged back to escape her elbow smashing into his stomach.

"Ha, ha, very funny," she said dryly. "Leave it to the Alpha man to make fun of his poor, pregnant mate. Men should only know the pains and discomfort of bringing the next generation into the world."

Remus rolled his eyes and took his mate back into his arms. "I'm sorry, baby, I'm being an ass. It is kind of early for you, though. What's going on?"

Maddie took the eggs off the stove and poured them out onto a plate she pulled from the oven. "Michael called late last night, after you went to bed. They're gonna be back today."

Remus frowned, a feeling of unease coming over him. "What the hell's going on? They haven't been gone a week. Nobody comes home from their honeymoon early."

"You do know they went to Hawaii, don't you?"

"Yeah, I know where they went. You've been bugging me relentlessly to plan a trip for us after the pup comes."

"Don't you ever watch the news, Remus?"

He couldn't stop the growl from escaping. "Apparently not. What's going on?"

Maddie turned and growled back at her mate. "Don't growl at me, Mr. Morning Sunshine. If you'd paid attention to the weather, you would know that Hawaii is in the path of a rather fierce storm. He wanted to get Ariane away from the danger so he got in touch with one of his former clients, one who just happens to own a private jet. They'll be back here this morning."

Remus grinned. "Must be nice to have friends in high places, or at least friends with money."

"I'll say." Maddie giggled. She placed his plate on the table and pulled his chair out. "Sit, eat, oh, great wolfy one."

Remus sat down and then stared up at his mate. "All these irreverent names you've assigned to me need to stop, woman. The pack's gonna think I don't have any control over my own mate."

"Well, excuse me, Mr. Alpha Wolf, Sir. Wouldn't want anyone to question your masculinity, now, would we?"

Remus sighed at her words and then winced when she slammed a glass of orange juice down on the table in front of him. He cleared his throat. "Uh, baby, aren't you eating?"

She looked at him like he'd just suggested she committed some kind of crime. "No, your grace, I wouldn't be able to keep it down."

"But don't you—" A knock at the door interrupted Remus's words. He glanced at Maddie. "It's Koril. I asked him to come by this morning."

Shrugging, Maddie went and opened the door. “Good morning, Koril. Please, come on in.” She stepped back, allowing the large man to enter.

“Good morning, Alpha Femm, Alpha Remus,” he greeted.

“Maddie, Koril, I’ve asked you to call me Maddie. There’s no reason we have to be so bloody formal all the time.” Maddie stalked over to the stove and turned the burner on under the teapot. “Do you want some tea, Koril?”

“No, thanks, Alph, um, Maddie. I would love a cup of coffee, though.”

The slam of the teapot against the stove’s burner had both men jumping. “Well, I’m sorry, but we don’t have any damn coffee.” She turned without another word and stomped out of the kitchen.

Koril glanced over at Remus, his face a mask of horror. “I’m so sorry, Remus. What did I do?”

Remus chuckled and shook his head. “Pregnancy hormones.” He figured that should be enough to explain everything.

Koril’s eyes got big as saucers, staring toward the door where Maddie had disappeared. “I’m never gonna mate,” he mumbled.

“Good luck with that.” Remus laughed. “Excuse me a minute.” Remus got up and went to answer the ringing phone. “Hello?”

“Remus, we found her, or rather, she found us,” Ethan said.

“Is everything all right?”

“Everything’s perfect, bro. We’ll be there in a little while to fill you in on everything. She’s not involved with Kaugh’s plans. You don’t have to worry about that anymore. Everything else I would rather tell you in person.” Ethan’s voice lowered. “We’re keeping her, Remus. She claimed both of us last night.”

“I’m happy for you, Ethan, for both you and Latan. We can talk more when you get here.” He smiled. “And, Ethan, tell her I said welcome to the family.” He hung up the phone and glanced over at Koril. “You can be the first to congratulate me on the mating of my brothers.”

"Ethan and Latan mated?" he asked, surprise in his voice.

"Yeah, they've come over to the dark side," Remus said with a smirk.

"I didn't even know they'd been seeing anyone. Who are the females?"

"Our new schoolteacher, Tania."

"Wait, the same schoolteacher you've had us checking out?" Koril looked puzzled. "Which one of them mated her?"

"They both did," Maddie answered, walking back into the kitchen.

"Both of them? They both mated the same wolf?"

"She's not a—" Maddie cut off Remus's words, slapping her hand across his mouth.

"I don't think that's our secret to tell, do you?" she asked.

Remus pulled her hand away and thought for a moment. "Actually, I think it is, Maddie. Koril's responsible for security and the safety of all the members of the pack. He can't protect her if he doesn't know the truth."

For just a moment, Maddie looked unhappy, then nodded. "Okay, I guess that would be for the best. I just wish they could be here to tell their own news."

"Understood, baby." Remus turned his attention to Koril. "Tania's only half wolf, the other half is feline. She shifts into a cat, not a wolf."

"A cat?" Koril asked, his eyebrows rising.

"Yeah." Remus laughed. "A cat, as in the one that tried to eat Taynor's finger and, as I recall, tried to carve her claws into your leg."

Maddie giggled. "Do tell. I miss all the fun."

Koril glared at her for a moment and then turned his attention back to Remus. "The cat we thought was her pet?" he asked.

"Yep, not her pet at all. It was her, all along."

"Look, gentlemen, as interesting as all this is, I need to be going." Maddie walked over and leaned down to kiss Remus.

"Sure, Maddie, we can leave whenever you want." Koril snapped to attention and walked to the back door.

"We?" Maddie asked, an angry light entering her eyes as she stared over at the pack's security chief.

"Uh, yes," he said, glancing around the room and fidgeting. "I'm your new bodyguard."

"Is that so?" she drawled. "And what would make you think I need to be guarded?"

Koril glanced at Remus. "Because Alpha Remus told me to remain at your side any time you leave this house until further notice."

"Of course he did," she replied, gritting her teeth. Her eyes shot daggers at Remus. "Well, we certainly can't go against the wishes of his royal Alphaness, now, can we?" She leaned down and yanked on his ear. "I'm in a hurry right now, but we'll definitely talk about this later, oh, great fuzzy one."

Remus groaned when he heard Koril snickering. "Maddie, it's for your protection, and it's not up for discussion. When you get home, I'll tell you everything so you'll understand."

Maddie gave him a little smile and strode over to the door. Koril quickly opened it and then followed her out after shooting a desperate look over his shoulder to Remus. Remus could hear his mate laying down the rules she expected Koril to follow as the door closed behind the unhappy man.

* * * *

Melissa unlocked the door to Michael's new office and stumbled wearily inside. She'd finished her business in Houston two days faster than she'd thought possible and couldn't wait to get back to her new home. She'd thought about calling Mali, to tell him about her change of plans, and then decided to just surprise him.

Smiling at the thought of the new love in her life, Melissa dropped her bag by her desk and hurried upstairs to check out her new apartment. Reaching the large room, she stopped and looked around. Frowning, she walked over to the small bathroom and glanced inside. "What the hell's going on? It doesn't look like he did anything." Deciding she needed to call her lover, Melissa headed for the stairs and heard the door downstairs open. "Damn, I forgot to lock it," she groaned.

"Sunshine, where are you?"

Melissa's heart skipped a beat when she heard the voice of the man she'd grown to love. *Oh, my God! I'm in love with him!* Hurrying, she raced down the stairs and across the room, throwing herself into his open arms.

"Sunshine, what're you doing back so soon?"

"Mali, why haven't you done anything on my apartment?" Melissa laughed when both of them spoke at the same time. "Sorry, I didn't mean to interrupt you."

"You don't have to be sorry, just tell me everything's okay."

"Sure, everything's great. I finished closing up all my business sooner than I thought I would, so here I am." She smiled up at him.

"Why didn't you call me? I would've picked you up at the airport."

"I wanted to surprise you, so I took an airport limo back."

Mali nuzzled his face into her neck and inhaled deeply. Melissa trembled when he licked from her collarbone up to the area behind her ear and then tugged on the lobe with his teeth. "I've missed you, Sunshine, missed you so much." He drew her chin upward and captured her lips with his, licking, then gently biting, her bottom lip before plunging his tongue inside her mouth. Their tongues slid together in an erotic dance, his hands tightening around her waist, pulling her closer to his warm, hard body.

He caught her hips, urging her closer, and ground his erection against her stomach. Large hands moved to her back, skimming along her spine, then curling over her neck, tangling in her hair. She felt herself pushed up against the wall, her wrists anchored above her head with one of his hands. His lips abandoned hers, working their way down her neck as she squirmed in pleasure.

Dark eyes came up to gaze into hers right before he bent his head and sucked her nipple through the material of her blouse and bra. Melissa groaned sharply, her knees buckling, her body trying to slide to the floor. Her loud gasp echoed through the room when Mali thrust his knee between her legs, pressing against her throbbing mound, effectively stopping her descent.

"Mali." She gasped when he transferred her wrists to one of his hands and brought the other one down and pinched her swollen nipple. Not stopping there, he guided his fingers down, snaking them into her slacks, and rubbed her clit through the silk of her panties. Her hips jerked, pressing toward the caressing fingers.

"I want you, Sunshine, want you now." Mali growled softly and then picked her up, encouraging her to wrap her legs around his waist. Quickly, he started for the stairs, Melissa nearly lost in a haze of desire. They both froze when they heard the door open, and then laughter filled the room behind them.

Mali growled menacingly, causing Melissa to giggle, before he turned around. Appalled, she stared into the grinning face of Michael's sister, Maddie, and a man she'd never seen before. Immediately, she began to struggle, trying to make Mali put her down.

His arms tightened, and a low growl came up from his chest. "Mine," he snarled.

Melissa froze for a moment and then smacked him on the side of his head. "Put me down, Neanderthal, now," she demanded. Mali glared at her while Maddie laughed even harder behind her. Melissa felt herself blush furiously as her large lover let her slide down his body, her breasts raking across his chest, the hardness in his jeans nudging her clit. She didn't know when she'd ever been more embarrassed.

"Hey, Maddie," she said, refusing to meet anyone's eyes. "What are you doing here?" Melissa pushed Mali's hands away and walked over toward the door.

"I'm here to meet Michael. This is our friend, Koril."

"Nice to meet you," Koril mumbled. "Hey, Mali, how's it going?"

Melissa looked back at Mali in time to see him nod and then turned her attention back to her best friend's sister. "Maddie, he's not due back for another week, at least."

"Oh, you're so wrong, my good friend and faithful companion of my brother. They're coming back today in order to avoid a nasty storm that's about to hit Hawaii." She gave Melissa a wicked grin. "Good thing we interrupted you. They're due in any minute, and they might've gotten an eyeful."

Mali growled, low, startling Melissa. She turned, gave him a small growl of her own, and then narrowed her eyes when he laughed.

"Did everything go all right with the sale of your condo?" Maddie asked.

Melissa turned back around, determined to ignore the way her heart beat faster for the man behind her, and smiled at Maddie. "It couldn't have been better. The buyers wanted a quick closing and even offered to buy the excess furniture I didn't wanna bring with me. I made a killing."

"That's great, honey! You should get Michael to design you a house and have it built on the mountain. We could be neighbors." Maddie smiled.

Melissa felt like screaming when she heard a low growl behind her again. She couldn't figure out what was making him act so weird. "No, I think I'll just stick with my apartment for now. I'm not ready to be a homeowner just yet. I need to spend a little time here, make sure I'm happy, and that I'm gonna stay." She jumped when Mali's arms came around her, pulling her tightly back against his body.

"What're you doing here, Koril? You looking for me?" Mali asked, holding Melissa around her waist.

"No, I, um…" He glanced at Melissa. "I'm just doing Remus a favor, giving Maddie an escort today." Before he could say anything else, the door opened.

"Michael," Maddie squealed, right before she threw herself into his arms.

"Well, hell." Michael laughed as he swung his sister up into a hug. "Are we having a party? The gang's all here."

"No, we're not having a party, and the gang's not all here. Do you see Remus anywhere?" Maddie scowled at him and then turned a smile toward her new sister-in-law. "Come here and give me a hug, Ariane." Throwing her arms around the young woman, Maddie sighed. "It's so good to see you. I'm glad you came back early so I wouldn't have to worry about you when the storm hits."

"It's good to be home, Maddie. Hawaii was great, but I missed everyone here." Ariane looked over at Michael. "I didn't give him a single moment of grief when he suggested we hit the road early."

Michael walked over and shook Mali's hand, gazing for a moment with a surprised look at the arm held tight around Melissa's waist. "Hey, Mali, it's good to see you again." He glanced around the office. "Everything looks great. Did you get everything done that Melissa wanted?"

"Not exactly," Melissa replied before Mali could say anything. "He's still working on the apartment upstairs." She glanced up at him over her shoulder and wondered about the smirk on his face.

"No problem," Michael replied. "Take all the time you need. I'll pay for Melissa to stay at the bed-and-breakfast no matter how long it takes." Grinning, he nudged her arm with his elbow. "Don't I get a hug from my new partner?"

"Absolutely." Melissa smiled. She wiggled away from Mali and threw her arms around her best friend. "It's good to have you back," she whispered, and then squeaked when Mali's hands pulled her away, back into his arms.

Michael laughed and then turned back toward the door. "Koril, isn't it?" He walked toward Koril with his hand out. "We met at our wedding."

"Yeah." Koril shook the hand offered. "Welcome home, man. And you, too, Mrs. Barrows." He nodded toward Ariane.

"Come on, Koril, you've known me for a long time. It's Ariane, and it always will be."

"Welcome home, Ariane." He smiled.

"Now that we're here, how about I take everyone to lunch?" Michael asked.

"Michael, wait," Ariane said. "Lunch is great, but I have to go to the bank first. You wanna wait here for me, or should I meet all of you at the diner?"

"Actually, I need to stop by the bank today, myself." Koril looked at Maddie. "Why don't you wait here with everyone, and I'll walk down to the bank with Ariane. It'll give you some time with Michael," he glanced over at Mali and smiled, "and Mali and Melissa time to pull themselves together."

"Very funny, man," Mali growled. "Go on to the bank, and get your butt back here. I'm hungry."

Laughing, Koril held the door open for Ariane. "After you, married lady."

Ariane gazed over at Melissa and grinned. "It's great to see you, Melissa. I'm gonna want details when I get back, and you know what I'm talking about."

Michael laughed as Koril left with his wife and then walked over and put his arm around Maddie. "Honey, I meant to say something before the wedding, but I never got the chance. I would never hurt your feelings, you know that, but you're getting a little chunky. Been dipping into the Ben and Jerry's a little too much lately?"

"You're such an ass." Maddie smirked. "I'm almost tempted not to tell you you're gonna be an uncle."

"I knew it," Michael cried, swinging her up into his arms.

"Maddie, that's wonderful." Melissa had pulled away from Mali, wanting to walk over to congratulate Michael's sister, when the door opened suddenly. A tall, dark-haired man with a horrible scar on his face walked in. She froze, a scream bursting from her throat when she spied the small gun clasped in his hand. He raised his arm and fired one shot at Michael, followed quickly by a second one to Maddie. Melissa watched her friends slump to the floor as the man turned the gun in her direction. He took aim at Mali, who'd started to pull his clothes off, and fired. Melissa slumped to the floor, pretending to faint.

* * * *

Kaugh walked into the small office, Marty and Calvin close on his heels. He glanced at Sean as he aimed the gun toward the unconscious woman on the floor. "Forget it, Sean. My guess is, if she fainted, she's not a shifter." He looked at the other three bodies on the floor. "Nice work," he exclaimed. "Well, they certainly made it easy for me. Brother and sister together. How much more perfect could it be?"

"What about this dude?" Sean asked, nudging with his foot. "He shifted before he even got his clothes off. Do we take him, too?"

Kaugh sighed. "No, sadly, we don't have room for another male. I'm much more interested in having the genetics of the brother and sister to work on. Don't waste time, gentlemen." He watched as Marty picked up Maddie and Sean and Calvin picked up Michael. "Gently, please, we don't want to damage the specimens."

"Any danger of them waking up?" Marty asked.

"No, the darts had a small dose of the shift inhibitor, as well as a tranquilizer. It's enough to keep them down for at least six hours and to keep them from shifting for a day." He smiled, feeling like he'd just won the lottery, and followed his men out the door, closing it softly behind him.

* * * *

Melissa squeezed her eyes shut and tried desperately to control her breathing. *Maybe if they think I fainted, they'll go away.* She felt a tear trickle down her cheek. *They shot them, Michael and Maddie. Oh, God, they shot Mali.* Listening carefully, she tried to memorize everything they said and then stifled a cry when she realized they were taking Michael and Maddie with them. Relief flooded her mind when she heard that tranquilizers, instead of bullets, had taken down her friends. Her body tensed when the door opened, her breath catching in her throat. She lay perfectly still, listening to the sounds of the men moving around, and then trembled in reaction to the click of the door and the silence that filled the room.

For several long minutes, Melissa remained perfectly still, not completely sure the men had really gone. Finally, summoning courage from deep inside, she opened her eyes and peered toward the front of the office. Her shoulders slumped, and fresh tears streamed down her face when she didn't see Michael or Maddie lying on the floor where she'd seen them fall. Taking a deep breath, she rolled her eyes to the side, needing to see the man she'd fallen in love with.

Eyes widening, breath catching in her lungs, Melissa scrambled to her feet and began backing away slowly. Never taking her eyes off the floor, she continued backwards until her body came in contact with the office wall. Frightened, she gazed at what should have been Mali's unconscious form. Lying on the floor was a huge, brown dog dressed in the same type of T-shirt Mali had been wearing earlier. A pair of jeans was on the floor by the animal's feet. Melissa did the only thing she could think of. She opened her mouth and screamed at the top of her lungs.

* * * *

Koril smiled down at Ariane as they walked along the sidewalk toward Michael's office. "You seem happy now."

"Hmmm, I'm deliriously happy, Koril. Michael's the best thing that ever happened to me."

"Have you seen your uncle yet?"

"No, but I talked to him last night. He's having dinner with us tonight."

"How does he feel about Michael?"

She laughed. "A lot better since Michael found his wolf. He never really had anything against him. He just wanted me to have a traditional mating with the protection of a pack."

Koril narrowed his eyes. "Would you've mated with him if he'd remained human?"

"In a heartbeat," she sighed. "I love him, all that other stuff is just icing on the cake."

"If that's cake, I'm giving up dessert," he snorted. "I've been watching Maddie and Remus the past few days, and nothing would compel me to go through the hell they do."

"Maddie and Remus are having problems?"

"Not really problems, but she's been a little more, well, I would say, high strung since she got pregnant."

"Maddie's pregnant!" Ariane cried.

"Damn, maybe I shouldn't have said anything. Just let them tell you on their own, okay?" Before she could respond, Koril heard a blood-chilling scream coming from the office several doors down. He grabbed Ariane's arm and pulled her to a stop. "Stay here until I come for you," he ordered. Not waiting to see if she obeyed, he raced down the sidewalk and threw open the door to Michael's office.

Koril took in the sight before him and bit back an expletive. Melissa's screams were coming from the back of the room where she stood, plastered against the wall. Mali was unconscious on the floor, in his wolf form, and there was no sign of Maddie or Michael. He strode quickly over to Melissa, took her by the shoulders, and shook her firmly. “Calm down, Melissa. Tell me what happened,” he demanded.

Her screams stopped abruptly as she stared up at Koril, her eyes wide and unfocused. “They took them,” she whispered.

“Who took them?”

“I don’t know.”

“Melissa,” he yelled, shaking her furiously. “Where are Maddie and Michael?”

Trembling violently, Melissa gazed toward the door. “A man came in, and he shot them.”

Koril growled down at her pale face. “What man?”

She shivered and wiped at the tears sliding down her cheeks. “I don’t know,” she cried.

Taking a deep breath, Koril lowered his voice. “It’s okay, everything’s gonna be okay. Can you tell me what he looked like?”

“Tall, dark hair, bad scars on his face.”

Koril recognized the description of Kaugh’s man, Sean Cross. “Wait, you said *they* took them. How many were there? What did the others look like?”

“I think there were three others, but I’m not sure. I never saw them.”

Confused, Koril raised her chin to gaze into her eyes. “You’re doing good, honey, real good. If you didn’t see them, how do you know they were here?”

“Voices, I heard the voices.”

“All right. Let’s back up. Tell me what happened after the man with the scar came in.”

“He walked in, and he had a gun in his hand. He shot Michael and Maddie, and then turned the gun toward Mali. When it fired, I dropped to the floor, pretending to faint.” She looked up at him with a vacant stare. “I took self-defense classes in Houston, and that’s what they told us to do. She said it might fool them into thinking you were unconscious, and they would leave you alone."

Koril glanced over at Mali and frowned. "He can't be dead. He would've shifted back to human if he'd died."

Melissa glanced over at the animal on the floor. "Mali's gone. When I heard them leave, I waited for a while, then got up. Mali had disappeared, and that dog was just lying there. Is it dead?"

"That's not a dog, honey, it's a wolf," Koril snorted, "and he's not dead. He can't be." He walked over to Mali's still form and bent down to examine him. His eyes immediately focused on a small yellow dart sticking in his shoulder. Carefully, he pulled it out. "You said he shot Michael first, and then Maddie?" he asked.

"Michael was shot?" screamed Ariane.

Koril turned toward the door and groaned. Ariane was standing inside the office, her face white as a sheet. She growled low, her eyes glowing red, claws extending from her fingers. "Calm yourself, Ariane." He held up the dart. "They were shot with tranquilizer darts."

"Where's Michael?" she growled.

"Michael and Maddie were apparently tranquilized and taken. From Melissa's description, I would say by Kaugh and his men."

"Who the hell is Kaugh?" She came closer and stared down at the wolf. "Is that Mali?"

"Yeah, it is."

"I don't understand. He should've shifted if they shot him with a tranq. I mean, even if they killed him, he would've shifted back to human."

"It's an inhibitor," Melissa mumbled.

Koril glanced up at Ariane and then walked over to take Melissa into his arms. "What's an inhibitor, honey?"

Melissa took a deep breath and gazed up into his eyes. "Right before they left, one of the men asked if there was any danger of them waking up. Another man said no, the darts have a small amount of the inhibitor and a tranquilizer in them."

"Damn," Koril snarled.

"Oh, my God! Is it permanent? Will he not be able to shift back?" Ariane asked.

"I don't know." Koril ran his hand through his hair.

"No," Melissa added. "He said the shot would keep them out for at least six hours, and they wouldn't be able to shift for a full day." She looked over at Mali. "Is that really Mali?" she asked, tears making her voice husky.

"Shit," Koril groaned. "Yeah, it's Mali. Listen, honey, there's a lot we need to tell you, but not right now. I need to concentrate on getting Maddie and Michael back. You need to hold it together for me." He glanced at Ariane and pulled out his cell. "I'm calling Remus. He needs to know what happened, and he can explain to you about Kaugh."

"He's gonna go ballistic," she said, coming to put her arms around Melissa.

"He deserves to." Koril closed his eyes as he waited on his Alpha to answer his phone. "I failed him, failed to protect my Alpha's mate. He should put me to death."

"No," Ariane cried.

Koril sighed when Remus answered the phone. "Alpha Remus, I've failed you."

* * * *

"I don't understand why the Council purposely kept me in the dark about her mission here." Remus glared at Ethan and Latan. "Am I not to be trusted anymore? Don't they think I can handle my own territory?" Angrily, he pushed back from the table and began pacing in the roomy kitchen. His brothers and their mate had arrived earlier and spent the last hour explaining what Tania's assignment entailed.

"Alpha, I'm so sorry," Tania began.

He stopped his pacing and pulled her to her feet. "No, you've nothing to be sorry for, and I told you to call me Remus."

She squealed when Remus lifted her in a hug, leaving her feet dangling a few inches off the floor. "If it helps, I don't think it had anything to do with trusting you or your abilities as an Alpha." She sighed as he lowered her back to the floor. "They decided it would be better for my cover to have only one contact in the area. There would be less danger of my identity being discovered that way." She gave him a sheepish look. "They picked Vanard because, well, he, um, he has a friend on the Council."

Remus frowned. "You mean he received special consideration because of this friend?"

"Not exactly," she hedged.

"Come on, Tania, give," he growled, and then glared at his brothers when they jumped to their feet. "Chill out, bros, you know I would never do anything to hurt your mate, but her evasive answers are driving me crazy!"

Tania grimaced as her mates chuckled and returned to their seats. "I'm sorry, I guess I'm trying to be diplomatic, and it's not really in my nature." She returned to her seat at the table and smiled when Ethan and Latan scooted closer to her chair. "Vanard wasn't given all the information about my job. I mean, they only wanted a contact in case I disappeared. He only knows that I work for the Council. His friend, and please don't ask me who it is because I won't tell you, said Vanard was the perfect choice because he, um, he, oh, hell, he wasn't smart enough to figure anything out on his own." Tania groaned and hung her head when all three men threw back their heads and laughed.

"Man, oh, man, does the Council have Vanard pegged or what?" Latan smirked.

Ethan shook his head and grabbed Tania's hand to press a kiss against her palm. "Don't look so sad, baby. Nobody's holding anything against you."

Latan reached over, put his hands around her waist, and pulled her onto his lap. "He's right, pretty lady, you've got nothing to be sad about." He raised her chin with one finger and gazed into her eyes. "Come on, let me see a smile." When she grinned, he leaned forward and gave her a swift, hard kiss.

"My brothers are right, Tania. The only people I'm angry with are Vanard and the members of the Council. I'd reported the situation with Kaugh to all them, and they let me waste a lot of time worrying about you when we could've been working together."

"You've been worried about me?" She bit her lip. "You thought I was working with him, didn't you?"

"No, absolutely not," Ethan cried.

"No way, love," Latan declared.

"Yes, I'm ashamed to say, I believed you had to be involved with him in some way. Hell, we kept hitting roadblocks when we tried to find out anything about your background." Remus took her hand in his. "But the important thing is that I know the truth now." He pulled her out of Latan's lap and hugged her tightly. "Welcome to the family, little kitten."

Remus released Tania and glanced at his brothers. "I need to call Maddie and get her butt home. We need to plan a party to celebrate your mating in style." He turned toward the phone when it began to ring.

"Maybe that's her now." Ethan laughed.

"Well, he did say the word *party*." Latan smirked.

Remus shook his head at his brother's antics. "Hello," he answered, and then stilled at the sound of his pack mate's voice. "What's wrong, Koril?" He looked at Ethan, who'd come to stand by him, and then glanced over at Latan, who had his arms around their mate. He knew they were picking up on his anxiety through their family bond. Anger and panic warred inside him as he learned what had happened at Michael's office. "Don't do anything on your own. Get Ariane, Mali, and Melissa to my house as soon as you can, and we'll organize from here. I'll call everybody in." He hung up the phone and closed his eyes in anguish.

"You want me to call and round everybody up?" Latan asked.

Remus blinked back his tears and gazed over at Latan. He knew their wolf hearing had allowed them to hear both sides of his conversation, so he had no need to repeat what Koril had told him. "Call Vanard and tell him to have everyone meet at the Pack House in two hours."

"What about your guards?" Tania asked. "I've spent the last few days avoiding the wolves you have watching Kaugh and his men. Where were they when all this went down?" Latan looked at Ethan, who in turn gave Remus a puzzled look.

"See if you can reach Brenner and have him check it out," Remus ordered.

"That won't work," Ethan argued. "He said he wouldn't be back for a few days."

"Damn, then have Vanard send one of the men to check on them. They should've been in the woods behind Kaugh's office." Remus bent over and put his hands on his knees. For a moment, he let the fury race through his body, and then he rose up and punched the wall next to the telephone with his fist, leaving a small hole in the drywall. "Well, hell," he chuckled, "now I'm in trouble. Maddie will skin me alive when she sees what I've done to her wall."

"We'll get her back, bro," Ethan promised.

"Before he hurts her, or Michael?" Remus asked. "What the hell kind of Alpha am I? Again, I've failed to protect my mate and one of my wolves, no, two of my wolves. You heard him. He said Mali's unconscious and still in wolf form. For all we know, the damage could be permanent. He could be stuck in shifted form for the rest of his life." His voice lowered in pain. "They shot my mate, my pregnant mate, with whatever the hell it is. What's it gonna do to my son?" he cried.

Ethan put his arms around his older brother. “Come on, man, pull it together. We need to come up with a plan for rescue and implement it. You can fall apart after we get her furry butt home.”

“We have to find them first, Ethan,” Remus yelled.

“We already know where they’ll be taken,” Tania said, quietly. “The cottage in the woods that Kaugh purchased.”

“Damn, of course. I’m not thinking clearly.” Remus looked at Ethan. “We need the blueprints of that place. I know it has a basement, but we need to know the exact layout.”

“You don’t need the plans,” Tania interrupted. “I was in it yesterday after they moved in a bunch of equipment. I can tell you everything about the place.”

“Damn it to hell, you went back there alone,” Latan cried, giving her a little shake.

“Baby, are you trying to get yourself killed?” Ethan asked. “Why couldn’t you’ve trusted us? We could have—”

“Lay off her, both of you,” Remus demanded. “You can chastise her later, hell, I’ll help hold her down for you to spank her ass, but right now, we need to hear what she has to say.”

Tania gave him a wide-eyed look and cleared her throat. “They fortified the place with double locks on all the inside bedroom doors and bars on all the windows. There are two large and two small rooms underground, no windows, and the only access is the stairs that lead down from the kitchen.” She swallowed hard and closed her eyes. “One large room is full of equipment and a small fridge with medical vials of something. The other one has two metal cots bolted to the floor with leather straps attached to the frame. The two small rooms are empty.”

“Son of a bitch,” Remus bellowed.

“Remus, calm down,” Ethan pleaded.

“You calm the hell down. He’s gonna strap my mate to a damn bed like an animal and do God knows what to her. What the hell are we gonna do now?”

"The place is easily defendable, in a small clearing with heavy tree cover on three sides and a stream on the fourth." Tania hesitated, and then continued. "I could easily sneak in and make my way downstairs and unlock their doors. After I released their restraints, Michael and I could surprise them from below at the same time you mount an attack on the house. The element of surprise could work."

"No," Ethan and Latan cried simultaneously.

"Yes," Tania responded in a quiet voice. "It's my job, and I won't walk away from it. It's the last one I'll ever do for the Council if I'm gonna be your mate."

"You'll really give it up, stay here with us for good?" Ethan asked.

Tania smiled at both her mates. "I love you guys, both of you, very much. I wanna be with you. Make a life with you. I just can't ignore my last responsibility, especially since it involves Maddie. Try to understand."

"All right, baby, we'll go with you to protect you." Ethan spoke like it was a done deal and she had no choice.

"You can't," Tania replied.

"Why the hell not?" Latan's face had taken on an angry, red sheen.

"Your wolves are too big to sneak in. I can fit through the bars on the windows, plus the big guy with the bushy beard likes me. If I'm caught, he'll just think the stray cat is scrounging some food."

Everyone was quiet for several moments, and then Remus walked over to Ethan. "This is your decision. I'm not gonna order her to do this. She's your mate, and you need to be okay with whatever goes down." He watched his brothers stare at each other and knew they were discussing their options across their family mind bond. He didn't know what he would do if they refused to let her help in the rescue.

Finally, Ethan sighed and took Tania's hands in his own. "All right, baby, we'll do this your way this time. But the minute we have

Maddie home, you're turning in your resignation to the Council. Deal?"

"Deal." She smiled.

Remus was about to suggest they sit down and put together a preliminary plan when he heard a pounding on the front door. All three brothers went swiftly toward the front room. Throwing open the door, Remus stared in shock. Koril stood, struggling under the weight of Mali's wolf, while Tehran waited behind him with an unconscious Melissa clasped against his chest. Ariane stood quietly at the bottom of the steps. He stood aside as Ethan rushed forward to help Koril carry Mali into the house. "What the hell happened to Melissa, and what are you doing here, Tehran?"

Koril glanced over his shoulder. "I called him from Michael's office. I didn't like the way Mali was breathing. I thought a doctor should check him out before I moved him."

"And Melissa?" Remus asked.

"I'm afraid I'm to blame for her condition," Tehran spoke up. "She was quite hysterical in the aftermath of everything, so I gave her a sedative to calm her down. She'll sleep for a few hours now."

Remus nodded and stepped back, pointing down the hall. "Put Mali in the first room on the right and Melissa in the second." He hesitated. "Tehran, come back after you get her settled. I've got a couple of questions I need answered."

"Will do." Tehran carried the sedated woman down the hall and disappeared into one of the bedrooms.

Remus looked at Ariane and held out his arms. She walked into his embrace without a word. "I need you to sit with Melissa until she comes around. Will you do that for me while I get our family back?" Without a word, she turned and followed Tehran down the hall.

Remus walked back into the kitchen and waited for the others to join him. After a couple of minutes, Tehran walked in and sat down at the table with him. "Is she okay?" he asked the pack's doctor.

"She'll be fine. I left Tania and Ariane watching over her."

"Did Koril tell you they gave Mali something that keeps him from shifting even when he's unconscious?"

"Yes, but I have to say, I've never heard of any such drug."

Remus swallowed hard. "Maddie was probably given the same thing. Will it hurt the baby?"

"I'm sorry, Alpha, there's no way to know without running some tests on the drug itself. I wish I could say more, but I don't wanna give you false hope."

"I understand, but I had to ask. I guess you don't know if Mali will be all right either."

"His vital signs are stable, and if what Melissa heard is true, he'll be back to normal this time tomorrow. However, if the tranquilizer wears off in a few hours, you're gonna have one pissed off wolf on your hands, one that can't shift back to human. He may need," he coughed, "supervision, until the other drug disappears from his system."

"Understood, I'll leave a guard here with you when we leave. I want you to stick around and keep an eye on them, make sure they stay healthy." Remus looked up as Koril came through the door, followed closely by Ethan and Latan. "Okay, guys, we need to get over to the Pack House and coordinate this rescue plan with everyone else."

Koril moved forward. "I got a call from Sortee a few minutes before we got here. He watched them carry Maddie and Michael into the cottage a little while ago, right before they brought in Elcor and Janis, also unconscious."

"They were assigned to watch Kaugh's office and follow him if he left, weren't they?" Remus growled.

"Yes, Alpha. I don't know if they've been shot with the same drug, or killed." Koril lowered his head and bared his throat in submission.

"Forget it, Koril. It's not your fault." Remus glanced around. "Let's get moving. The faster we get our plan organized, the faster my mate will be home."

Chapter 7

Maddie drifted toward consciousness, the sound of her name breaking through the silent void she'd been floating in. A pounding in her head kept her eyes closed while she struggled to lift the dead weight of her arms. *What's wrong with me? Am I sick?*

"Maddie, wake up!"

She recognized Michael's voice and slowly tried to turn her head in the direction she thought it came from. "Michael," she whispered. Slowly, she opened her eyes and then immediately closed them, groaning softly.

"Honey, you're gonna be okay. The dizziness only lasts for a couple of minutes, and then it's not so bad. Try to open your eyes for me, please."

Determined to find out what had happened to her, Maddie opened her eyes again. Swallowing hard, she waited for the room to come into focus. What she saw made her wonder if she was still asleep, having a nightmare. Michael was lying on a bed a few feet away, dressed in something that looked like a hospital gown. There were large, black bands around his arms, stomach, and legs, literally holding him prisoner on the thin mattress. Fearful for his safety, she tried to sit up, to go release him from his bindings, only to discover the same type of straps held her tightly.

"Are you all right?" he asked.

She glanced over at the concerned look on his face. "I think so. Where are we?"

He sighed. "I don't know. There hasn't been anyone around since I woke up. Do you remember what happened?"

Maddie thought carefully. "We were at your office, waiting for Koril and Ariane to get back so we could go to lunch. Do you think they're here somewhere?" she asked fearfully.

"There's no way to know. I've tried reaching her with our mate bond, but it's like she's not there."

Concentrating, Maddie tried to hear Remus's thoughts. "No, I can't hear Remus, either."

"Yeah, well, it gets worse. I can't bring my wolf."

"What!"

"I've tried over and over again to shift, and I can't find the magic. Give it a try."

Reaching down, deep inside herself, Maddie searched for the magic that would allow her to shift into her wolf. A tear escaped her eye when she felt only emptiness. "What's happening, Michael? What've they done to us?"

"I don't know, babe. A man walked through the door and shot us with something."

Maddie gasped. "What about the baby?"

"Calm down, honey. We don't know anything for sure, so let's not assume the worst. What about your other gift? There are a couple of glasses on that table over there. See if you can get mad enough to move them."

"I won't have any trouble getting mad." Maddie snorted. She stared at the two glasses and thought about her baby being in danger. After several minutes, she cursed loudly. "Nothing's working."

"Okay, you tried, now we just need to calm down and think of something else." He was quiet for a moment and then turned and frowned at his sister. "Maddie, I need to ask you something that doesn't make any sense to me."

"Okay." She laughed harshly. "Whatever it is should fit right in with everything that's happening today. Oh, God, how long do you think we've been here?"

"I don't think much time at all. It doesn't feel like I've been lying on this bed for long."

"Okay, what did you wanna ask me?"

"What happened between you and Dr. Constantine?"

Maddie gasped and peered over at her brother. "What made you ask about him?"

"Look, I remember the day he came with me to the cabin. He wanted to take you back to his clinic, and Remus arrived and talked him out of it. Then he was killed in a car accident a couple of days later."

"Okay, I didn't hear a question in there anywhere."

"Since I woke up from my little enforced nap, I'm remembering a totally different scenario. I don't remember everything perfectly, but I can picture being on a road with you in his car in front of me. There were dozens of wolves blocking the road, and Remus was there. Constantine was trying to take you off the mountain, and Remus and the wolves stopped him. I don't know where these thoughts are coming from, but they seem awfully damn real."

"That's because they are real, Michael. Constantine was an evil man. He knew about the shape-shifters on the mountain and about our family history in particular. He'd been doing research on me all the years Dad left me locked up in his clinic. When he found out I'd mated with Remus, he became desperate to get me back under his control. I think he knew I would be able to find my wolf, eventually."

"But why do I remember all the wolves on the road?"

"Constantine was kidnapping me. Remus and the pack had to forcibly stop him from taking me off the mountain."

"Why didn't I remember any of this before now?"

Maddie didn't like the hurt tone in his voice. "You didn't know about the shape-shifters at that point, and I didn't think you were ready to find out. To keep our secrets safe, Remus had the Elders alter your memories of the day. We always knew it would be temporary and, someday, the truth would come out." She sighed. "I'm really sorry it had to be like this."

"What happened to Constantine, Maddie? The truth," Michael asked coldly.

"I can't answer that except to say that the pack took care of the problem."

"Did Remus kill him?"

"I don't honestly know, Michael, but I don't think so. At least not personally. He had the problem handled, which is what Alphas do. He never told me the details, and I never asked."

"Damn it, Maddie. You let them fuck with my brain," he yelled.

"Don't be an ass, Michael. Your brain was never in danger. They gave you a hypnotic suggestion to alter the way you remembered one afternoon, a suggestion that couldn't even be permanent."

"I don't appreciate—" Michael's words stopped when they heard someone walking outside the door. "Someone's out there," he whispered. The sound of locks thrown sounded loud in the small, enclosed room.

* * * *

Vincent Kaugh listened to his associates argue as he gathered the supplies he would need to begin his workup on the sibling test subjects presently unconscious in the other room. "Gentlemen, we need to remain focused on our primary goal. Calvin, did you get the sensors placed around the compound?"

"Yes, sir. They're all operating perfectly. There's no way a human, or a wolf, could slip in without setting off an alarm."

"Excellent! That doesn't mean we can be lax about standing guard. Set up a rotation so that someone is always watching the two doors into the house." Kaugh finished collecting the necessary blood vials and then reached into the refrigerator and grabbed a container of the inhibiting serum.

"What about the two shifters we've got upstairs?" Marty pulled a gun from his shoulder holster. "You want me to get rid of them?"

"No, absolutely not. I don't want them harmed in any way."

"What are we gonna do with them?" Calvin asked.

"They're prime specimens, Calvin. We can use their DNA back in the lab for crossbreeding." Kaugh looked over everything on his cart. "Looks like I have everything I need for now. I'm going to be busy for a while with some preliminary blood work and a few other simple tests. Keep a close watch, and let me know if you see anything unusual." He motioned for Sean to come forward. "Help me move this equipment into the other room."

Sean's face broke into a huge, evil grin. "Happy to give you a hand, doc."

"You sure that's wise, Dr. Kaugh? He's already been mouthing off about what a looker the female is," Marty said in disgust.

"Not to worry, I don't plan on leaving him alone with her."

Sean scowled, pushing the loaded cart toward the door. "Why don't you mind your own damn business, Marty?"

Kaugh laughed and followed the big man out into the hall. Taking a deep breath, he reached up and threw open the first of the two bolt locks on the door. Excitement filled him as he reached for the final lock, visions of his work racing through his mind. Swinging the door open, he stepped inside and stopped short at the angry gazes of the brother and sister strapped to the beds.

"Who the hell are you people?" Michael demanded to know.

Ignoring him for the moment, Kaugh moved farther into the room, allowing Sean to push the cart through the door. "Put it between the beds, against the wall."

Sean followed the instructions and then turned and stared down at Maddie. His gaze wandered to her legs, lying bare against the mattress. "You sure are a pretty little thing," he drawled, trailing his finger from her ankle up to her thigh. "It sure was fun putting you in this hospital gown."

"Get your hands off my sister," Michael yelled, struggling furiously against his bindings.

"Save it, wolf boy," Sean said with a laugh. "You're not getting out of those straps anytime soon."

"Enough." Kaugh sighed. "Sean, leave us, and shut the door behind you." He watched his associate turn toward the door, his hand sliding down Maddie's leg as he walked away. The young woman shook violently, tears streaming down her face.

"Sure you wanna be left alone with these freaks, doc?" Sean asked.

"Get out!" Kaugh jumped at the slamming of the door and then pulled a chair over so he could sit between the two beds. He reached over and took Maddie's hand, tightening his grip when she tried to pull away. "It's all right, Maddie, no one's going to hurt you." Pulling a handkerchief from his pocket, he reached up and dried the tears from her face and then sighed as fresh ones fell. "Please don't cry, my dear. Sear was lying to you. He wasn't in the room when I changed you into the gown. I'm a doctor, and I would never violate your privacy in such a way."

"You really are crazy, aren't you?" Michael snorted. "You don't think kidnapping violates our privacy?"

Kaugh looked over at the angry young man and tried to think of what to say. It would be easier to conduct his research if he had their cooperation. "I'm truly sorry for the way you had to be brought here, but we really didn't have any choice."

"Who are you?" Maddie asked quietly.

"Oh, I'm terribly sorry." He smiled. "My name is Dr. Vincent Kaugh. I was a friend and colleague to Richard Constantine."

"Oh, my God," Maddie gasped.

"What the hell do you want with us?" Michael growled.

"Truthfully, Michael, I didn't really want anything with you. I'm much more interested in your sister."

"Why?" Maddie whispered. "What do you want from me?"

"To continue Richard's research, of course. I want to find a way to control your inner beast, and then, we're going to create some new species of shape-shifters."

"You're crazy," Maddie cried, beginning to pull at her restraints.

"I should probably let you know, you won't be able to shift into your wolves."

"What did you do to us?" Michael groaned.

"Simple, my dear boy. I've developed a formula that inhibits your natural ability to shift. If given to you in your human form, you're unable to bring out your wolf. The same is true in reverse. I can hold you in your wolf form indefinitely with daily injections. I'm also experimenting with a drug that will be able to bring your wolf on command, my command, that is."

The blood drained from Maddie's face, and fresh tears poured from her eyes. "Michael, the baby," she cried.

"Hush, little girl. It'll be okay," Michael promised, glaring at Dr. Kaugh.

Kaugh looked from Maddie, over to Michael, and then back to Maddie. "You're pregnant?"

"What will it do to my baby?" she sobbed.

"It shouldn't do anything," he said, thoughtfully. "The serum doesn't even have a lasting effect on adult shifters. You have to be re-injected every twenty-four hours to maintain the effect. It doesn't have any effect on humans, and since a shifter doesn't gain the ability to shift until puberty, I don't see a problem."

"But you don't know for sure, do you?" Maddie closed her eyes and trembled. "I've never encouraged my mate to do violence, never wanted to see him embrace his beastly nature." She raised her head and glared daggers at the doctor. "But I'm gonna be there cheering him on when he rips out your throat."

Kaugh chuckled and then reached to pull his equipment cart closer. "I'm not going to worry too much about that, Maddie. We're not going to be here long enough for him to be a problem, and he'll never be able to find you once we leave." Efficiently, he wrapped a rubber strap around her arm and pulled it tight to bring out the vein. He held her still while he jabbed a needle into her skin.

"No," Maddie cried out, trying to pull away from his steely grip.

"Relax, girl. I'm just drawing some blood. The hard part is over, and the needle's in. Just be still so it doesn't come out, or I'll have to stick you again." He proceeded to fill five different vials and then deftly removed the needle, placing a bandage over the puncture. Kaugh picked up a small package from the cart and ripped it open. Quickly, he swabbed her thigh with alcohol and then picked up a filled syringe from his supplies.

Regret rushed through him as he stared down at the struggling female. "I'm sorry, Maddie. This is going to hurt a little. It stings going in, and there's nothing I can do about it."

"Get away from her," Michael pleaded.

"Stop," Maddie screamed as the needle pierced her skin. She groaned loudly as he depressed the plunger, the thick, brown serum slowly entering her muscle.

"There," Kaugh soothed, wiping the injection site with the alcohol once more. His eyes traveled to her face in alarm when her body went slack. Looking closely at her eyes, he frowned.

"What's wrong with her?" Michael strained to peer over at his sister.

Maddie appeared to be in a catatonic state, oblivious to what was happening around her. Kaugh checked her vitals and shined a penlight into her eyes. Finally, satisfied, he turned to Michael. "She'll be fine. She's withdrawing, mostly out of fear, I would imagine. She could even be trying to contact her mate telepathically." He laughed. "You might want to explain to her when she wakes up that the serum will block that process, as well as her telekinetic ability. Basically, she's having an adult version of a child's temper tantrum."

"If you're only interested in Maddie, why did you bring me here?" Michael asked.

"The research on Maddie goes back for years, and it makes her participation in the experiment to control the wolf shift mandatory." Kaugh picked up the rubber strap and placed it around Michael's arm. "The other work we're doing, creating a new species of shifter, needs male DNA, specifically, sperm."

"Son of a bitch!"

Kaugh laughed. "No need to worry, my boy. We collect it under medical conditions. It's not like I'll be asking you to go in and deliver it in person to a female cougar."

"You really are insane." Michael winced as the needle slid into his vein. "You're really trying to mix the shifters together?"

"Not anymore. We've already accomplished that, with less than perfect results."

"What does that mean?"

"We haven't been able to control which hereditary traits are passed on to the offspring. With all participants being only half animal, the resulting children were too docile."

"So, why are you continuing?" Michael groaned as he injected the serum into his thigh.

"I've decided the answer could be to eliminate the human factor in one of the subjects."

"Wait, you're trying to mix a wolf shifter's sperm with a wild cougar to make a cub?"

"Exactly, the offspring should have enough human characteristics to be susceptible to orders, while still retaining the cunning, strength, and survival instinct of its animal parent."

"What could possibly be the reason for such insanity?"

"Don't look at me like I'm off my rocker. This project was introduced, and is being funded, by our dear old Uncle Sam."

"You're lying," Michael declared.

"No need to, it doesn't matter if you believe me or not. You're no longer Michael Barrows. You've just become a file number in a US Government research project." He pulled the top of Michael's hospital gown down and began to attach electrodes to his chest. "We've got some more simple tests to run, just enough to get a baseline on both of you, and then we'll be transferring out tomorrow or the next day."

"Where are you taking us?"

Kaugh hesitated for a moment and then smiled. "I don't guess it matters one way or another if I tell you. We have a facility in Canada where we do most of the genetic research now. You and your sister will be moved there to be with the other subjects." He pulled the cart closer and flipped one of the switches. "This isn't going to hurt. I'm only running a few EKG strips on you. Then," he said, glancing over at Maddie's still form, "I think I'll run an ultrasound to find out more about her baby. I don't want any surprises coming up."

* * * *

Melissa stretched out, slowly wakening. Her eyes focused on the pale blue curtains hanging at the window, and she frowned. *Where the hell am I?* Sliding up in the bed, she let her gaze wander around the room. A tendril of fear raced up her spine as the memories of the morning came flooding back. She tensed when the door suddenly opened and then breathed a sigh of relief when she recognized Ariane.

"Hey, lady, it's good to see you awake. How're you feeling?" Ariane walked over and sat on the chair beside the bed.

"Scared, confused, angry, not necessarily in that order." She pushed the comforter away and got to her feet. Dizziness overwhelmed her, the room seeming to move on its own.

"Whoa," Ariane cried, jumping to her feet to grab Melissa's arm. "Not so fast, my friend. Give yourself a couple of minutes to adjust."

Melissa sat down on the bed and glared up at the wife of her best friend. "What the hell happened?"

"What do you remember?"

She thought for a minute. “You and Michael, coming home early. I remember Maddie coming to the office, and a strange man with a gun.” Melissa’s heart began to race. “He shot everyone, everyone but me. I played dead,” she whispered. She was quiet for a moment, and then her eyes shot to the younger woman’s face. “He took them, Maddie and Michael.”

A look of pain appeared in Ariane’s eyes and then disappeared so fast Melissa wasn’t sure she’d really seen it. “They were kidnapped. Remus believes by some doctor that wants to do research on them.”

“Why would someone want to do research on Maddie and Michael?”

“Uh, well, they’re the same as Mali.” Ariane was clearly getting uncomfortable with the conversation.

“The same as Mali,” Melissa repeated. Then a memory came back, and her eyes widened in shock. “Koril said the dog, I mean, the wolf, was really Mali.”

“That’s right,” she said, a tremor in her voice.

“Where’s Mali?” Melissa demanded to know.

“Relax, he’s here, and he’s okay, but still unconscious. The doc’s with him in the other bedroom.”

Melissa struggled to her feet. “I wanna see him.”

“Melissa, I’m not sure that’s a good—”

“Now,” Melissa argued.

Ariane shrugged. “Okay, but Remus isn’t gonna like it.”

“I don’t really care at this point what Remus likes or doesn’t like.” She followed Ariane out the door and down the hall to the next room. Before they could enter, a man she vaguely remembered came walking down the hall.

“Melissa, you remember Tehran, don’t you? He’s the pack’s physician.” Ariane smiled at the older man.

“Hello again, young lady. Are you feeling better?” He raised his hand toward her face and scowled when she jerked away, out of his reach. "I wouldn't hurt you, Melissa. I just wanted to check your pupils to make sure all the medication is out of your system."

Frightened, Melissa turned to Ariane. "Nobody's checking anything until I see Mali for myself." Ariane stepped aside and held her arm out for Melissa to go inside. After a brief hesitation, she walked into the darkened room. Her breath caught in her throat when she spotted the large, hairy animal lying on the light-colored sheets.

Ariane walked over to the bed and laid a hand on the animal's head. "He's fine, Melissa, just sleeping."

"I remember they said they'd shot everyone with some kind of tranquilizer and something else. Some kind of inhibitor." Melissa walked over and stared down at the silent beast. Hesitantly, she laid her hand on his side and trailed her fingers through the soft hair. "You said Maddie and Michael are like Mali. You mean, they're wolves, too?"

"That's right, we all are."

Melissa looked up at Michael's wife in surprise, a thousand questions running through her mind. "I don't understand any of this." She moved closer, sat on the side of the bed, and then took Mali's paw into her hand. "He spent so much time with me, and even claimed to love me. Why would he do that if we're so different? How could he hurt me like that?"

Ariane came and put an arm around Melissa's shoulders. "Honey, he wasn't trying to hurt you. He does love you. You're his mate."

"What?" Melissa cried, her hand freezing on Mali's body.

"Remus told me that Mali recognized you as his life mate. He would've told you himself, but Remus wouldn't let him."

"Why not?" she asked bitterly.

"He thought it might be easier for you if Michael explained everything. He didn't want Mali to scare you off before the two of you could mate."

Melissa stood and backed slowly toward the door. "So, let me get this straight. Mali wanted to be with me, but Remus said he had to wait until Michael came home to talk to me." She looked at Ariane. "Is that an accurate description?"

"Uh, yeah, that's right. It's a little more involved than that, but basically, that's what happened."

Tears welling in her eyes, Melissa gazed at the wolf one more time and then turned and rushed out the door. Pushing past the doctor before he could say a word, she ran into the bedroom she'd awakened in, slammed the door shut, and locked it behind her. Crying, she flung herself on the bed and buried her face in the pillow.

Ariane's voice came through the door. "Melissa, are you okay?"

"Go away and leave me alone," Melissa yelled, listening to someone trying to open the door. The noise stopped, and she heard a loud sigh coming from the hall.

"All right, I'll leave you alone for now. I'll be close if you need anything." Ariane's voice sounded sad.

Melissa rolled over and stared up at the ceiling. *If he'd really loved me, he would've told me the truth.* Her eyes felt heavy, her body weak. Struggling briefly to stay awake, she finally succumbed to exhaustion and allowed her eyes to close. Her last conscious thought caused tears to form in her eyes. *I've got to find a way out of here and off the mountain before Mali wakes up.*

* * * *

Remus looked around the table at the members of his pack and growled softly. "Are we clear now?" He tried not to let his anger bleed into the meeting, but the phone call he'd taken from Ariane had raised his angst to a new level. He'd fucked up royally, not allowing Mali to claim his mate, and now, Melissa could very well run away.

"I'll take a group of wolves and cover the area just across the stream," Taynor spoke up. "Koril will take his men and cover the west side of the house, and Lanicor will take the east." He glanced over to Remus. "That leaves the south, facing the kitchen window, for you and your brothers."

"Right," Remus continued. "We'll cover while Tania sneaks in through the kitchen."

"How the hell's she gonna do that?" Taynor asked, sounding a little annoyed.

Remus realized that nobody had told the men about his brothers' mating or about Tania's special abilities. "Be respectful of my brothers' mate, Taynor." He smiled at the collective gasp that traveled through the room. "Yes, that's right. My brothers have formed this pack's first tri-mating."

Taynor looked over at the mated trio and frowned. "Well, I'm happy for you guys, I really am. But that doesn't explain why she'll be the one sneaking in. Why would you risk a female like that?"

Tania jumped to her feet, practically hissing in her human form. "I'm not just a mated female, you pompous, chauvinistic pig. I'm more than qualified for this mission, probably more so than any of you here."

"All right, everyone calm down." He glanced at the newest member of his family and had to bite his lip to keep from smiling. "Tania, please take your seat." He was grateful when she only shot him an annoyed look before sitting back down between his brothers. "Tania has unique abilities that make her perfect for what we're doing."

"How's she gonna get in?" Lanicor asked. "I understand there're bars on the windows."

"You're correct, but she'll have no problems getting in. Our newest pack member isn't a wolf." He looked at her apologetically. "I'm sorry, little sister, but they need to know the truth so they can watch out for you."

"That's okay, Remus. I understand." Tania leaned over and pressed her cheek against Latan's shoulder, while taking Ethan's hand and hugging it to her chest.

"If she's not a wolf, then what is she?" Vanard asked.

Remus narrowed his eyes and glared at the head Elder. "You're the last person I thought would ask me that."

"He didn't know." Tania raised her head and frowned at Remus. "He only knew part of my background, but he never saw me shift."

"Alpha, I—"

"Never mind," Remus interrupted Vanard. "Tania shifts into a small black cat." He watched as all the eyes in the room turned toward the small woman. "She assures me she'll have no trouble fitting through the bars on the windows."

"Well, hell, girl. You must make a pretty damn small cat." Taynor smiled and then quickly closed his eyes. "Shit, tell me you're not the cat that I caught at our last group meeting."

Tania laughed. "You mean the one you called a *puddy tat*?"

Taynor groaned and hung his head. "Yeah, that would be the one." He chuckled. "As I recall, you got even with me." He grinned. "And if I remember correctly, you have really sharp claws."

Remus laughed with everyone else and then glanced at the clock. "Listen up, people. Once Tania's inside, she'll make her way to the basement where we believe Maddie and Michael are being held. She'll shift, release them from their restraints, and then head back up the kitchen stairs. She already knows the layout from earlier reconnaissance."

"How will we know when she's achieved her goal?" Lanicor asked.

"She'll appear in the kitchen window as a sign, and I'll give the all clear to move in. I'll give her twenty minutes tops, and then we're going in anyway." He gave them a grim look. "Be on the lookout for Elcor and Janis. They disappeared this morning. This is a search-and-destroy mission. I want no prisoners. Collect all the research data, and then get out. I'm planning on destroying the place after we get our family out. Any questions?"

"Did you clear all this with the Council?" Vanard asked, a worried look on his face.

"Any important questions?" Remus growled. After a moment of silence, he pushed back his chair and stood. "Then, gentlemen, it's time to lock and load."

Ethan chuckled as he stood up and joined his brother. "Remus, you're definitely watching too much late night television."

* * * *

Melissa's eyes flew open, her breath catching in her throat as she tried to focus in the dark room. For just a moment, she struggled in confusion, and then the memories of the past day came rushing back. She pushed to the side of the bed and started to stand as an overwhelming need to get away assaulted her senses. Grabbing her shoes up from the floor, she started toward the door and then stopped suddenly when it swung open.

"You're awake!" Ariane smiled and walked farther into the room. "Tehran thought you might be out until morning after the sedative he gave you. Sorry for using a key, but we thought it was prudent to check on you. How are you feeling?"

"Much better," Melissa said, warily. "Any word on Michael and Maddie?"

Ariane ran her fingers through her long hair. "No, nothing yet."

As Melissa watched, tears began to leak from Ariane's eyes. "It's gonna be okay, Ariane. I'm sure everything will work out." She squeezed her shoulder then ran a hand up and down her back in a comforting stroke. "I know. Remus will bring them back. I have faith in him and the others."

Melissa cleared her throat. "How's Mali?"

"He's doing great. The tranquilizer wore off about two hours ago, and he's just been pacing ever since. Tehran's not sure how long it'll be before he can shift, but he's hopeful he'll be back to normal in the morning."

"Yeah, I remember the men saying something about it lasting twenty-four hours." She walked a little closer to the door. "I'm gonna get out of here, Ariane."

"What? No, you can't," she cried, walking closer to the door.

"Stop!" Melissa held out her hand, trying to keep the other woman back. "I have to, don't you understand? You're all family, and I don't belong here." She sighed, struggling to keep her tears from falling. "I just wanna go somewhere I can feel safe."

"Melissa, you're safe here. No one here will ever harm you. You're Mali's mate, and the pack protects what's theirs."

"I'm nobody's mate," she said, gritting her teeth. "I can't take any more of this. I've got to get out of here." Melissa turned toward the door and froze. A large brown wolf sat on its haunches right inside the door. "Mali," she whispered.

Ariane turned and looked at the large animal. "Yes, that's Mali." She laughed. "He's been having a fit to get in here. I thought Tehran was gonna have to resort to tying him to the bed so you could get your rest." She walked slowly toward the door. "Relax, Melissa. I promise he won't hurt you. With you being his mate, he's driven to be near you. Just let him lie close, and he'll be just fine. It'll help keep him calm until the other drugs wear off."

Melissa watched, incredulous, as Ariane walked out of the bedroom, closing the door behind her. Her gaze moved to the large animal that watched her avidly with round, dark eyes. She started when he lumbered to his feet and began stalking toward her trembling form. "Stay," she groaned, her hand thrown out to stop his forward motion. When his progress didn't slow, she backed toward the bed, not stopping until she felt the mattress against the back of her knees. Exhausted, she sank down on the firm surface.

"Damn it, Mali," she sighed, "how could you keep this from me?" He padded over to the bed and nudged her leg with his snout. Soulful, sad eyes held her gaze as he laid his head on her knee. After a minute, she held her breath and tentatively placed her hand on his head. She grinned when he closed his eyes, let out a deep breath, and wiggled closer to her legs. Her fingers scratched behind both his ears, before sliding down his back, gliding through the soft strands of hair. "You're so beautiful," she whispered. "I'm gonna change my name to Alice 'cause I've definitely fallen down the rabbit hole."

Mali opened his eyes and let out what sounded suspiciously like a snort of laughter. Melissa was about to chastise him for the sound when he moved back and then jumped up on the bed. Alarmed, she scooted back toward the headboard, watching him uneasily. She breathed a sigh of relief when he settled down on the bed, his head between his front paws.

"Ariane says I'm your mate, but I don't even know what that means. It sounds serious, almost like a marriage." She ran her hand over the warm, furry head. "Why didn't you say anything? How could you let Remus dictate our relationship? God, Mali, I loved you. I still love you, but I feel betrayed, and not just by you. Hell, my own best friend never said anything to me about what he was. But you, I trusted you, and you let me fall in love without knowing the truth," she sobbed. Mali moved forward and snuggled closer to her body. Leaning forward, he licked the tears from her cheeks before running his long tongue across her lips.

"Ugh." She laughed, pushing at his head with her hands. "Get off of me, you overgrown flea bag. You're not getting around me that easy." Melissa moved down in the bed and threw her arm around Mali's wolf body. Burying her face in his silky hair, she wondered what the morning would bring. "I love you, Mali," she whispered.

* * * *

Tania leaned back against Latan and watched the other wolves from the pack head into the woods to move into their positions on each side of the small house where they were holding Maddie and Michael. She looked up as Ethan came to stand in front of her. He tugged on the long strands of her hair, tilting her head back farther, and then cradled her face between his hands. "I love you," he whispered, and then kissed her hungrily, his tongue sliding against her own. She couldn't help whimpering into his mouth. Latan pressed his heat to her back, his lips trailing down her neck.

Ending their kiss, Ethan brushed his lips across her temple and turned her to face his brother. "I love you," Latan growled. His fingers tangled in her hair, yanking her head back and twisting it sideways to cover her lips with his. He kissed her roughly, nipping at her bottom lip. She moved closer and rubbed against his erection while Ethan pressed against her butt. A groan escaped when he pulled away from her lips. "Be safe, and don't take any unnecessary chances." Latan gave her a light kiss and allowed Ethan to pull her away.

"Be careful, baby. Remember, we love you, and you've got a lot to live for. You're not alone this time. You've got the whole pack behind you." He pressed his lips to hers and gripped her arms tighter. "We're gonna follow behind you at a safe distance, but if we hear anything unusual, you can expect we're gonna come barreling in."

Remus walked over, pulled her away from his two brothers, and gave her a hug. "I'm your Alpha now, and it's really gonna piss me off if anything happens to you." He grinned down at her. "You don't wanna piss me off, trust me." His face turned serious. "If you can't get them out safely, abort the mission, and get your furry little butt back here, pronto. Don't take any chances with your safety. Do you understand?"

"Yes, Alpha, I understand perfectly. Don't worry, I'm not a rookie. I know what I'm doing, and I'll get them out."

"Okay, then get moving." Remus stepped back, giving her more room.

"I love you guys, both of you, very much." Tania gave her mates one last look and then let her coat slide down her arms. She was naked underneath. Closing her eyes, she reached for the magic she carried inside and felt her body begin to tingle. In the flash of an eye, she was standing on all four feet, looking up at the giant men of her new family. "Meow," she purred softly.

"Damn," Remus mumbled. "I never would have believed it if I hadn't seen it for myself."

Laughing inside, Tania turned and raced toward the woods, thoughts of taking out Kaugh for good feeding her adrenaline. She slowed down as she got closer, dropping down to crawl along the ground. They were looking for wolves and humans, not something as small as a cat. Her black coat blending in with the dark night should make her difficult to spot.

Reaching the clearing, Tania stopped and listened. Hearing nothing and sensing no movement, she raced across the lit area and hid under the bushes next to the house. Her tiny feline heart beating furiously against her chest, Tania peeked out from her shrubby haven. Not spotting anyone, she looked up and then jumped onto the ledge outside the kitchen window.

Glancing inside, she was pleased to see the kitchen was empty. The metal bars felt cold as she squeezed through them into the kitchen. She made her way cautiously along the counter and was about to jump to the floor when she heard a toilet flush. Not wanting to encounter anyone, she sprang from her perch and then raced across to the open door that led to the basement stairs.

Hurrying down the steps, she paused twice to listen for any sounds from below. Reaching the bolted door to the room with the beds, she reached out with her mate bond and informed them that she'd reached the basement safely. Shifting back to human, she quietly unlocked the door and then slipped inside the darkened room, shutting the door behind her. Reaching over, she flipped on the lights.

"What the hell?" Michael cried. "Who are you? What are you doing here? Where the hell are your clothes?"

"Shh, be quiet," she ordered. Moving swiftly, she released Michael's restraints and then turned to set Maddie free. "I'm Latan and Ethan's mate. We're getting you out of here. Remus is waiting outside. All we have to do is shift and head out the back door. The pack will take care of these guys."

"We can't," Michael argued.

"What do you mean?"

"They gave us something that's keeping us from bringing our wolves."

"Damn, I was hoping Melissa hadn't heard correctly." She helped Maddie stand and tied her hospital gown behind her. "All right, change of plans." She raised her shields to prevent her mates from hearing her thoughts. "Remus and his brothers are right outside and can protect you once you get out the door. I'll shift and let them chase me out the front."

"No, I can't let you do that." Michael growled and ran his hand through his hair. "I'll distract them, and you get Maddie out the back."

"While I appreciate the sentiment, big guy, it's better my way. I can shift, and they've got no hope of catching my little butt." She frowned at the Alpha Femm. "Are you all right, Maddie?"

"No, she isn't," Michael growled. "Kaugh gave her a sedative when she got hysterical about the baby."

Tania put her arms around Maddie and hugged her tight. "It's almost over, sweetie. Your mate's outside, anxious to get you home where you belong." She looked up at Michael. "I'm gonna shift, and the two of you follow me quietly up the stairs. We don't wanna be discovered until you're about to run out the back door. Be ready. As soon as they chase me through to the front, you go."

"How can you be sure they'll chase you and not just shoot you on sight?" Michael asked.

She grinned. “Easy, they won’t consider me a threat.” Before they could question her further, Tania shifted into the small black cat she called Kit.

“Holy shit,” Michael gasped, pulling Maddie closer to his side. He opened the door slowly and peered outside. “All clear,” he whispered.

Tania stepped out into the corridor and led them toward the stairs. She climbed slowly, Michael and Maddie right behind her. At the top, she peered around the corner and spotted Marty leaning against the sink. She was relieved to see him. Of the three men who worked for Kaugh, he was the least likely to do her harm. The crazy man wanted to take her home and adopt her as a pet.

Taking a deep breath, she strolled out into the kitchen, making sure the big man noticed her.

“What the hell?” Marty exclaimed. “Well, hey, kitty. Did you come to see me?”

Tania watched him walk toward her and then raced past him down the hall toward the front of the house. She breathed a sigh of relief when she heard him follow behind her. Reaching the living room, she raced toward the barred window and felt a sharp stinging pain in her left side. Stumbling, she fell to the ground and looked up into the face of Vincent Kaugh. *I hope Maddie and Michael made it out,* she thought, right before she fell into a black void.

* * * *

Kaugh entered through the front door with Sean and heard Marty’s voice coming from the kitchen. Before he had a chance to call out to him, a black cat came running across the floor. Something triggered in his memory. “Shoot it,” he yelled.

Sean raised his gun and shot toward the running animal, hitting it on the side, just above its back leg. “Okay, so why did you have me knock out a damn cat?”

Kaugh walked over and peered down at the struggling feline and then smiled. "Because she's not a damn cat, Sean. She's a shifter, and we've met before." He grinned and picked up the unconscious animal. Glancing out the window, he tensed. There were wolves converging on the house, and he could see Michael running across the clearing carrying Maddie. "No," he screamed.

"What's wrong, boss?" Calvin had come out of one of the front bedrooms, his gun clasped in his right hand.

Kaugh grabbed the tranquilizer gun from Sean's hand and looked up at Marty. "You imbecile, they're getting away." He turned to Sean. "You and Calvin take the front and use the bullets this time." He started toward the kitchen.

"What are you gonna do with it?" Marty asked, pointing to the cat.

"Take it to a vet and have it put to sleep." Kaugh chuckled.

"But it's just a cat. Can't you just let me take it home?"

"You really are too stupid to live." Kaugh raised the gun and shot a dart into the bushy-bearded man. As he watched, Marty's eyes rolled back into his head right before the big man dropped to the floor. Without wasting another second, Kaugh turned and headed for the kitchen stairs.

* * * *

Latan looked at Remus and growled. "I'm telling you, something's wrong. I can't read her anymore."

"All right, we move in now." Remus pointed to Sortee. "Go let the others know we're going in two minutes." He looked back at his brothers. "That'll give everyone time to get in position."

"I think she's blocking us on purpose." Ethan frowned. "There's something going on she doesn't want us to know."

"I'm gonna turn her ass red when we get her home," Latan promised. "She's got to..." His voice quieted when they heard a commotion coming from the clearing. Not waiting for Remus's order, he rushed toward the house, Ethan right on his heels.

It looked like the wolves had converged on the property at the same time, scaring the men who were standing watch. As Latan got closer, he saw Sean Cross taken down by Lanicor and his men, while Calvin Ames lay unconscious or dead at Taynor's feet. He was about to go inside the house when his Alpha grabbed his arm.

"Wait," Remus cried. "This was too easy, and Kaugh and Dyer are still missing." Before he'd finished his sentence, Michael came through the back door, carrying Maddie in his arms. Remus rushed forward, meeting him halfway across the clearing, and took his mate from her brother. "Baby, are you all right?"

"She's okay, Remus. They gave her a sedative a couple of hours ago, and it hasn't worn off yet." He looked around. "Where's Ariane?"

"Back at the house with Mali and Melissa." He glanced at Ethan. "I'm taking her out of here. Bring Tania back to the house when she comes out." Without another word, he stalked off with his mate in his arms.

"Where is Tania, Michael?" Latan tried to conceal the fear coursing through his body.

Michael turned and glanced at the cabin from the cover of the trees. "She'll be coming out the front. Since we couldn't shift, she got them to chase her through the front of the house so we could get out the back. Do you know she turns into a kitten?"

"Yeah, we know." Latan snorted. "She's our mate."

For a moment, Michael looked stunned, and then he grinned. "That's what she said, but I didn't really believe it. I don't know why I'm surprised, guys. This family never does anything normal." He slapped Ethan on the back. "I'm happy for you. Now, I'm gonna go put my mate's mind to rest."

Latan watched as Michael hurried off and turned his attention to Ethan. "I can't just sit here and wait. I'm going in." He hurried toward the house, Ethan hot on his heels. They stopped outside the door, and Latan looked inside. Not seeing anyone, he walked in, listening for anything that would tell him where their mate was. A sound behind them had him turning toward the stairs that led down to the underground rooms. Moving quickly, he ran toward the open door and looked down in time to see Kaugh hurrying down the last few steps, a black cat draped across his arm.

"Tania," Ethan screamed as both brothers rushed down the steps.

"Too late." Kaugh smirked as he threw open a dead bolt lock on a door at the end of the hall. Before they could stop him, he slipped through the opening and then slammed it closed behind him.

"No," Latan cried, hearing the sound of locks thrown. He pulled furiously on the door, now locked from the other side. "Where do you think it goes?" he asked Ethan.

"Shit, this side of the house faces the creek. Maybe it somehow leads down to the water."

"Come on," Latan yelled, racing back up the stairs. He could hear the sounds of Ethan's feet on the wooden steps. The sight of Marty Dyer's body lying on the living room carpet didn't even slow the men down. When they reached the clearing, Latan called for several of the pack's wolves to follow him. They all raced down to the stream but could not find any sign of Kaugh, or Tania.

"I'm gonna break down that door and see where it goes." Latan spared a glance for his brother and headed back to the house. Stopping at the wood pile outside, he grabbed up the ax and headed back to the basement. In the living room, he found two of his pack mates examining Marty Dyer.

"He's alive, Latan. Do you want us to get rid of him?" Sortee asked.

He thought for a moment. "No, take him back to Remus. We may need to find out what he knows about Kaugh's plans." Turning, he motioned for Ethan to follow him, and they made their way back to the locked door where Kaugh had disappeared. It took less than five minutes for the two brothers to hack their way through the thin wood door.

"It's a damn tunnel," Ethan exclaimed.

Latan didn't respond, just started walking down the darkened passage. About twenty minutes later, they reached the end, where they found another door locked from the outside. Angrily, Latan raised the ax and began to chop at the wood. It took longer this time, the door being twice as thick. Finally, he broke through and, with Ethan's help, found himself standing near the stream, apparently some ways from the main house.

"Look." Ethan pointed. "Tire tracks. He had himself a damn escape route."

"Damn it," Latan growled, throwing the ax to the ground. A feeling of fury rolled over him, and then calm settled. He looked at his brother. "I wanna talk to Dyer and see if he knows where Kaugh would take Tania." Without waiting for a response, he started back up the narrow tunnel to the house.

* * * *

Kaugh looked down at the small black cat and smiled. "Didn't you think I would remember you, little cat?" His attention returned to the road. "I missed you after they took you away. You were my shining glory until you shifted the first time." He frowned down at the silent bundle of fur. "Then you made a fool out of me with your little puny body and soft sounds." Slowing down, he glanced down the road to make sure there weren't any cars visible and then turned onto the main highway. "I know a lot of people who would give big money to get their hands on you, Tania, but that would be too easy. You've screwed me over for the last time, little one. You cost me my new subjects, and that's something I just can't forgive. I don't know how I'm gonna get my hands on Maddie again."

Pulling over to the side of the road, he parked and reached for a case on the backseat. Glancing first in the rearview mirror, he reached into the bag and pulled out a filled syringe. Grinning, he leaned over and injected the contents into Tania's hindquarters. "Okay, missy, now you're stuck in that furry little body for at least twenty-four hours, and maybe longer, since the dosage was meant for a much larger wolf."

Glancing around, he got back onto the highway and headed toward Kenyan. "I'm gonna drop you off at the vet's tonight, little girl. Then, I'm gonna ask them to have you put down tomorrow." Kaugh laughed and shook his head. "I just wish I could be there to watch you sweat all night, knowing that needle's coming at you tomorrow, and there's not a damn thing you can do about it."

* * * *

"He caught her," Maddie cried, and then collapsed into Remus's arms.

"Shh, baby. It's okay." Remus cuddled her close and locked his gaze on Latan. "What happened?"

"We don't really know. He carried her out over his arm, unconscious. There was a tunnel from the basement rooms that led to the stream. From the tracks on the ground, we know he had a car there, waiting."

"You know for a fact she's just unconscious? Can you sense her with your bond?" Remus sat down and placed Maddie on his lap.

"She unconscious," Latan growled. "I won't consider any other possibility."

"Okay, bro, she's unconscious. How can we help?" Remus wiped the tears from Maddie's face and kissed the top of her head.

"I had the men bring Marty back here. I need him awake so I can ask him some questions." Latan's hands fisted at his side.

Remus sighed and glanced at Tehran. “The doc pulled a tranquilizer dart out of his side. According to him, it’ll be hours before we’re able to bring him around.”

“Damn it, wake him anyway. I don’t care if it kills him.” Ethan slammed his hand on the table, knocking a glass onto the floor.

“No matter how much I want to be able to help, there’s no way I can bring him around for at least six hours. There’s nothing I have that can neutralize the medication they used.” Tehran paced in the large kitchen.

“In six hours, she could be anywhere,” Latan moaned. “What are we gonna do, Ethan?”

“I’ll tell you what we’re gonna do,” Remus said. “Taynor, get some men on each of the roads out of this county. Get at least two up to that hotel where they’ve been staying.” He looked around the room. “Lanicor, go down to their office and see if anybody shows up there.”

Maddie pushed away from Remus’s arms and stood by his chair. “Tehran, you go sit with Marty and do whatever you can to speed things along. If nothing else, you’ll be there the second he starts to come around. I can’t stand the thought of something happening to that sweet girl.”

“But—” Tehran began.

“You heard the Alpha Femm. Get to it.” Remus punctuated his command with a hearty growl. He turned to Koril. “Did you bring all the data from Kaugh’s lab?”

“Yes, Alpha. There were two computers and a rack of disks. We brought those, plus all the vials in the fridge. We thought they could be used to create some kind of vaccine against the inhibitor.”

“Excellent, now take some men and destroy the place. I don’t want anything left but a hole in the ground.”

“Right away.” Koril glanced at Brenner and nodded, and then the two men left by the back door.

“Okay, gentlemen,” Remus stood and walked toward the door, “put your heads together. Where would Kaugh take an unconscious cat that wouldn’t look suspicious to the other people around him?”

Chapter 8

Tania blinked and turned her head in a half circle. *Where am I?* Still in her feline form, her gaze took in the bars in front of her. Trapped in a long rectangular cage, there seemed to be only one way out. She struggled closer to the opening and peered out.

"So, you're finally awake." Kaugh's face appeared on the other side of her prison door.

"Hsssssss!" Every hair on her body stood up as she backed farther into the safety of her cell.

"Don't hiss at me, you stupid cat." Kaugh laughed. "Your time's almost up, little girl. I wanted you to spend the night at the animal hospital contemplating your early demise, but I guess the dosage I gave you was too much." He pulled up a chair and sat down. "Bet you never thought your last home on this Earth would be a pet taxi." He chuckled. "Don't bother trying to shift. I've given you a second dose of the inhibitor." Kaugh leaned in close. "I'm gonna take you to the local vet and have them put you down like a stray, feral cat. And there's not a damn thing you can do about it."

Tania froze, unable to believe what she'd heard. *A pet taxi isn't very strong. I should be able to break it.* She closed her eyes and concentrated on searching for her inner magic. *I can't shift! What about the bond? Latan? Ethan? Can you hear me? Please, somebody, I need help.* Her legs slid out from under her as Kaugh picked up the carrier. Her small body rolled back and forth as he made his way across the room.

"Time to go, little kitten." He whistled as he walked out the door.

The small cat braced herself as she swayed back and forth. *The only chance I'll have to get free is when they transfer me to a cage. I'm gonna have to be ready to move.*

* * * *

Mali sighed as he watched the woman he loved more than anything sleeping on the bed beside him. His body tensed as a familiar tingling began in his stomach, followed by a painful clenching of his muscles. *Yes,* he cried inside, watching his human limbs form. He raised a trembling hand to cup his mate's cheek, needing to feel her skin against his own. "Sunshine, wake up."

Melissa turned toward his body, her face snuggling into his caressing palm. After a moment, her eyes fluttered open, and then widened in shock when they focused on his face. "You're back," she murmured. "Are you really here? I'm not dreaming?"

"I'm here, and I'm not gonna leave you again." His arms slid around her waist, pulling her flush against his chest. "I love you, Sunshine. I wanna spend my life with you. We can have a family together. You'll never want for anything, and I'll protect you for the rest of your life."

"Why didn't you tell me the truth, Mali? Why didn't you tell me what you are?"

He lowered his eyes, ashamed of the way he'd handled their relationship. "Part of it was because Remus asked me to wait. He said it would be easier on you to hear about us from someone you loved and trusted."

Her hand came up to stroke his face. "I love and trust you. Don't you know that?"

"I wanted to believe that, more than you know. No one ever loved me before, and I guess I didn't know how to react. I've been so afraid of scaring you off."

Melissa took a deep breath. “I’m not afraid of you, Mali. I love you, very much. I wanna be with you always, but I need to ask some questions.”

“Of course. What do you wanna know?” His arms tightened, and he placed a gentle kiss on the top of her head.

“Ariane said I was your mate. What does that mean?”

“You’re the other half of my heart. All shifters have someone, somewhere, that’s their perfect complement. Without that person, the shifter feels like something’s always missing. I knew the minute we met at Michael’s reception, and I scented you, that you were the missing piece of my soul. The feeling will only grow stronger once we mate.”

“Uh, don’t wanna throw a monkey wrench into your explanation, but we’ve already mated, several times, if I remember correctly.”

He chuckled. “Different kind of mating, Sunshine. Although it does involve sex, it’s more than that.”

“I don’t understand.”

“Once you agree to be my mate forever, we’ll make love. During the peak of our passion, I’ll bite you on the shoulder and take in a little bit of your blood at the same time I inject an enzyme into your system. That will tie my scent to you for life.”

“Wait… You’re gonna bite me? That’s just so weird.” She giggled, sounding a little hysterical.

Mali buried his face in her neck and growled. “Not weird, but very erotic. You’ll really like the way it feels, and the small scar it leaves becomes an erogenous zone.”

She pushed back and gazed into his eyes. “For real?”

“Oh, yeah,” he replied, kissing the tip of her nose.

“I won’t… I mean, it can’t… There’s no way I can.” Her face turned beet red.

“No, Sunshine. You won’t turn into a wolf after I bite you. That’s only in the movies.”

“Sorry,” she mumbled, refusing to meet his eyes.

"Don't be, it's a valid concern. I understand. There is more, though."

"Okay, I'm listening."

"Once I inject the enzyme, several things can happen, at least, that's the theory. I don't know anyone else whose mate was human, so everything is speculation." He paused and thought about his words. "A psychic connection, or bond, will form between our minds once we've mated."

"You'll be able to read my mind?" she asked, eyes widening.

"It goes both ways, Sunshine. You'll be able to read mine as well. We'll always know what the other is feeling. There's also a chance your senses will get a boost. You could end up with better vision, or hearing. We won't really know until after the mating."

Melissa thought for a moment. "What about our children? Will they be wolves?"

"It's possible, because they'll be half wolf. They'll have the shifter gene, but it may take mating with a full-blooded shifter to bring out their wolf. That's how Michael and Maddie found theirs. Their father was a half-breed and their mother human. Neither of them found their wolves until after they had a full-blooded shifter's DNA introduced into their system. That's why you won't turn into a wolf after I bite you. You don't already have wolf DNA inside you."

Melissa was quiet for a minute, running her hand up and down Mali's arm. Finally, her gaze moved up to meet his. "Okay, I'm ready."

"What? What do you mean?" He didn't want to take a chance on misunderstanding what she wanted.

"I'm ready for you to make me your mate." She leaned over and kissed his lips. "I love you, Mali. I wanna be your wife, I mean, mate, more than anything."

He hooked his finger in her belt loop and pulled their hips together and then used a finger to raise her face. "I want you to be my mate, and my wife. Will you marry me, Melissa?"

"Yes," she cried. "I love you so much."

She moaned into his mouth as their lips met for a brief, sweet kiss. He savored her softness as he licked at her mouth, his tongue tracing her lips then licking them open. Gentle kisses grew into deeper ones, their lips parting, tongues tangling together. Her hands were warm, sliding up his chest before her arms wrapped around his neck.

Mali threaded the fingers of one hand through her hair, while the other roamed down her stomach and over the swell of her hip. Grinding his erection against her denim-covered mound, he licked the roof of her mouth, enjoying the soft groans vibrating against his chest. Bringing his hand up, he swiftly undid the buttons of her blouse and pushed it off her shoulders. He cupped her breast, his fingers teasing the nipple through the white silk fabric of her bra. "You're so responsive," he whispered, watching the nipple harden beneath his fingers.

Removing his hand from her hair, Mali undid her jeans and shoved them roughly down her hips, taking her panties with them. Worshiping his mate, he kissed every inch of the hot, silken skin as he undressed her. Throwing her clothes to the floor, he moved back up her body, trailing his tongue between her breasts as he inhaled her sweet scent. Flipping open the front fastening of her bra, he peeled it from her body and dropped it over the side of the bed.

He groaned, watching Melissa lick her lips, and then buried his face in her neck. His lips found a sensitive spot, his tongue coming out to lick the silky area, wanting to taste more of her skin.

Melissa's hands slid down to his shoulders, her fingers drawing little circles on his heated skin. Her hands stroked the hair on his chest and stomach. "I love the way your hairy chest feels against my skin," she groaned. His cock throbbed as her fingers crept to his waist and then stopped, her face blushing, her eyes dropping.

"Touch me," he whispered, guiding her hand down to where his erection pushed out at her. Melissa grabbed his cock and started stroking slowly, her fingers sliding along his shaft. "Suck me," Mali begged, and then froze when her hand stilled.

Mali groaned in pleasure when she rubbed her cheek against his throbbing cock. She lapped at the distended head before exploring him thoroughly, her tongue tracing the veins and dipping into the slit. He could hear animalistic growls and, with a start, realized they were coming from his own throat. Melissa moved farther down and ran her tongue over his testicles before sucking them into the heat of her mouth.

"Enough," he growled as his hands swept slowly down the silky length of her body and pulled her up. "I don't wanna come that way. I wanna be buried in your sweet pussy." His mouth moved to her shoulders and then back up her throat to her mouth, his lips catching hers in a fierce, hard kiss. One hand stroked down her back and cupped her ass as she burrowed closer. He licked and nibbled at her neck and then kissed her again, coaxing her tongue into his mouth. His tongue stroked along her lower lip before thrusting deep into her mouth to taste her essence.

The feel of her breasts against his chest excited him, the points of her nipples digging into his skin. He ran a fingertip down the valley between her breasts before closing one large hand gently around the large globe. His thumb ran over the nipple before his fingers began fondling and pinching. Bending, he took the small nub into his mouth and suckled, his teeth closing around the hardened tip. His heart pounded against her chest in rhythm with hers. Her small cries of pleasure fed his soul.

Mali laid her back on the bed, settling his larger body over hers and pushing her legs far apart. He planted a kiss at the top of her dark curls, his fingers tangling in the silky hair. "You're already wet for me," he moaned. His hand smoothed up her leg, the flat of his tongue sweeping through her pussy before it zeroed in on her clit. Flicking his tongue across the tiny button, he trailed his finger through her cream and down to her puckered opening. Her fingers clenched in his hair when he took her clit between his lips and sucked.

"Mali," she cried out, her legs trembling on each side of his shoulders when his finger breached her sphincter muscle and sank into the forbidden opening.

"I need my cock in you, now!" He crawled up her body and plunged into her fiery heat. His hips began thrusting slow and deep, his mate wiggling beneath him. Groaning, he pulled out and lightly smacked her thigh. "Get on your hands and knees, Sunshine." Scooting back, he helped her turn over and positioned her on the bed. Moving up between her spread legs, Mali dragged his tongue up the curve of her spine. He lifted his hips and aimed his cock at the tight, dripping entrance before him. Slowly, he guided his shaft back inside her. His eyes slid closed, and he thrust upward, her sheath tight and hot around him. Writhing beneath him, she made a groaning sound deep in her throat.

"I love you," Mali whispered. Gripping her hips, he thrust into her quivering body over and over, harder and harder. With one hand still on her hip, he reached around and found her clit, his fingers plucking, and stroking.

"Mali," Melissa cried, her pussy convulsing around his throbbing cock.

A hoarse yell burst from his throat as his climax rushed through his body, his canines dropping in preparation for claiming his mate. Mali deposited his seed deep into his mate as he sank his teeth in the soft skin of her shoulder. Her body jerked as a second climax raced through her system.

Sated, he collapsed gently on her back, his cock still hard inside the walls of her twitching pussy. After a moment, he carefully disengaged from her warmth and pulled her into his arms. "You're mine," he growled. He claimed Melissa's mouth with his lips, tongue, and teeth.

"Forever yours," she whispered.

* * * *

Carrying Tania, Kaugh walked into the small animal hospital and looked around. “Hello, anybody here?”

“I’ll be right with you,” a voice called out from one of the back rooms. After a couple of minutes, a young man walked up to the front desk. “Can I help you?” He glanced at the carrier in Kaugh’s hands.

“Yes, you can. I’m sorry to say I’ve got the unpleasant task of having a dangerous cat put down. Can you take care of that here?”

“Absolutely, no problem.” He reached below the counter and pulled out some papers. “You’ll need to sign a release. The fee’s based on the animal’s weight.”

“It shouldn’t be much, then. She’s pretty small.” Kaugh set the carrier on the counter and began to fill out the necessary form.

The young man peeked through the bars at Tania. “That’s a dangerous cat?” he asked skeptically.

“Meow, meow, meow, meow,” Tania cried.

Kaugh chuckled. “Don’t let her looks fool you. She attacked my brother’s kids for no reason, and I can’t have her around like that.”

“Okay.” He shrugged. “I’m not the vet, and he won’t be here until tonight. Did you want to witness the procedure?”

“Not necessary, young man. I’m sure I can trust you to take care of the problem.” He handed over the signed form. “How much do I owe you?”

“It’ll be thirty-five for the euthanasia. Did you want us to dispose of the body, or will you pick her up?”

“Meow, meow, meow, meow!” Tania’s cries were getting louder and more frantic sounding.

“Hmm, I think I’ll pick her up tomorrow. That way I can see to a proper burial.”

“Meow, hsssssss!”

“Boy, it’s almost like she knows what we’re talking about.”

"They say animals are very perceptive. What time tonight will you be putting her to sleep?"

"The clinic closes at eight, and he always does stuff like this after we're closed."

"Then I'll be back in the morning to pick up her body and the carrier. You can just leave her in it for now. She'll be happier in her final hours in something she's familiar with."

"Hey, man, that's pretty decent of you. Most people don't think of the animal's comfort if they're fixing to have them put down."

Kaugh headed for the door. "I'm thinking of your comfort, too, son. If you try to take her out, she just might bite you and escape. I can't have that happening. I'll see you in the morning." He left, the door automatically closing behind him. Making his way to his car, he laughed. "That's one less problem in my future." Smiling, he drove down the street and checked into a small hotel on the highway. He wanted to be there bright and early the next morning to pick up Tania. Then, he was heading to the lab in Canada. He would have to figure out another way to continue Constantine's research.

* * * *

"Why hasn't he been able to wake him?" Latan yelled. "It's been over sixteen hours."

Remus looked at his brothers and felt deep sorrow. The longer it took to get a lead on Tania's whereabouts, the less chance they had of getting her back unharmed. "Try to hang on, Latan. Tehran's sitting with him, and he'll let us know the minute he's conscious."

"We have to find her, Remus, and soon. There's no telling what he'll do to her," Ethan sobbed.

"Remus," Tehran called, rushing into the kitchen. "He's waking up."

"Finally," Remus growled. He headed down the hall toward the bedroom, his brothers close on his heels. He walked into the room and stood over the bed.

"I gave him a stimulant about a half hour ago. He's coming around, but I can't guarantee how lucid he'll be." Tehran stepped up and slapped Marty's cheeks. "Wake up. You need to wake up, Dyer. We need to talk to you."

Marty Dyer's eyes opened. He looked around the room, his gaze stopping on the two wolves that sat by his bed. A look of horror came over his face.

"Don't worry about them, Marty. They won't attack unless I tell them to." Remus had left several wolves guarding their prisoner. Some of them had elected to remain in their wolf forms around the unwelcome man. "Look at me, Marty." He waited until the man's gaze returned to his own. "Where did Kaugh take Tania?"

Marty looked puzzled and tried to talk. His voice came out rough and weak. Clearing his throat, he tried again. "I don't know what you're talking about."

"Could he have been shot before Kaugh took her out?" Ethan asked.

"He might just not know what the doctor had planned. Marty, who shot you with a tranquilizer?" Remus asked.

"Dr. Kaugh," he whispered.

"Why did he shoot you?" Remus reached down and shook Marty's shoulders when his eyes dropped shut. "Why, Marty? Why did Kaugh shoot you?"

"I wanted the cat. I don't know why that upset him so much."

"Where's the cat now?" Latan demanded.

"She was such a cute little thing," Marty mumbled. "I just wanted to take her home and love her, let her love me."

"Where's the damn cat?" Ethan growled.

"He said he was gonna take her to a vet and have her put to sleep." Marty's eyes filled with tears. "I just wanted to love her."

"Marty, do you know which vet?" Remus asked.

"No, he didn't say." His eyes closed as he dropped back to sleep.

Remus jerked his head toward the door, motioning for his brothers to follow. He walked quickly back to the kitchen and then stopped in the doorway, surprised to see Mali and Melissa sitting at the table. "Mali, are you feeling better?"

"I'm feeling great, Alpha." Mali jumped up, pulling Melissa to her feet. "Alpha, uh…"

Remus sniffed the air and smiled. "No need to explain, Mali." He walked over and pulled Melissa into a hug. "Welcome to the pack, Melissa. I know you and Mali are gonna be very happy."

"Thanks, Remus. That means a lot to me. I know I've got a lot to learn, but I wanna make Mali a good wife."

"You will." Remus grinned. "When this crisis is over, we'll throw a big party celebrating your mating."

"What's the latest on Tania, Remus? Can we help?" Mali asked.

"We're getting to that now. Stick around." Remus looked up as Michael and Ariane came into the room. "Are you fully recovered, Michael?"

"One hundred percent, Remus. Is Maddie doing okay?" Michael hugged Ariane close to his chest.

"She's getting there. Right now, she's sleeping." Remus stepped closer to his brother-in-law. "I need you to get on the phone or the Internet and find me the nearest vet."

"Wait, I can answer that," Melissa said. "When I first came here, I was pretty lonely and thought about getting a cat. I wanted it to come from a professional, instead of someone's home, so I could be sure it was healthy. The closest animal facility is about forty miles from here in Kenyan. When I visited, they didn't have any kittens to adopt. The next closest is over seventy miles."

Remus breathed a sigh of relief and glanced at his brothers. "I don't think he would go any farther than Kenyan. He would want to get rid of her as quickly as possible." He looked at Melissa. "Get on the phone and try to reach someone there. Ask about a stray black cat. Get them to wait on putting it down until you see if it's yours." He turned to Mali. "I want you and Michael to stay here with the women. I'm leaving Tehran and the guards in the back bedroom with the prisoner. Don't take any chances while we're gone."

"Come on," Ethan yelled.

"Okay, everybody move. Koril, get the emergency clothes packs and have four of the men carry them. We can make better time if we shift."

* * * *

Tania lay on the cool, smooth floor of the carrier, her body trembling. It had been hours since they left her alone in the darkened room. She'd tried repeatedly to shift and call her mates, with no success. She would have only one chance at escape when they came to give her the shot that would end her life. Startled, she rose to her feet when the door opened and the lights came on. Two men came walking into the room, one of them the man that dealt with Kaugh. *I guess this must be the doctor. Damn, now I've got to get away from two men instead of one.*

"Sorry, little kitty." The doctor gave her a sad look. "I hate this part of my job." He moved to the cabinets on the wall and began collecting supplies, laying them on the metal table in the center of the room.

"Meow, meow," Tania cried. Her breath caught as she watched him draw up fluid into a syringe. She'd never felt so much fear.

Sighing, the doctor placed the syringe on the table and walked over to the carrier. Peering inside, he frowned. "You're awful small to be considered a danger."

"Meow, hsssssss." Tania couldn't help hissing, growling, and showing her teeth.

"Well, I guess that answers my doubts." He chuckled. Tania watched as he donned a pair of thick rubber gloves that reached his elbows. "All right, little lady. It's time."

Tania backed into the corner, hissing and spitting, swiping at his hand with her claws as he reached for her tiny body. Not deterred, his hand kept coming until he was able to grip her tightly around her midsection. He slid her toward the carrier's opening where his other hand waited to catch her in an even firmer hold. Just as he pulled her free from her prison, the door to the room flew open, slamming into the shelves on the wall behind it.

Tania saw the doctor's head jerk toward the noise and felt his hands loosen their hold. Taking the opportunity, she wiggled free and jumped toward the floor. He made a wild grab to catch her. His hand closed around her back leg, and then she felt it jerk away.

* * * *

Ethan grabbed the bag of clothes from Koril and quickly donned a pair of jeans and a T-shirt. "Hurry up," he whispered, watching Remus and Latan pull on a similar outfit while he slid his feet into a pair of sneakers.

"Everyone, wait outside," Remus ordered. "Only the three of us are going in." He walked around the building and opened the front door. A young man was sitting in a chair behind the desk, talking on the phone.

"Sorry, we're closed. You'll have to come back tomorrow." He motioned toward the door and went back to his conversation.

"Do you have a black cat here? One that was brought in to be put to sleep?" Ethan growled.

Frowning, the boy ended his call and stood up. "Yeah, we had one brought in this morning, but you're too late."

"What do you mean, too late?" Ethan cried, gripped with a fear he'd never experienced before.

"Sorry, man. The doc's in the back now. He's been back there long enough to finish it. Hey, wait," he called out. "You can't go back there."

Ethan ignored him and threw open the closed door. He scanned the room and quickly moved toward a man pulling something out of a pet carrier. As he got closer, he could see Tania's struggling form. He reached the table in time to see his mate jump toward the floor, the doctor's hand catching her by the leg. His hand shot out, grabbing the man by the wrist. "Don't touch her," he growled, tightening his grip until the doctor flinched.

"Tania," Latan cried.

Ethan turned in time to see their mate jump into his brother's arms. He glanced down at the table and shuddered at the sight of the filled syringe. Tearing his eyes away, he walked over to Latan and cuddled Tania between them. "It's okay, baby, we've got you."

"Meow, meow." Tania purred, and rubbed her head against both men's arms.

"Relax, pretty lady," Latan crooned. "Tehran says the drug should wear off in one to three days, depending on how much he gave you. You won't be able to shift until then, but we'll keep you safe."

"Yeah, baby, you're never getting out of our sight again." Ethan smiled as she settled down in Latan's arms and closed her eyes. His mate was home.

"Guess she's definitely your cat." The young man from the front office had walked into the room. "You need to get her a collar or something, man. She was brought in as a stray."

Tania rose up and growled. Her claws extended while the hair on her back stood up.

"The dude that brought her in said she attacked his brother's kids."

"Could you tell me what this *dude* looked like," Remus asked.

"I can do better than that. He's supposed to come back in the morning to pick up her body."

"Calm down, honey. It's okay," Latan soothed. Tania was hissing and growling at the young man.

"Koril, get in here," Remus yelled. When Koril walked through the door, Remus pulled him aside. "Kaugh is due back here in the morning. That means he's close by."

"Don't worry, I'll find him," Koril promised.

"Hey, man, you don't need to go to so much trouble. I can tell you where he is."

"Where?" Ethan snarled.

"Dinah's Motel, just down the road. I saw his car when I went to dinner. He's parked down by the last cottage on the left."

"You sure it was him?" Remus frowned.

"Yeah, no doubt about it. We don't get many Avis rental cars in town."

"I'll check it out." Koril frowned. "What do you want me to do here in town?"

Remus looked up as Taynor walked through the door. "Bring him back to the compound, and we'll talk to him there."

Taynor laughed. "Why don't we dump catnip down his pants and turn Tania loose on him?

"Hey," Latan cried. Tania jumped from his arms and padded over to Taynor. She purred loudly, rubbing in and out of his legs, and then turned and ran over to jump back into Latan's arms.

The doctor chuckled. "I think she likes that idea."

Koril stared at Latan, watching him snuggle Tania, and smirked. "I thought you hated cats, Latan."

Tania hissed, her body tensing.

"Now, pretty lady, you're not gonna hold that against me, are you?" Latan bent and kissed her furry paw. Tania rubbed her head against his chin and then turned and sank her teeth into his thumb.

"Eeekk," he squealed as she jumped from his arms to his brother.

Koril laughed. "Guess that answers that."

* * * *

Tania woke with two sets of tender, nuzzling lips against her neck. Smiling, she stretched her arms out languidly, her hands coming to rest on two masculine chests. "I guess this means I'm human again." She chuckled.

"Open your eyes, baby," Ethan pleaded.

"Yeah, we wanna see those beautiful, green eyes." Latan nipped her ear with his teeth.

Slowly, her eyes opened, focusing on the two handsome men leaning over her. Before she could say anything, Ethan leaned forward and pressed a kiss against her lips. After only a moment, he deepened the kiss, his tongue sweeping through Tania's mouth. Latan rubbed his morning beard against her as he kissed his way down her belly, his bristly whiskers abrading her tender flesh. Ethan broke the kiss, leaving Tania dizzy and wanting as he pulled slowly away. He descended on her neck, biting and licking the sensitive skin around his mating mark.

Between the sensual assault on her body and the erotic thoughts coming across the mating bond, Tania was losing control fast. "Stop," she cried, placing a hand against each of their chests and pushing gently.

"What's wrong, love?" Latan smoothed the hair away from her face.

"Are you okay, baby?" Ethan raised her hand to his lips, kissing the fingers tenderly.

Tania squeezed his hand and ran her fingers along Latan's cheek. "I'm fine, and nothing's wrong." She felt a flush move up her neck. "I just didn't wanna get carried away before I get a chance to take a shower."

"You wanna stop and take a shower now?" Ethan frowned and shot his brother a questioning look.

"Yes, I need one now. I've been stuck living as a cat for almost four days. Licking my fur just doesn't do it for me, guys. There's no way we're gonna be intimate unless I get up close and personal with my bodywash."

Latan laughed and ran his hand down her side. "I'm all for a shower, pretty lady." He wiggled his eyebrows. "I'll wash your back if you'll wash mine."

"Uh, no, thanks."

"No?" His eyes narrowed, his hand stilling on her hip. "Why the hell not?"

She sighed. "Come on, guys. Give me a break. This is like a reunion for us, and I don't wanna have it in the shower." Leaning over, she placed a light kiss on Latan's cheek and then turned and repeated the caress to Ethan. "I want us to make love right here, in your bed." She looked around the room. "Are we gonna keep using your room, Ethan?"

"Actually, Latan and I have been talking about that. If you're agreeable, we'll turn the downstairs den into one large bedroom for all of us. We can use any of the bedrooms up here if we want any private time with you."

"That sounds perfect. Now, be good boys and sit tight. I'll be really quick in the shower. You could make yourselves useful and change the sheets while I'm gone. No matter what I do, I can't seem to stop from shedding."

"Yes, your majesty. Your wish is our command." Ethan laughed.

Latan swatted her naked ass as she climbed from the bed. "Hey, what's that for?"

"Consider it a preview of your punishment to come."

She frowned. "And just what am I being punished for?"

"For shielding your thoughts from us during the rescue," Ethan growled.

Tania gulped and then gave them what she hoped was a beguiling smile. "I didn't mean to shut you out."

Latan laughed. "Don't even go there, woman. Go on and shower, and then get your ass back in this bed. It's gonna be a while before we let you up again."

Liking the sound of that, Tania saluted them and then walked into the bathroom.

* * * *

"Who are you calling?" Maddie asked. Sipping tea at the kitchen table, she looked at peace with the world.

"The deadly duo." Remus smirked. "I wanna check on Tania." He listened while the phone rang.

"Hello," Ethan answered.

"Hey, bro, just wanted to see how things are going."

"As of this morning, we're all human again."

Remus smiled at Maddie and gave her a thumbs-up. "That's great, Ethan. Why don't the three of you come over tonight for dinner? I'm trying to get the whole family together for a celebration."

"Sounds good. How's Maddie?"

"She's fantastic, which is one of the reasons we're celebrating. Tehran ran some blood work and did an ultrasound yesterday. It doesn't look like the drugs had any effect on the babies."

"Uh, did you say babies?"

"Damn it, Remus. You promised not to tell anybody," Maddie groaned.

He chuckled and returned his attention to the phone. "I guess you heard that."

"Yeah, sounds like your ass is in trouble again."

"It's true, the test showed two babies instead of one. I'm gonna have a pair of sons."

"For real? You know they're boys?"

"Well, not exactly. You know Alphas always have sons first. It's tradition, so they can take over for me. The babies were facing each other, so there's no way for Tehran to know for sure."

Ethan laughed. "From your lips to God's ear, bro. I hope you're right. Tell the little mamma-to-be I said congrats, and we'll definitely be there tonight to help you celebrate."

"All right, bro. Tell Tania we're glad she's better, and we'll see you later."

"You got it. Goodbye."

Remus hung up the phone and smiled at his mate. "I'm sure you heard they're coming tonight."

"That's great, everybody accepted."

"Did you ask Mali and Melissa?"

"Absolutely! As far as I'm concerned, they're family now."

He walked over and pulled Maddie to her feet. "Are you gonna let me tell everyone else about the babies?"

"You mean I could stop you?" She snorted. "You can tell anyone you want, wolf man, but you need to stop saying they're sons. You're gonna feel awfully foolish when they turn out to be girls."

"Bite your tongue, woman. Fate wouldn't do that to me. We'll have our sons, and then you can have as many daughters as you want." He gave her a quick, hard kiss.

Maddie laughed, and strolled toward the bedroom. "Careful how you tempt fate, wolf man. Payback can be a real bitch."

* * * *

Tania gasped when she walked into the bedroom, a towel wrapped around her naked body. The heavy blinds were closed and lit candles now stood on the dresser and the tables beside the bed. The scent of vanilla drifted through the room. The sheets had been changed, and the covers were folded neatly at the foot of the bed. She could hear romantic music playing softly, helping to set the mood. Her mates appeared tense, poised at the foot of the bed, looking as if they might pounce any minute.

Ethan rose, walked over, and wrapped her in his arms, rocking gently side to side. "I love you so much, baby. I was so scared when we couldn't find you."

A pair of arms surrounded her from behind, loosening the towel so it dropped to the floor. Tania trembled and ached with unsatisfied desire as Ethan's cock swelled against her tummy and a hard, warm body pressed against her back. Crushed between her two mates, she could feel their hearts beating against her back and chest while arousals poked her from the front and back.

Ethan cupped her chin and gazed down into her eyes. She reached up and pulled his head down to kiss him. His lips opened wide, tasting her deeply, devouring her mouth. Tania flicked her tongue at his, wanting to absorb his taste.

Warm, calloused fingers feathered up her sides and then circled around to cup her breasts, the thumbs rubbing lazily back and forth across the nipples. She groaned and pressed back against Latan when he dragged his mouth along the sensitive skin of her neck and shoulders. Cream oozed onto her thighs when he nipped his mate mark with his teeth.

One of Latan's hands fell away from her breast to grip her hip tightly. Her eyes flew open when a pair of warm lips claimed the abandoned breast. Ethan licked and nibbled and then pulled her nipple deep into his mouth while Latan pinched the other side between his thumb and forefinger, plucking at it gently.

Tania let her hands wander over Ethan's chest. His hair was wiry and dark, a rough, sensual treat for her palms. She pinched his nipples and teased them with her thumbs. He began to rub her arms with his big hands while she let hers explore his hard frame.

Stepping away from the two men, Tania faced them both. She left one hand tangled in the hair on Ethan's chest while she trailed its mate across Latan's shoulder and down into the dark whorls of hair around his pecs. He stepped closer and rubbed his swollen cock against her hip. Her hand wrapped around his shaft, squeezing softly. She peered up at Ethan through lowered lashes and found him stroking his own cock, his gaze locked with her own. Pushing his hand away, she wrapped her fingers around his thickness and sank to her knees before the two men.

Tania leaned close and swirled her tongue around the head of Ethan's erection. Cupping his testicles, she gently squeezed each one in turn. Leaving her hand to caress his sac, she turned her attention to Latan. "I wanna taste you," she whispered. Scraping her nails lightly across his scrotum, her hand closed around his length. She ran her tongue up the underside in a long, slow swipe and then flicked it rapidly at the base of the crown. She could feel the vibrations slide along Latan's skin when he moaned. She watched him carefully as she opened her mouth wide and took him in deep. Her lips extended down the shaft until she felt his pubic hair tickle her nose. His eyes rolled back in his head, his fingers sliding through Tania's hair until they caught in the band holding her ponytail. With one jerk, he tugged it loose, sending her long hair cascading around her shoulders.

Turning, Tania grinned and sucked half of Ethan's length down her throat. His hips thrust up a bit, forcing his cock a little farther into her mouth. She opened wide, swallowing around his hardness. Slowly, she stroked Latan's satiny, steel length while she sucked rhythmically on Ethan's massive erection. Each of her mates had his own distinctive scent and taste, and she would never be able to choose between them. She let Ethan slip free and licked lower, pressing her tongue just behind his balls to the small bit of flesh between them and his ass.

"Enough," Ethan cried. He yanked her to her feet and scooped her into his arms. "It'll be over with before it starts if you keep that up, you little minx." Chuckling, he walked over and tossed her onto the bed. Both men immediately crawled up beside her. Ethan caressed her stomach and then raked through her feminine curls and spread her lips apart.

Latan kissed up from her oversensitive breast to her neck and chin to cover her mouth with his. Her arm looped around his shoulder in a loose hug, her hand exploring his muscled back. His tongue probed deep, licking the roof of her mouth and mapping out the interior. Warm fingers gripped her hip, splayed wide over her naked skin. Slowly inching up, he cupped her aching breast.

Ethan ran the tip of his finger along her slit and then worked it inside. "You're so wet," he groaned. Spreading her legs farther, he began rubbing her clit with two fingers, setting her insides on fire. He pinched the tiny, pulsing bundle of nerves between his thumb and forefinger and tugged and then inserted two fingers into her tight passage. Tania ground her pussy against his hand.

Latan's fingers plucked gently at her nipples, hardening them more than she thought possible. Each tug sent a bolt of electricity down into her needy pussy. His lips clamped over one stiff point and sucked hard. His teeth closed around the sensitive spot, gently pulling away from her body and then laving away the sting. "I wanna get your nipples pierced, Tania. Think of what it would feel like to have us tugging on the little rings, the sharp, steady pulls on your breasts." She was too breathless to reply to his words.

Ethan moved and finally slid between her waiting thighs. He massaged her clit with his thumb as he spread her pussy lips wide with two thrusting fingers. "You're so pink and pretty, dripping with honey. Is all this for me, baby?" His moan vibrated against her core as his tongue stroked in and out. She could feel her pussy pulse, the cream dripping down toward her ass. Her hips lifted against him with each thrust of his tongue, the sensual assault between her legs turning her gasps into moans that filled the room.

"Fuck me, please," she cried out. "I want you inside me, filling me."

Seizing the opportunity, Latan pulled her up in the bed, clutched her hips, and helped her straddle his body. His hands curved over the bare flesh of her hips, stroking the skin repeatedly. Tania hovered above his straining cock, teasing him with the promise of her heat. “Don’t tease, pretty lady. I wanna fuck you so bad.” Smiling, she placed the head of his shaft at her entrance and then slowly lowered herself until his balls met her butt cheeks. Tightly clenching her muscles around his cock, she ground her pussy against him. Holding her in place with his hands on her hips, Latan groaned harshly and rammed into her. Tania released a keening moan, her head falling back on her shoulders.

Ethan reached down and kneaded Tania’s ass, a cheek in each hand, squeezing gently. “I wanna fuck this tight ass of yours, baby.” She wiggled her bottom to entice him and then felt her cheeks part. A gentle finger slid down her butt crack and spread it, a cool breeze blowing over her heated flesh. “I’m gonna spread these cheeks and rim this sweet little hole.” She shuddered as he kissed his way down her spine. He ran his fingers over the tight hole and then traced the ring of muscles, drawing little circles against the puckered skin.

Latan’s hands began idly playing with her breasts, tweaking the already turgid nipples. His long fingers trailed down her belly and rested at the top of her mound. She rotated her hips, deliberately clenching her pussy muscles, and delighted in his hoarse growl. Probing gently between her legs, he found her clit and began drawing circles around the tiny nub, flicking it with the tip of his finger.

Ethan reached for the tube of lube he’d left on the table by the bed and then squeezed a generous amount into his hand. She watched as he coated several of his fingers before applying the rest to his cock. When he moved back behind her, she pushed her ass toward him, anxious to feel both her mates in her body. Tania moaned and arched into his touch when Ethan’s finger penetrated the tight muscles of her ass. She trembled as he worked the slick oil into her opening, adding a second finger. Her hips began to move with the rhythm of his thrusts.

A third one inserted brought a gasp with the first twinge of pain. "Shh, baby, it's okay. Take a deep breath."

She grunted when he pulled his fingers out and then sucked in a breath when she felt his cock lining up between her butt cheeks. Her fingernails dug into Latan's arms as Ethan slowly pushed the crown of his cock through the tight ring of muscle. He pushed in steadily until she felt his body against her ass and then pulled partially out. Groaning, he wiggled his hips and thrust back in. His hips began to move slowly, thrusting into Tania's ass. "God, baby, you're so tight."

Latan slowly withdrew and then slid back into her, alternating his thrusts with Ethan's. "Is he thick and hard inside you?" he whispered.

"Oh, Latan, I feel so full," she cried. She felt stretched beyond her wildest imagination, filled to overflowing. They continued to pound into her, faster and faster, snatching her breath away. Familiar tingles began forming low in her abdomen, making her hold tighter to Latan. "I'm so close," she groaned. Latan tugged on her clit and, with a loud moan, she shattered. She convulsed over him, straining as they pumped hard within her.

"Yeah, baby, come for us." Ethan pounded into her ass hard. His body shuddered, and with a deep moan, he came, his seed shooting into her depths.

Latan drove one final time into her body and came, hips thrusting as he rode out his orgasm. His fingernails scraped down her back, his body shaking as he cried out her name in a hoarse voice. She could feel the warmth as he filled her body with his semen.

Together, the two men rose as one and sank their canines into their mating marks, claiming her again as their own. The slowing tremors of her orgasm catapulted into a cataclysmic event. She screamed out both their names and then collapsed against Latan's chest.

"Are you okay? We didn't hurt you?" Ethan pressed a kiss against her back as his softening cock slid from her ass.

"No," she groaned. "You didn't hurt me. I feel great." She chuckled. Latan grabbed her hips and lifted her free of his cock. She could feel the fluids leaking from her body as he laid her on the bed between them. "We didn't use a condom," she whispered.

"We don't want to use them, baby." Ethan smoothed his hand across her stomach. "Nothing would make us happier than to have children with you."

"Even if you don't know what they'll be?" She held her breath, waiting for their answer.

Latan turned her face toward him. "They'll be ours, and we'll love them no matter what."

With tears in her eyes, she moved closer to kiss his lips, thrusting her tongue deep into his mouth to taste him. After several moments, she pulled free and turned to Ethan. Repeating the kiss, she felt Latan snuggle up and spoon into her back. "I love both of you very much, and I wanna have a family with you. I guess I'm just scared."

Ethan hugged her close. "Nothing to be scared of, baby. We'll take each day one at a time."

Closing her eyes, Tania let herself dream of the possibilities of her future.

* * * *

"Well, come on in and join the party." Maddie stepped back and let Mali and Melissa in the front door. "Go on back, everyone's in the kitchen." She followed them through the house, trying to remember the last time she felt this happy.

"Well, if it isn't the newlyweds." Michael got up and hugged Melissa and then turned and shook Mali's hand. "Haven't seen you guys for a couple of days. What've you been up to?"

Ariane giggled and came over to give Melissa a big hug. "What do you think they've been up to? Same thing we've been up to would be my guess."

"Hey, guys, how's life treating you?" Ethan smiled up at the newly arrived couple. He pulled Tania down on his lap and then grinned when Latan scooted his chair close and draped her legs over his thighs.

"We can't complain." Mali smiled. "Looks like the three of you are doing pretty good. Did, uh, Remus run out of chairs?" he asked, a smug look on his face.

Tania rolled her eyes. "Very funny, big man. My mates are still a little paranoid, and this is about as far away from the two of them as I'm allowed."

Remus laughed. "Must be hell going to the bathroom!" He winced when Maddie smacked him on the back of the head.

"Remus, that's just gross." She motioned for everyone to take a seat. "Before we eat, I wanna make an announcement." A grin broke out when she saw Ariane and Melissa take up similar positions on their mate's laps. She turned and gazed up into Remus's love-filled eyes. "You wanna do the honors?"

He smiled and hugged his mate close. "We have official word that Maddie and I are having twins." He chuckled and pulled her even closer when everyone stood to offer their congratulations.

"Wait, everyone, if I could have your attention." Michael whistled loudly and clapped his hands. The room quieted, and everyone turned toward Ariane and Michael. "My mate and I would like to make this an even bigger celebration by announcing that we're also going to have a baby."

"Michael," Maddie squealed. She rushed over and threw her arms around her brother's neck.

"Hey, don't cry, sis. This is a good thing." Michael wiped the tears from her face.

She turned and kissed Ariane's cheek. "I know it's a good thing. These are happy tears." Everyone laughed when she turned and buried her face in Remus's chest.

"How about we sit down and eat this wonderful food before it gets cold?" Remus motioned toward the table and picked up his mate.

"Remus, put me down," she demanded. Maddie sighed when he placed her in a chair at the head of the table.

"Stay, little momma-to-be. You've done enough work today. We'll handle things from here." She watched, incredulous, as he and the other men brought the food over from the stove.

"Tania, I got a call from your boss yesterday." Remus took his seat beside Maddie and smiled at his sister-in-law.

"Her ex-boss, if you don't mind," Latan scolded.

Tania scowled at her mate and then turned to Remus. "What the hell did he want?"

"To see if I could influence you to tear up the resignation you apparently faxed to him this morning. The foolish man thought I could intimidate you into continuing to work for the Council." Remus chuckled.

Tania looked embarrassed. "I'm so sorry, Remus. I don't know what to say."

"No need to say anything, honey. I set him straight about my family working undercover in the future." He grinned. "I think he got the message."

"Was he upset about the outcome of all this?" Tania asked.

"No, he wasn't upset. Of course, it helped that we turned Kaugh and Dyer over to the Council and didn't kill them outright." Remus began filling Maddie's plate with food. "They were the only ones left alive."

"Ethan told me about that. What made you decide not to get rid of them?"

Remus looked thoughtful for a moment. "He told me that a lot of the shifters rescued from the lab were having problems. If they can persuade him, Kaugh could be invaluable in finding medical answers for the problems he helped create. It seemed a fair solution as long as they keep a close watch on him. Of course, they're hoping he'll tell them where the Canadian lab is. I let Dyer live because he gave us the necessary information to find you."

Tania raised her glass. "Well, here's to the National Council keeping their word."

Remus raised his glass and then looked over to his mate. "What's wrong, baby?"

Maddie wiped at the tears running down her cheeks. "I was just thinking about Grandfather's journal. He wanted me to embrace my Wolfen Heritage." She looked around the table at her family and smiled. "I think he would be very happy at the way we've not only embraced it," she glanced at Tania, "we've changed it."

She stilled when she heard her grandfather's voice in her head. *I'm proud of you, Maddie. Enjoy your Changed Wolfen Heritage.*

Epilogue

Months Later

"Push," Tehran cried. "You're almost there, little mama. The head's coming now." Tehran eased the newborn from its mother's body and grinned as the child's lusty cries filled the air. Working quickly, he suctioned the baby's nose and mouth and then deftly tied off and cut the umbilical cord. Gently, he laid the naked, screaming infant on its mother's chest. Smiling, he turned his head and looked at the new father. "Better let them know something before they come to find out what's taking so long."

"Right," he mumbled and bent down to kiss his mate. In a daze, he walked out the door and down the hall. Stopping outside the waiting room, he gazed through the small glass window at his new, expanded family.

Smiling, he watched Remus and Maddie cuddle their five-month-old twins, Victor and Eloise. Remus had gotten the son he wanted to carry on his name. Too bad Maddie would never let him forget Eloise was born first.

Tania stood in the corner of the room, wiping the faces of the two boys she and her mates had adopted. She'd told the family about her unhappy childhood growing up in the Council's home for children, and Remus had suggested they might want to make life easier for some other abandoned shifter child. The result of his talk had been the addition of Eric and David to the family. They were ten and twelve years old, respectively.

Latan and Ethan were standing behind the other couch, gazing down at the baby sleeping in Ariane's arms. Michael was tucking a pink blanket around their one-month-old daughter, grinning like a fool. They'd named her Kilana, after Ariane's grandmother.

Sighing, he pushed open the door and stepped into the room.

"Well?" Maddie asked.

Mali pulled the hospital cap off his head and smiled. "It's a boy!"

THE END

www.missymartine.com

ABOUT THE AUTHOR

I was born, and raised in the great southern state of Tennessee. In my youth, I studied nursing, and spent several happy years working in the hospitals there until I branched out into medical management in 1980.

In 1998 I was managing a medical supply house in Chattanooga, when I met the love of my life. The only problem facing me then, he lived way out in Oklahoma. You see, we had met in a chat room!

He romanced me daily with love letters, flowers and phone calls. It wasn't long before I uprooted myself, and moved west to join him. We married in 1999, and then continued our fantasy romance all over the world. Together we have traveled in almost all of the Continental United States, and taken trips to Canada and China.

We moved to Minnesota in 2003, where my life was changed forever by a series of small strokes. For someone who had owned her own business, and worked twelve hours a day, being incapacitated was pure torture. The strokes damaged a part of my brain that helps controls speech, and for a long time I couldn't communicate what was in my mind, to my lips. I could read however, and I became an avid reader of romance novels.

Strange as it sounds, the strokes did not keep me from voicing my opinions. I discovered that I could type my thoughts, almost as fast as I once spoke them. It was then that I started writing long, lengthy newsletters to my family and friends. I got all kinds of compliments on my amusing tales of our everyday life.

It wasn't long before my husband was encouraging me to find some kind of outlet to occupy my time, something that was challenging, and rewarding. I was already obsessed with reading about romance, and I began to think I could probably write a good, romantic story. My husband heartily agreed with me. With that encouragement, I began writing my first book. I wasn't really convinced that anyone else would find it interesting, but he pressed me to take a chance and send it in to a publisher. To my surprise, it was accepted, and now I'm able to share it with readers everywhere who like a "happily ever after" story.

Now, I'm living in California with my, still romantic, husband of twelve years, and our boys. Our boys consist of Beau, Midnight, and Bubba, three male cats that allow us to live with them and serve them at their leisure. I continue to write almost daily, hoping that someone, somewhere will get the same enjoyment from reading my stories, that I get from writing them.

Also by Missy Martine

Ménage Amour: *Table for Three*
Siren Classic: A Wolfen Heritage 1: *Discovering Her Wolfen Heritage*
Siren Classic: A Wolfen Heritage 2: *Denying His Wolfen Heritage*

Available at
BOOKSTRAND.COM

Siren Publishing, Inc.
www.SirenPublishing.com

LaVergne, TN USA
09 February 2011
215839LV00006B/148/P

9 781610 342346